Doctor Samaritan

ELIZABETH SEIFERT

Doctor Samaritan

ÆONIAN PRESS

Leyden, Mass. 01337

For Richard in Idaho

Doctor Samaritan

I ❀❀❀❀❀❀❀❀❀❀❀❀❀❀❀❀❀❀❀❀❀❀❀❀❀❀❀

IT was a fine, blue-hazed October evening, and any man in his right mind should walk along even a city street with thoughts about something other than angiograms, narrowed coronary arteries, and collateral circulation. Any young man. Thirty-one was young. Lately the newspapers had gone on record as the mid-forties being *young*. So Redding Cahill, at thirty-one, was very young.

Then why did his feet ache, and his back? Why did his eyes burn, and his thoughts turn to the troubles of his troublesome patients, instead of . . . ?

He touched C'ele's doorbell, pushed on the flat gray door, and stepped inside.

"I'm never going to get married," he announced, not really caring if anyone heard him, "because I am mortally sure I would have to live in a garden apartment."

The dark-haired girl on the couch looked up at him questioningly, smiling, and he bent over to kiss her cheek.

"Every one with a terrace space or a balcony," he added, sitting in the room's only armchair. C'ele couldn't afford to live alone and buy furniture too.

Red's eyes flicked to the curly-headed blond woman

who sat on the floor, changing the diaper of a baby. A little girl . . . Red frowned. Why wasn't C'ele alone?

C'ele smiled at him.

And Red nodded. "Women in curlers," he continued his growling complaint. "Those fat, enormous rolls surrounding their heads. Capri pants, too, in all the improbable colors. Can't you buy Capri pants in anything but chartreuse, shocking pink—and stripes? Dear God, the *stripes!*" He put his hand to his head, and C'ele chuckled.

"Red—" she attempted.

"They ventured to flirt with me," said the big young man. He wore brown slacks and a light-blue jacket. His hair was cut very short and his eyes were deep-set. "Those women in pink curlers. The dogs all yapped at my heels—when they weren't doing worse things. The kids, too, and then there were the young girls—fourteen, sixteen—with the damnedest eye make-up. They looked like coal miners who haven't washed well."

Quickly C'ele got up from the couch and came to him. "Red, dear," she said firmly. "Stop talking a minute."

He looked up at her. "Why?" he asked directly.

She laughed. "Well, for one thing, I want to introduce you to Sharon."

Red's glance slid toward the kitten-faced blond girl on the floor and then focused on the kitten-faced child. "How old is she?" he asked, his voice rough.

"Oh, Red!" cried C'ele.

"I meant the baby."

"Well, she's twenty months old, and Sharon—she's Mrs. Frieze—she went to school with me. Business school, I mean."

"How are you, Sharon?" asked Red, not caring—and showing it. He got up, knelt beside the child, and took one of her pipestem arms in his fingers. "Name's Caroline?" he asked, glancing at the mother.

The young woman laughed. "How did you know?" she squealed.

"Inevitable," said Red. "For the past two years or so half the girl babies have been named . . . What does she weigh?"

The baby protested peevishly when Red held her firmly and pulled the pink dress down from her shoulder. "She's perishing thin," he muttered.

Really the child looked ill. She had a bad color, and her right shoulder and arm seemed tender.

"Has she had a fall?" Red asked the mother.

"He's a doctor," he heard C'ele explaining.

"Oh, I see," said the blond girl. "Well, no, not lately she hasn't had any falls. When she was real little—once she even fell off the table."

Now Red was unbuttoning the small frock and taking it down from the chest and shoulders.

"Red!" C'ele protested.

He glanced at her. Then, "She has a lump here on her chest," he told the mother.

"I know. She's always had that."

"Hmmmmn," said Red. He stood the child away from him, took his thermometer case from his pocket, and held it out. The baby reached for it with her left hand. Red tried to get her to extend her right arm. She could move that arm, but she seemed to prefer using the left. The right shoulder was swollen, and Caroline whimpered when Red touched it. There was no redness.

The doctor got to his feet and walked about the room.

"Why don't you go on, if you want to?" C'ele murmured to her friend, wanting Sharon to leave. Red, a surgical resident, didn't get enough free time to spend it looking at puny babies. Anyone could see that Caroline was tiny for her age, but, heavens, Sharon dragged the kid along everywhere she went! Fed her Cokes and cheese bits, probably spoiling her for regular meals, if any. . . .

C'ele stooped to pick up the toys and the diaper bag.

"D'you take her to the clinic over at the hospital?" Red asked Sharon. His tone was gruff, and she resented it.

"Well, no, I don't!" she cried. "There's nothing wrong with her!"

"Agh!" Red growled. "Of course there's something wrong with her. I can think of at least three things that could be wrong with her. She should weigh more—a lot more. She looks sick, and probably she is sick. So why don't you take her to the clinic and prove me mistaken? Eh?"

Now Sharon was deeply offended. The baby was all right, she told C'ele. She bruised easy and was a fussy eater, but she was *not* sick! "You and your doctor friends!" she said resentfully as she went out through the front door.

C'ele turned back and faced Red accusingly. "You're just a—a nuisance!" she told him, kneeling down to brush cookie crumbs from the carpet.

Red kicked off his shoes and stretched out on the couch. "I can think of three reasons—no, *four*," he said, "why that baby should be taken forcibly to the clinic."

C'ele sat back on her heels. "What do you mean *forcibly?*" she asked.

"Just as it sounds. Forcibly. That woman is killing her baby, and there are laws against murder."

C'ele stood up and came to him. She touched his cheek. "Are you serious?" she asked. One could not always tell about Red. He could stage a long and elaborate gag.

4

But this evening she believed he was serious. He said that he was. "I should have been able to take that baby away from her silly mother," he cried. "I should have taken her kid to the hospital—for the care she obviously needs."

"Oh, Red!"

"I mean it, C'ele. That child won't *live* unless—"

"But if that's true," cried C'ele, becoming alarmed, "couldn't you have taken her? You're a doctor."

"Would you want some doctor on a bus to decide that you needed to have your tonsils out and then be free to take you—?"

"Oh, that's silly! That's different!"

Red nodded. "Yes," he agreed soberly, "it is different."

"But for a child, couldn't you do something?"

She sat down on the edge of the couch, and Red put his arm around her slender waist. "I did do something," he said. "I told the mother. Beyond that I cannot go. There are laws. Bad laws, admittedly, but . . ."

C'ele stroked his cheek, wanting it to crease into a smile. She treasured the hours which Red could spend with her; she did not want him being preoccupied by a whiny, unattractive child who had just happened to be in the apartment when he came in.

"Do you have to be a doctor all the time?" she asked, showing her annoyance.

Now Red smiled at her. "Yes," he said, "of course I do. Why? Don't you like it?"

He was not going to trick her! "I'll go stir up some supper," said C'ele. She went toward the little kitchen, knowing that Red watched her. After a little he would follow her out there, and she would find things to talk about other than his doctoring.

She did find them, but Red remained thoughtful during

the meal which she managed to get together. He might as well have eaten in the cafeteria for all he noticed her food. And her efforts at light conversation. He answered her—yes, he liked hard rolls. Certainly he thought Vince was good company. And, no, he didn't believe the gossip about the supe's leaving to open a nursing home. He was spooning chocolate ice cream into his big mouth when he blurted, "I think that child is being abused!"

C'ele looked up, frowning.

"Maybe even beaten!" he added.

"You mean Caroline?" C'ele asked in amazement.

"I mean Caroline. She has every sign of repeated trauma. Of course there could be a malignancy—that lump on her rib cage—leukemia—or maybe even a metabolic disturbance—but, offhand, I would bet on consistent and repeated beatings."

"But, Red!" cried C'ele. "Then you are going to have to do something about it! Aren't you? You *will*, won't you?" Her eyes were round, dark, and pleading.

But Red shook his head. "There's a 1 cm. lump on her chest," he mused. "On the anterior end of the ninth rib—a bony halo, I would say. The right shoulder and arm—I'd say that the periosteum was stripped and has been torn. Even the legs show evidence of healed trauma."

He was talking to himself. C'ele worked in the records room of the hospital complex, but Red knew that these terms were little more than words to her. However, she did know that if Red was so upset, there must be a good reason. He wasn't chief Neurological-Surgery resident without knowing a lot about doctoring. The hospital word was that Cahill was exceptionally good.

"You must know a way," she cried in panic, reaching across the table to shake his arm.

6

He glanced at her. "The best thing I can think of," he said, "is for you to try to persuade your friend to take that baby to the hospital clinic."

C'ele shook her head. "We're not that kind of friends," she said. "Sharon happens to live in this neighborhood. I meet her now and then—on the street, or in the supermarket. She's a flighty thing. I've met her husband only once. We're not *friends*, Red!"

"But you could look her up. She knows that you work at the hospital. You could tell her—"

"What *you* should have done, this afternoon," said C'ele, "was just to take the baby to the hospital, see that the necessary things were done for her—and—and if she has been mistreated, you could have reported the parents to the police!" C'ele sat back in her chair and smiled triumphantly at Red.

He grinned. "As easy as that, eh?" he asked.

"Well—couldn't you?" she demanded.

He was lighting a cigarette and shook his head. "Nup!" he said. "I couldn't even begin to do that."

"But, I can't see— Look!" She pushed the dishes out of the way, put her arms on the table, and leaned toward the big man. "Suppose you had found that child—Caroline— injured at the side of the highway, after a car wreck, perhaps, wouldn't you have done something for her?"

Red pursed his lips and looked at the ceiling. "Yes," he admitted. "If I had come along—after an accident—I could have taken an injured child to the hospital."

"But you did come upon her, by chance, in my home."

"Ah-huh. And I found a child with the signs of previous and repeated injuries. But, no, C'ele, your Caroline is not comparable to the child on the highway, to an emergency case. I did everything in my power for Caroline when I suggested that the mother should take her to the clinic."

"Well, I think she needs more!"

"So do I. And you, perhaps, could do more. But not me. I'm a doctor, and doctors have to be especially careful."

"But that isn't right!"

"Yes, it probably is right. Anyway, it is a legal rather than a moral point. Because there are laws governing what a doctor may or may not do, and when he doesn't obey those laws, lawsuits follow."

"But if those laws say you can't protect a child you know is being hurt, those laws are wrong, Red! Dead wrong!"

She watched Red's face as he smoked his cigarette, without speaking. He was the rugged type of man; his face was square, the skin on it like fine-grained leather; his hair would have been blond, but, cut as short as he wore it, it took on the same light tan tone of his skin. His eyes were blue and deep-set. His cheeks could crease deeply when he smiled or knot—as they did tonight—into lumps before his ears. Red Cahill was not a pretty-handsome man, but women turned to look at him a second time, and men admired him. He had thick, strong shoulders, strong arms and hands; he was tall and flat-waisted. . . .

Cecilia Davidson was in love with Red Cahill and hoped against hope that he loved her, that he would.

Tonight his thoughts were on anything but the slim, dark-haired girl who had served supper to him and wanted to talk about things far removed from his profession. But if he could think and talk only about a mistreated child, then C'ele would talk about that. And wait until he was ready for fun, for foolishness, or even, and rarely, a cozier moment.

Now he mashed the end of his cigarette into the square glass tray and frowned across at C'ele, not seeing her at all.

8

"The laws are wrong," he said slowly. "In your Caroline's case they are."

"Don't call her *my Caroline!*" protested C'ele. "And isn't there anything we can do?"

Red's eyes focused on her. "You and me, C'ele?" he asked. "No. Not as things stand. You could mention the clinic to your friend, say that all children need regular checkups, shots . . . Then, if she should bring her in, or even take her to a doctor, the parents might be charged with neglect and the baby made a ward of the court." He frowned. "Maybe," he said thoughtfully. "Sometime, maybe, even new laws could be, and will be, passed."

He kept that idea, and Caroline, in his mind for the rest of their evening, which was not the pleasant one C'ele had hoped it would be. Red had few enough times when he could relax, away from the hospital, away from the work he did and the calls made upon him. She was sorry to have this free time squandered.

When he was off duty, he needed a lift and a change. C'ele sometimes could give him that lift—and always she wanted to do what was good for him, to please him.

So she was sorry.

He seemed to know that she was, and when it came time for him to leave, he kissed her.

He walked back to the hospital, not hurrying. He knew exactly how long it took for him to walk from C'ele's to the Center, to check in, to go to his room and be there to go on call exactly at ten.

So he walked at a steady pace, thinking. He turned the corner and went past the parking lot. The hospital lobby was bright. He checked in, spoke to the nurse at the desk, and waited for the elevator, talking to those who spoke to him, not thinking much about what he said.

Upstairs the halls were dim, with spots of light at the station and at the elevator. O.r. was dark. He went on to his room, belatedly conscious that he would have enjoyed a walk through the park on that half-cool, half-warm autumn evening, regretting that he had not even relished the short walk from C'ele's. Poor girl, he had ruined her evening, too, because of his preoccupation with a child who was one of a thousand children right here in this city. No man, no doctor, could care for them all. Let this one doctor save his strength and mind for those he could help.

He snapped on the light on his desk and closed the door behind him. Some effort had been expended to make the room attractive. The walls were a soft green, his bedspread and window curtains were rosy beige, the steel furniture was silver-gray.

Red took off his blue jacket and hung a fresh white coat where he could reach it in a minute. On his desk there was a letter, plastered with special-delivery stamps. He smiled a little. It would be from his mother, who often sent her letters to him special delivery. The hospital had learned to discount their air of urgency.

Red sat down in the chair, took the letter in his hand, and reached for something with which to slit the envelope. He would read his letter and then go to bed.

He did read it, grinning; the letter contained the usual things. His mother was a sweet person, generous, preoccupied with the life she led in the East. Red's father had died when he was in med school; his mother had married again, a rich man who liked to travel, to entertain, and to dwell among other rich men.

Red put the letter into a tole container at the back of his desk; one of these days he would answer it, and if he did not, his mother would call him.

He snapped off the light and lay down on the bed. Now on call, he was back on duty as of midnight, and a job would surely come up for him. The nurse would open his door and speak his name, "Dr. Cahill?" and speak it again, "Dr. *Cahill!*" Then she would come in and shake his shoulder; he would groan, turn over, look up at her resentfully, get on his feet, put on his white jacket—and go—out . . .

He was trained to sleep when and how he could lie down on a bed. Tonight he could only drowse and wake again to his thoughts.

Thoughts of that kitten-faced child, Caroline. C'ele had agreed that she could and would try to persuade the mother to bring the little girl to the clinic.

It was Red's guess that he would never again see the baby.

But there would be others, helpless, neglected, mistreated. This big hospital center got them all.

And something might be done for some of them.

2 ❋❋❋❋❋❋❋❋❋❋❋❋❋❋❋❋❋❋❋❋❋❋❋❋❋❋❋❋❋

"IT does *not* snow on Halloween!" pronounced Dr. Cahill, watching the last patient wheeled out of o.r. He pushed his face mask down, his cap up and back.

"You should look out of the window, Doctor," said Polly Ferris, preparing to follow the cart.

"I'll do that, when I have the strength to find a window."

"You're tired," said the nurse who came to untie his gown.

"Aren't you?"

"Sure." Her voice was cheerful and her step quick as she walked away from him.

Red shuffled on to scrub, through it to the small room where he could write his report, drink a cup of coffee, and talk a little to those of the o.r. team who might come in. The place was cluttered with gear, but the doctors liked it.

Vince Sebaja was in the room before Red, and he reached into the cupboard for the mug marked with Dr. Cahill's initials. Dr. Enns came in almost at once, his gray hair ruffled, his hands rubbing together. The younger men greeted the Chief with friendly respect, and their eyes brightened when Polly followed him. They all liked Polly and were glad to have her back at work.

Red put down his pen, opened the door, and beckoned to an orderly who would take his report to the chart desk. *Now* he could drink his coffee, lean back against the table, and talk . . .

But—

He growled below his breath.

"All those *d*'s, Doctor!" protested Polly.

Red grinned at her and stepped to one side to allow Iserman to come on in. What he wanted was anyone's guess. Iserman was a resident in Internal Medicine, but he had a way of being everywhere at once. Now he had some question to put to the N.S. Chief. He stood before the taller man, face lifted, body arched. Dr. Enns answered him quietly, and by all rules of usual procedure the little doctor should have then departed.

But not Kenneth Iserman. In that great hospital *he* was called "Doc." He cherished his profession; he leaned upon it. He never signed his name—to anything—without the prefix which marked him as a doctor. This was a hospital joke of which he was imperturbably aware.

Dr. Sebaja could talk endlessly about the psyche of the small man given authority.

Little Dr. Iserman was competent, no more. He would never be a chief resident; he would not be a success in private practice.

"House doctor in a retirement hotel" was the niche that his co-workers designated for him.

Meanwhile they endured him in the big hospital complex where they all worked. Today they endured him in the small o.r. anteroom up on Neurosurgical. Dr. Enns, Chief of Service, Dr. Polly Ferris, anesthesiologist, Dr. Sebaja, P. N. resident, there as consultant, Dr. Cahill, senior resident in Neurosurgery—four doctors who had worked hard for several hours and now wanted to unwind, rest a little, before they must go on with their duties or face another emergency. They did *not* want to listen to Dr. Iserman tell about his recent drive to Chicago, the traffic problems, the way a truck had crowded him. . . .

"I'm going to look in on Bernie," said Dr. Cahill loudly, setting his mug down with a thump.

He strode out into the hall.

In less than ten minutes he came back. Dr. Iserman was gone. Red grunted and filled his coffee cup. "Where did you hide the body?" he asked.

"Dr. Enns suggested that he might be needed on Medical."

"And Iserman couldn't argue with that! Well, I guess that is what makes a man Chief. Brains."

Dr. Enns laughed with the others. He had a good team on N.S.

"I'm glad I came back to work," said Polly comfortably. She meant that she had missed this sort of talk. This sort of professional loyalty, interdependence, respect.

"We're glad you're back, too," Red told her warmly. "You are very good at the gas machines."

Polly rinsed her cup at the sink. "I had better be," she said. "With the retraining I took."

She wiped the cup with a paper towel and put it up on the shelf. "Of course," she added reflectively, "sometimes I am homesick for the house, my deep easy chair, the kids, and the dog. If I really did have my druthers, I suppose I'd be there instead of here."

Red looked surprised. "Then why come back to work in

14

this rat race?"

Too late, he caught Enns's frown. The question *had* been bald. But Polly only laughed.

"I had to come back," she said frankly. "My kids are college age, and my husband is no good."

Even Red was shocked. "I'm sorry I asked," he mumbled.

Polly grinned at him. "You would have found it out sooner or later," she said. "It always helps to get the facts down on the history sheet. I'm glad I had a profession to take up. When I married— You see, Red, that was one of those romance things. You know?"

Red shook his head. "I hope to know some day."

"Oh no!" said Polly. "The rose-colored glasses get broken, the cloud nine dissolves into sleet and rain, the flowers around the cottage door get choked with weeds . . . You be wise, Red, when you decide to marry. Or at least thoughtful." She threw the paper towel into the bin. "And," she added, "put on a starchy-white coat before you go out into the wards again. In that low-necked T shirt you look like a prize fighter's trainer."

Red was startled, but he laughed. "Well—thanks," he said. "I guess."

The others in the room were smiling. They could see that Polly was going to be a help in many ways. Setting Cahill down occasionally would keep life interesting.

"When I was doing my brush-up," Polly told them, "there seemed to be a problem. Some students had to be reminded, and were reminded, not to attend clinics in jeans and tattered shoes. Once a chap even showed up in shorts."

"It was different in my day," said Dr. Enns.

"And in mine," Polly agreed. "I have one of those medical school photographs, and it shows us up to be so respect-

15

able, both in clothing and facial expression, that we look positively middle-aged. And I know we were no older than the classes now!"

Dr. Enns smiled at her. "Maybe you look younger now than you did then," he said warmly.

Polly considered this. "Maybe I do. Now I wear the same shorts that Amelia does; twenty-five years ago I wouldn't have. Yes! That is a beautiful thought, Doctor! And thank you very much for it!"

Dr. Enns chuckled and went out into the hall. Red followed him by a half minute. He stopped in Recovery and checked on his patients, then he proceeded down the corridor, still in his T shirt and the loose trousers of o.r. He would go to his room and change—Polly was right. He should look the part.

But before he could reach his room he was waylaid by a little group coming out of one of the women's wards. A patient was going home, accompanied by a nurse, a husband carrying three potted plants, and an orderly with a suitcase.

Red crossed over to tell Mrs. Staires good-by. She had had a laminectomy, and her recovery was excellent. The doctor took over the handles of the wheel chair. "I'll go down with her," he told the nurse.

He should have changed, but now was the minute to give this woman a bit of courage to take home with her. It was important to let her talk to the doctor as the elevator descended, as Red pushed the chair along the corridor and out to the ramp. And all the way Mrs. Staires did talk to him, effusively. She called him a tower of strength; she indicated that he, and he alone, was responsible for her recovery and the recovery of all the patients on Neurosurgery. "It must be wonderful—a young man—to have such

16

ability and so much responsibility."

Red laughed and eased the chair down the ramp to the car which was waiting. "I wish you'd tell my girl some of the nice things you think up to say," he told Mrs. Staires. He lifted her into the car seat.

"I'd like to meet your lucky girl," Mrs. Staires told him warmly. "Oh, good-by, Doctor. And thank you! *Thank you!*"

Red smiled, stepped back, and watched the car drive away. Then he started back into the hospital, seeing himself reflected in the glass of the wide door. "Wonder what a starchy-white coat would have got me," he said, half aloud. He began to walk fast.

Time was a-wastin'. It was almost five and there were things to do—rounds to make, orders to write, a bite of supper to eat.

A party had been planned for that evening; the "gang" was going to a restaurant, to eat pizza and drink a little wine—or beer—to dance, talk, and have fun. Red was taking C'ele. He would be on emergency call after six; his date with C'ele was for "around eight." He might make it. . . .

He began his rounds, a pleasant doctor, brisk, liking his work, liking his patients. And at five-thirty an emergency came in. A boy had been shot accidentally by a gun put on the floor of a car. This boy and his brother, in the back seat, had got to scuffling . .

It was a nasty, tedious job, just picking out the buckshot. The chief danger was to the eyes. More work would need to be done tomorrow or the next day.

Red came out of o.r. to the news that a patient was "going bad." The night residents could and would attend to that, but the senior resident should know what was happening and what might happen. The matter took another twenty minutes. By then the family had arrived, and Red talked to them. He was released when his signal came through. He walked to the desk and picked up the phone.

"Dr. Cahill here," he said. "I was paged."

Dr. Enns wanted a conference of N.S. residents and interns at eight o'clock.

Well, there went his date! He didn't even have time to call C'ele. Dr. Enns nodded when he came in and began at once on the subjects which he had on hand. They were various—a matter of timekeeping, a matter of legibility on charts, an item of hospital gossip which had been traced to N.S., the frequent presence of an N.S. intern on other wards.

"We get visitors, too," said the junior resident.

They did. Dr. Iserman, for one. Red shifted his position in his chair and tipped it back against the wall.

"We do get visitors," agreed Dr. Enns. "But their freedom to visit is a matter for their Chief of Service. Now I come to the matter of giving a diagnosis prematurely either to the patient or to his family."

This was the reason the meeting had been called. During this current week someone had talked out of turn and trouble had been abundant. The senior resident was responsible for his doctors-in-training. Red paid close attention to all that was being said.

There were interruptions; doctors were called out and returned. Records were sent for. There was a bit of arguing. . . .

It was nine o'clock before Red could call C'ele.

"Don't tell me!" she said, her voice cool and clear. "You're going to be late!"

Red laughed. "It does look that way," he agreed. "But

Enns—"

"Your boss," said C'ele, a certain twang to her voice.

Red could feel his neck getting hot. "He *is* my boss, C'ele!" he said crisply.

"Yes. I *know!*"

There was a silence. Red thought he could wait it out. But he was the offender, the one to blame. C'ele had just been sitting there, waiting for him to show or the phone to ring.

He coughed. "I'm sorry," he murmured. "Do we still have a date?"

"Oh, sure," said C'ele. "I don't have any will power, either."

"Ten minutes," said Red, shrugging and putting the phone down. He got up from the chair—he was tired. But he'd said ten minutes. He changed, fast.

What with one thing and another—down in the parking lot someone had boxed in Red's car—he reached C'ele's apartment closer to ten o'clock than nine, and he expected her to have things to say. She did not. Not right away.

She was ready, a red coat over her white wool dress. She looked nice—C'ele always did—but she didn't want to stop for Red to say so. "I'm sorry we're late," she said when Red put her into the car seat. "It's a good bunch tonight, and you're on call, aren't you?"

"Emergency, yes. Clevie, the floor supe, won't call me unless she feels she has to."

"Isn't Enns still around?" she asked, putting a net thing over her hair. On her it looked good.

"He's around," Red agreed. "He always stays close by."

"With you always in his shadow," said C'ele plaintively.

"Oh, come off it, C'ele. I'm grateful Enns is the kind of

chief to stay on the job. The sun would be mighty hot if I'd try to stand out in it alone."

"But I'd like to see you do it, just once. Wouldn't you?"

Red pursed his lips and thought about that. "I don't know," he said slowly. "It seems to me, generally, that I am doing all right. I am still learning my trade; I need advice and instruction."

"When you're made senior resident, isn't it a sign that you've graduated?"

"A senior resident is given authority, responsibility, and plenty of headaches. In that respect it is good to have Enns on hand to help get me through and over them." Red was smiling. He knew better than C'ele the position of a senior resident and his need for a good Chief of Service. Red had such a man.

He drove with concentration, thankful that his mother had given him this good car. He cut through the park. There was some snow, but not enough to give trouble. The lights were haloed and sparkly. It was a pretty world.

It took exactly ten minutes to cross the park to the restaurant at the far side of it. Red had that time down to the second.

The party was in full blast when he and C'ele came in—twenty young people, talking loud, laughing; the noise of the orchestra a little too loud, its beat too insistent; the smell of hot bread, cheese, coffee, wine, and garlic, of course.

Red and C'ele were greeted with squeals and shouts. "Look, folks, here's Ben Casey at last!" yelped someone. People moved about, all friends. Most of them were interns and residents at the hospital; their dates were wives, sweethearts, with a new girl or two looking a little bewildered at the talk and the jokes.

Red was immediately as gay as anyone. He acknowledged his role as Ben Casey. "Only I smile!" he qualified.
"See? Teeth!"

He ordered his pizza—he was starved! C'ele?

Yes, she would eat now, too, while she had a chance, but
no anchovies, please.

Red wanted anchovies, sausage—the works! He got up
to kiss Sylvia Sebaja.

And when the pizza came, the coffee, the glass of wine,
Red talked.

"He's really a kook," he heard someone explaining to
someone else. "He can talk up a storm on any subject—real
crazy ideas he gets."

Red was having a fine time. He danced; he came back to
the table and made outrageous fun of one of the girls who
wore a full-skirted frock and, each time before she sat
down, flipped the skirts up and out of the way.

"We could charge admission if you'd sit on the room
side of the table," Red told her. "And use the money to pay
for some more wine."

His friends called him a kook and understood him. Dr.
Iserman disapproved of him. One of the strange girls—not
in medical work—asked her escort what sort of doctor Red
Cahill was.

"I'm only an intern," Dr. Damron reminded her. "And a
rotating one at that. I'm due to work soon with Cahill;
you'd better ask C'ele to tell you about him."

His girl—her name was Beverly—looked across at C'ele.
"Are you his wife?" she asked, wide-eyed.

"I'm not anybody's wife," said C'ele.

"But you'd know . . ."

"What kind of doctor Red Cahill is?" asked C'ele. "Oh,
sure, I know."

"In twenty-five words or less, C'ele," suggested Vince.

"I can do it in one word," C'ele told him. "And that word would be *big*. Capitals. B-I-G. Size, nature, doctoring. He's a big guy. Right, Vince?"

Vince shrugged and watched Red dancing with the girl who flipped her skirts.

"His patients adore him," C'ele told Damron's date. "Most of them do. Some, of course, are afraid of him."

Beverly was shocked. "Oh, not really!"

C'ele laughed. "No," she said kindly, "not really. Anyway, as a doctor, he's just a big store front."

Beverly was a pretty thing, with soft yellow hair and enormous blue eyes. Now she frowned over what C'ele had said.

"What does she mean, Cliff?" she asked her companion. "*Store front.*"

"I'll tell you," said C'ele. "I just meant that when Red works the chief surgeon is there behind him, always, putting out the merchandise."

On the small dance floor Red Cahill was whirling his partner until her full green skirts belled out. Beverly shook her pretty head. "I don't know what you're talking about, C'ele," she confessed, "but Dr. Cahill does seem to be a real kook."

"He is, really," said C'ele solemnly. "And I'm in love with him." Her face was serene.

"Then," said Beverly, "are you a kook too?"

"Oh, of course. And one day Red and I will have five or six little kooks. It will be just *loverly!*"

"I bet," said Beverly.

C'ele's eyebrows went up. She had expected something gushing and burbling. "It *will* be loverly," she said again, solemnly.

22

"But you aren't serious? I mean, shouldn't you remember that he's a kook? That could be very important in a marriage, couldn't it?"

C'ele pushed her chair back enough so that she could look down the room to where Red now was standing at the bar, talking to a group of people, all strangers to C'ele and probably to him.

"Red's not always a kook," she said slowly. "Beverly, he's not ever a kook when he is being a doctor. Never then. And the man I am going to marry is the doctor Red is. That is, I'll marry him if and when I can ever get him loose from Enns's gown strings."

Abruptly Vince Sebaja pushed the table away from him, to let him get up from the red-upholstered wall settee. Sylvia looked at him in protest, then she nodded.

Vince held his hand out to C'ele. "Let's dance," he said firmly. He was a tall man, not so "big" as Red. His hair was a dark cap, his skin was brown, his eyes were hooded. Now he was being insistent.

C'ele looked up at him. "This skirt is too tight," she said.

"We'll dance just the same," Vince told her sternly.

Now C'ele didn't bother to look at him. When he pulled her chair out, she stood up. She feared Vince Sebaja. She admired what the young man had done for himself; she knew better than almost anyone what it had meant for him to become a senior resident in Psychoneurology. She knew because—

She put her hand on his shoulder, felt his fingers close around her other hand, "I brought you out here," said Vince, bending so that his lips were at her ear, "to tell you to *shut up!*"

C'ele said nothing. She moved her feet and let Vince

23

guide her around the small floor.

"I don't think you should talk about Red," he said. "Not at all or to anybody. Almost anything you'd say could get him into trouble, you know. Or do you?"

Briefly C'ele lifted her eyes to look into Vince's face. "That Beverly—"

"Aghhh! It isn't Beverly! I'm thinking of all the scoop-ears about."

Yes, there were such ears. Iserman's, for one. And his wife's. Even the nice intern, Damron, might unwittingly repeat some of what C'ele had said.

"I'm sorry," she murmured.

"I hope you mean it," said Vince sternly. "Be sorry, too, that you brought Dr. Enns into it. After all, he is Red's sponsor."

"So?" C'ele's voice was cool.

Vince backed her into a corner and put his hands on her wrists so that she had to face him, though she would not look into his eyes. "So," he said roughly, "if Cahill is going to have trouble, let him get himself into it. He won't need your help!"

"But," C'ele gasped, "I don't want to hurt Red!"

"Then *don't* hurt him!"

C'ele drew her hands away from Dr. Sebaja's grasp. A tremor was rising within her, and she knew that he would detect it. He was a perceptive doctor and man. C'ele feared him.

Not because of any fault in Vince. But a year ago C'ele had told a big lie. A year year ago C'ele had met Red Cahill for the first time. A year ago she had had her first date with him, and she had lied to him. Vince must know that she had lied. Perhaps he also knew why.

Her reason had been good, but C'ele didn't want Red

24

ever to know that she had lied. Vince Sebaja was probably the only one who could tell him that she had lied and why. It was her reason for lying that shamed C'ele.

Red's immediate impact upon her had been tremendous. The big man with his clear, honest eyes, his ready smile, his kindly ways—she wanted such a man to be interested in her, but she had no hope that he would be. So she had lied about herself to him; she had answered his questions with lies—not wanting to. But she could *not* tell him truthfully about her background! Where she had grown up, about her family! That background, and that family, was a world apart from the world of Red Cahill.

And he would have no basis of interest in such things.

So she had told him—led him to think—that she was a college girl, ready now to earn her living in the records room of the big medical complex. To his question about her family she had shrugged. So—no family. All this was done on impulse, to impress an attractive man on their first date.

Now it often worried C'ele, this deception of Red. In a year she had come to know him well; their dates were about as frequent as a senior resident could manage. Had the deception been worth while? Was her picture of her background what had decided things between them? What about the day when he found out that she had deceived him? He might laugh about it; he might not. C'ele worried about these questions and their answers. Vince, a boy from her home town, knew the truth about C'ele, and he and Red . . .

"Red Cahill," Vince said now, "is my friend!"

Yes, indeed, Red was Vince's friend. The way men are friends together, with nothing able to change that fact. Once, months ago, worried about the things which Vince could tell, C'ele had tried her hand at drawing Red away from Vince Sebaja. She had quickly seen that she was on the wrong track. So . . .

If it were a matter between women, Vince would have immediately told his friend all about C'ele. But men were different. Vince knew that his background did not matter with Red. He probably thought that C'ele's true story wouldn't matter either. She hoped he thought that.

But she still didn't think that was the case between a man and a woman. Not between the man and a girl who wanted him to be securely her own. In a year's time C'ele's reasons for wanting Red Cahill had changed a little. Now it no longer mattered too much that this attractive man had—or would have one day—"pots of money." It did not even matter too much any more that he was attractive. "Cute" was the word she first had used about him. But her wanting him had not changed. Intently, completely, C'ele did want him, anyway she could get him.

And Vince knew that too.

Which made two of them worried.

3 ❀❀❀❀❀❀❀❀❀❀❀❀❀❀❀❀❀❀❀❀❀❀❀❀❀❀❀❀❀❀❀

THE snow which had fallen unseasonably on Halloween was added to during the following days. This doubled the emergency admittance rate at the big hospital, and a full percentage of all accident cases came up to Neurosurgery. Dr. Enns, Chief of Service, Dr. Cahill, senior resident surgeon, and Dr. Polly Ferris, anesthesiologist, along with the other residents, interns, nurses, orderlies, and aides, were, to quote Red, earning their keep.

On the black, cold morning when Red was awakened at four o'clock, his first thought, as he reached for the phone, was that they had a heavy surgery schedule and he needed his rest and sleep.

"Hello!" he barked hoarsely into the phone. "Cahill . . . "

He stiffened. "No!" he protested.

"How bad?"

He listened. He said thank you. Yes, he said, he would do as asked.

He put the phone down, and for a second he sat staring at it.

Then he bent over and put on his shoes. He still was

27

thinking about the heavy surgery schedule. How would he manage?

He dashed water into his face to waken himself. He went out on the floor, to the desk, and told the night supe. He asked for the o.r. schedule and studied it, head down, a frown between his eyes.

Then he reached for the telephone. He would call Polly.

It took awhile for her to answer. But when she did . . .

"Red Cahill here, Doctor. I had a call, fifteen minutes ago. Dr. Enns was in a car smashup at midnight, and—"

"Of course he's hurt! Listen, will you, Polly? I don't know many details. He was coming back from that talk he made at the University. Somehow he was involved in a wreck. He's in a hospital at Glen Owen—that's on the far side of the river, you know."

"Yes, he's hurt."

"No, not too badly that he couldn't ask them to send for me."

Polly's voice came in a rush of words. Red sighed and leaned against the counter. She was really upset.

"Yes," he said firmly, "I am going. I'll get things lined up here as quickly as I can, then I'll take off. I'll keep in touch—"

"Red," said Polly, "I want to go with you."

"Oh, now, look, Polly—"

"It won't be much out of your way for you to stop and pick me up."

He couldn't talk her out of it; he didn't have time to try, so he agreed. But he was shaking his head all the time he talked to the residents who would be in charge—they must explain to attendings, to patients, and, well, generally take over.

He didn't know how the wreck had occurred. Of course the roads were snow-packed. He didn't know how badly Enns was hurt. Yes, he would phone, if he could. He walked down the hall to change his clothes.

At five he was able to go down to his car; he picked Polly up at five-twenty, and they were on their way.

"It's about forty miles," Red answered her question.

No, he had had no further word. "I called you only to tell you about the changed schedule."

She nodded. "I'll not be any trouble to you, Red," she said softly.

He smiled at her. "I know you won't be."

Polly sighed. "He's a wonderful person, Red."

"Sure is. The best surgeon I've ever seen."

"But I meant as a *person.*"

"That, too. Yes. Though he keeps his ethical distance with chaps like me."

"You'd find out about him as a person if you ever needed his help."

"I do need his help—constantly."

"As a doctor."

"Yes." Of course he had meant that. A question flashed through Red's mind. Did Polly— Red glanced at her briefly.

She was a slender woman, this morning wrapped in a black coat, with a black scarf bound tightly about her head and throat. Her face looked drawn and pale.

"You're fond of Bill Enns," he said gruffly.

Polly shrugged. "What woman could help but be?" she asked softly.

Red hunched forward across the wheel. Well! Here was a thing! Dr. Enns . . .

His own situation pushed Polly's out of the way. "If

Enns is laid up for any time," he said, more to himself than to Polly, "the prospect is grim for me."

"You do lean on him, don't you?"

"Well, of course I do. He knows so much—he's *there* . . . "

And now he would not be.

It was six-thirty—a bit later—when they reached the town of Glen Owen and located the hospital. Polly showed every sign of sticking close to Red. She announced in so many words that she would not go off to some waiting room while he talked to the doctors and saw Bill.

"I'm a doctor too. Don't forget that."

Red did not forget it. He would not. She could, and did, follow him to the desk, then up to the surgery floor. The man who came to talk to them wore a gray gown. He was Dr. La Fleur, surgeon, and Chief of Medical Services at the hospital. He shook hands with Red, bowed to Polly, and said, "Come in here; we'll have coffee."

In here was a general utility room, squeezed into the floor plan. There was a sink and a shelf filled with vases. There was a hot plate and a carafe of coffee, a carton of paper cups. There were even a couple of chairs.

Dr. La Fleur said, yes, he would take them to see Dr. Enns. He was in fair shape—under sedation. "We have taken some X-rays, but, as you know, in an accident of that sort—"

"What sort?" asked Red sharply. He had a cup of coffee in his hand, but he would not sit down. He stood at the window and looked across the snowy hills to the brown line of the river. His muscles ached with their tenseness.

Dr. La Fleur glanced at his watch, then he told what he knew about the accident. There was a rise in the two-lane road, and Dr. Enns's car, coming up over it, had found, directly in front of him, this pickup truck stopped before making a left turn. Enns had thrown the wheel over hard. "That's how his wrist was broken. It was in a position of impact."

Red turned about and glared at the man. Polly put up her hand as if to hush him. Dr. La Fleur was doing all right. . . .

"Yes, that is bad for a man like him," the surgeon agreed. "To go on: he clipped the other car, then he hit the shoulder and skidded into a bank. The old man and he were brought here in the same ambulance."

Red made a growling sound.

"The other driver," the doctor continued, "was old. Seventy-five. That place in the road is bad—there have been other accidents. Left turns should be prohibited."

"Was he thrown out?" asked Polly. "Dr. Enns?"

"I—yes, he was. At least I think so."

"Good God, man!" said Red prayerfully.

"We—I was busy with the patients, Doctor. And this morning I have had no time to talk to anyone. I am telling you what I know."

Red muttered an apology. "It's just—"

"I understand. These things come on one and hit hard. Well, as you know, the roads were snow-packed. Dr. Enns's car came to rest against this bank. There were other cars following—people were good to him. Of course there was no doctor close by, but one of the women took off her fur coat and spread it over him. I think, before the ambulance came, someone laid him flat."

"Your ambulance?" asked Red tightly.

"No. We use a service."

"Undertaker?"

"Well, yes. The driver and his assistant lifted Dr. Enns to the stretcher and put it into the ambulance. His hip was dislocated, his wrist broken. There are abrasions on his face. His car was badly smashed . . . "

"And with a dislocated hip, amateurs—people being *good* to him!—laid him flat, then someone else 'lifted him to the stretcher' without splinting, I suppose?" Red paced the room, his face stormy. "No attempt at immobilization? Just dangle the limbs, and toss the whole mess into the wagon! There were fur coats to spread over him but no doctor within—how many miles, Doctor?"

Dr. La Fleur drank his coffee. "The accident took place about twenty-five miles away from here, sir." He spoke quietly. "We are the closest hospital. We do not have staff men available to answer ambulance calls. Dr. Enns was hurt —not critically, but seriously. His leg—his hip—*is* dislocated—"

Red groaned.

"Wasn't there a doctor closer?" asked Polly.

"Possibly. But I will point out that your Dr. Enns was unconscious. His car hit that bank with an awful smash. You are right that his leg might have been immobilized, though if a doctor had been riding in the following car, except for a splint, he could have done little more than the ambulance men did. They picked him up, they brought him here. We cleaned things up a little last night, took X-rays, and sent for his friends as soon as he was conscious enough to tell us who his friends were. And no doctor, on the spot, could have done anything else. Stop the bleeding, send for an ambulance—"

"That's all they'd do?" cried Red. He was frightened and angry. "Riding along the road, see someone hurt— doctors would just let the poor guy lie there! With no

32

attempt to straighten the limb or splint the hand?"

"Oh, a simple splint, maybe. But, no. A doctor—*especially* a doctor—would, or could, do little else!"

"That's crazy!" shouted Red.

Dr. La Fleur again looked at his watch. "Young man," he said firmly, "if ever you are in such a spot, *you* would be crazy to do more!"

Polly and Red spent a busy morning, during which they ate breakfast, saw Dr. Enns, talked again to the hospital doctors, looked at the X-rays, and phoned three times to their home hospital. They asked that someone from the orthopedic staff drive to Glen Owen. He did, and after a consultation it was decided to take Bill Enns home. He could be, and should be, cared for at the Center.

Polly offered to ride in the ambulance with him, and she did, Red's car closely following. He could see her comforting Bill, talking to him. Once she put her head down against the injured man's shoulder, the gesture tender.

Red shook his head and frowned. Polly Ferris had a husband—and two children. Of college age, she had said.

Bill Enns was unmarried and a swell guy.

But if things were as they looked to be . . .

What a day! What a day!

It had indeed been a day, and the next was another one, and the next, and the next. Dr. Enns underwent surgery and was, at his request, brought up to N.S. for rest and care. The senior resident caught up on his schedule and tried to meet each new thing as it came, feeling as if he lived and worked in the cone of a tornado; he tried not to think, or even talk, about Dr. Enns's accident. Sometimes he could not help going back over it in sickening waves of speculation. If that old man had not stopped, if there had been better on-the-spot care, if, even at the hospital, something had been done! A broken wrist, a dislocated hip—for a surgeon! Had one of the clumsy handlers dislocated that hip?

Dr. Enns was cheerful and sure that things would mend quickly.

Then, four days after the accident, the whole Center, and especially Neurosurgery, was thrown into a new turmoil. New X-rays had been taken, and Dr. Enns had been allowed to view them along with the Orthopedics man. Bill saw a crack in his hip. The Orthopedic Chief said he didn't think so. The Ortho resident said he wasn't sure . . .

But Bill Enns said there *was* a crack, and he wanted instant surgery!

The Center whirled in circles of fear, debate, hot arguments; old friends quarreled on the subject; Vince Sebaja and Red Cahill quarreled.

Polly Ferris shook her head. "Ten times a day," she marveled, "we solve such questions for our patients. Why should it be so difficult for one of the staff?"

"Doctors make the worst patients," said the supervisor. "Haven't you heard?"

The Chief of Ortho was a bit huffy, though he certainly wanted to do the best for Enns! He asked for a consultation. Enns agreed, and after more discussion an eminent orthopedic man was selected. The famous specialist was called.

Could, he asked, the X-rays be sent to him in Chicago? He would go by them; he was sure that Dr. Ebenloh could and had made a competent visual and contact diagnosis.

Dr. Enns accepted this. Red Cahill did not. The man could have made a trip of this sort—wasn't anyone interested in this particular patient?

It took Polly Ferris to get Red calmed down and re-store N.S. to something like functioning order. That floor, of all places, could not continue to be the wild shop it had been for the last five days!

If he were not already upset by this new development in his case, Polly would have appealed to Dr. Enns. As it was, she did speak to the Chief of Surgical Services.

"Dr. Cahill should know what his duties are," said that busy man.

Polly shook her head. "I am sure he does know, Doctor. But he is used to having Dr. Enns take the final responsi-bility."

"Yes. All right. I'll see what I can do."

What he did was to call a meeting of the Residents' Committee. And these staff doctors assembled the Center's residents, as was done frequently. That night Red almost decided that he could not make the meeting.

But eventually he did show up, standing near the door, leaning against the wall of the conference room, ready to go out again if called.

The Chief of Surgical Services took over the meeting, and after one or two items had been presented and dis-cussed, he mentioned the situation up on N.S. with the Chief of Service incapacitated.

"That unfortunate condition has recently affected Dr. Cahill and his assistants. It could, with equal suddenness, affect any of you men. Now, what is the procedure? What responsibilities are put upon the senior resident? What can and should be expected of the other doctors on the service?"

There was a lot of talk; many details were brought out and examined. The matter of rotating interns, the absolute-

35

final say on duty hours, split shifts . . . Red listened, not laughing when others laughed, but gradually accepting the fact that help was being offered to him.

At the end of the meeting he spoke with the Chief.

"You'll do all right, Cahill," that eminent surgeon told him. "Just carry on until Bill is able to resume. Other men are available to you. You have your regular list of attendings."

"Yes, sir."

"Of course you are responsible for surgery on N.S., but you have been. However, you are to ask for help if you need it."

Red went upstairs and found that the diagnosis had come in from the orthopedic specialist. If there was a crack in Dr. Enns's femur, it was hairline. The treatment for the dislocation of that same hip should be adequate to care for any break.

"Did it make Dr. Enns feel better?" Red asked Polly.

"Yes. He'd been asleep. Just turned over and went to sleep."

"Good." Red flexed his arms and shoulder muscles.

"Tell me about the meeting," said Polly.

Together they walked down the hall, tall, good-looking people in their white garments. They would get coffee and talk. Red talked first, Polly murmuring agreement. Of course, she said, he could handle the responsibilities put upon him; he was a well-trained man, in his third year of residency. All residents were well-trained. Dr. Enns soon would be available for advice; they had good attendings— most of them . . .

Polly refilled his coffee cup and sat gazing at the big man in his white coat. "I wonder," she asked thoughtfully, "if you have any idea, Red, of what it means to me to come back to work here in the hospital?"

"You like it. I know that."

"Yes, I do," said Polly.

"Maybe you should never have given up your career. I mean, other women marry and have children—"

"I know. But at the time I thought I was doing the right thing." She glanced up at Red. "I was pretty darned dewy-eyed, you know."

"And you don't do things by halves."

"No. No, I don't. Now," she said, speaking slowly, considering her words, "I think I appreciate my work more than I did when I was young, more than I would if I had not given it up for a while. It's more—more intense. The sounds, the smells—"

"Oh, bro-*ther!*" said Red.

"I know. But just the essence of the floor—alcohol, flowers, soup, rubber, hot cloth—and the way things look!" Her face glowed with eagerness. "I come upstairs every morning, and excitement fills me. The elevator door opens, I step out—and there's the shining floor, the lights, the nurses gathered at the station, the call board, a patient in a chair, a doctor walking fast, his white shoes flipping up and down in fast rhythm." Her hands illustrated.

"It's *life*, Red!" she said tensely. "And I had come to a place where I thought my life was over. At least, the thrill . . . " Her voice trailed away.

Red stood up, took her cup and his, and rinsed them at the sink. "Let's get back to that work you like so well," he suggested.

She smiled and walked out of the room ahead of him. "I'll peek in at Bill," she said.

Red watched her go down the hall. She was a fairly tall woman, slender, with a thick mop of red-brown hair. Her wide-set eyes were hazel brown and steady, her full-lipped mouth sensitive as a child's is sensitive, ready for hurt, for joy—and for wonder.

Dr. Enns would be glad to see Polly. By then the ward, the floor, the whole hospital, was pretty sure that Dr. Enns was in love with Polly Ferris. They were expecting her to divorce her husband and marry Bill. And everyone felt pretty good about it.

But Red Cahill frowned. He had become wary of deciding that anything would move along smoothly in an expected groove.

Those days Red frowned a lot, which was not like him, but understandable to most of his associates. The man was carrying a tremendous responsibility, and he felt the full weight of it. He could, and did, talk to Dr. Enns about things, bringing a chart to the bedside, asking advice on a development which must be handled—"The Millers want to take Judy home with a nurse. How about it?"

But that was not the same as having Enns on his feet, standing quietly observant in the background, always ready to move forward with a word of advice, of praise— or an equally ready word of sharp rebuke.

It was the difference which put Red into a blue funk which he recognized as not being any improvement over his first numb shock.

"I don't know what to think about myself," he confessed to Vince Sebaja on the day when he brought his lunch tray over to the table occupied by his friend, ready to make some sort of apology for anything he might have said in the excitement and stress of Dr. Enns's accident.

Vince brushed the apology away as accepted and really not necessary. "I recognized your delicate condition," he drawled.

"Er—yes," said Red, beginning to eat his soup, but lifting his head alertly at the first syllable from the enunciator.

"You can't imagine what it is like," he tried to tell Vince.

"I'll accept you as a clinical example," said Vince. Red frowned.

"How long has it been since you took some free time?" Vince asked. "This pie is terrible."

"The pie here is always terrible. They know we'll eat it anyway. How can I take free time, Vince?"

"You know," said his friend, leaning back in his chair, "you are getting to sound more and more like Iserman, the indispensable doctor."

"Agggh!"

"But you are, Red. And I can't see any prospect of that helping you, me—or Neurosurgery."

"I—well, I do feel responsible."

"Good. Fine. Don't you have some pretty good men on N.S.?"

"Residents, you mean? Yes, they're good. But—"

"So you're underfoot all the time. So they get no training in responsibility. So—is that what you are for? Besides, I hear your disposition has gone real sour. That you not only snarl, you *bite!*"

Red considered the lettuce leaf under his fork. "I chew 'em all out, regular," he admitted morosely. "I'm scared, I'm worried, and I take it out on anyone handy. You—or anyone else."

"Me," said Vince cheerfully, "I don't take it. The residents, interns, and nurses on your service have to take it. So why don't you spend an evening with C'ele?"

"C'ele?" Red looked up, surprised.

"Yeah, C'ele. The little girl with the big yen for you. Remember her?"

Red sighed. "I haven't even talked to her for two weeks. She'd know about Enns . . ."

"Yes. And in case she doesn't, you go to see her and tell her about him. She'll be fascinated." Vince stood up.

"But—" said Red. "Wait a minute, Sebaja. What can C'ele do for me or even find to say?"

"I'll bet she'll think of something," said Vince as he walked away.

Red shrugged and ate his gingerbread. But he would go to see C'ele! He did go.

He didn't phone first—something might come up. If she were not at home, he would return to the hospital where he really belonged.

But C'ele was at home. A lamp glowed behind the drawn curtains of her window; she opened the gray door immediately, taking down the chain and smiling to see Red.

"Well, come in, stranger!" she said gaily.

Red stepped inside and dropped his coat across the nearest chair. "I've been busy," he said, coming across to the couch.

C'ele curled up in the big chair. "Want a drink? Food?"

"Later maybe."

"Not on call?"

"No, but they know where to find me."

C'ele nodded. She wore a white blouse—a little frilly. There was embroidery or something on it. Her stretch pants were black, and on her they looked good.

"Vince told me to come over here, " Red said, stretching out his legs.

"Oh?" said C'ele. "Why?"

Red shrugged. "I think he was practicing his psychiatry on me. He evidently thought I should talk to you. Or that you should talk to me. Maybe you know what about."

He was not looking at C'ele. And there was something about his face—it looked a little stern, and his words, *Maybe you know* . . .

C'ele clenched her hands hard against the cushions of the chair. Fear swept over her in a cold and sickening wave. Vince had told Red about her! The truth was out.

She closed her eyes and leaned her head back, seeking a moment to think about what she would say, how she would say it. Vividly against her eyelids there came a picture of that home, as it would look to Red. The brick house built into the side of the hill, the portico which was formed by the jutting second story, the bricked floor of that porch, the wine barrel set out to dry and sweeten. The chickens that pecked among the dry grass of the yard and ventured up on the bricks. This cold weather her father would not be sitting on the porch, but his chair would be there. And C'ele could see him as he sat there in the summer—suspenders over his undershirt, his mustache ends a little stained, his thin cigar, the way he greeted his friends.

"Hi-ya, Coon?" he would call cordially. "How's the old woman?"

In C'ele's home town a man's wife, even as a bride as young as sixteen, became his "old woman." C'ele hated the term. She hated her father's coal-mining friends, his home, his undershirt . . .

Thinking of those hated things, not wanting to bring them into her neat living room, the color drained from C'ele's face. Maybe Red wouldn't care—about her home, about her father and the wine barrel. Maybe he wouldn't even care that C'ele had fibbed to him. Or would he?

At least he would think that she was silly. Which wasn't too bad, except that C'ele wanted him to like her. A lot.

Desperately she got up out of the chair, went to the

41

small kitchen, and got two cans of beer. She found some crackers and took a square of cheese from the refrigerator, then she came back to the living room and set the tray on the coffee table. She curled up beside Red.

He looked at her questioningly.

She cuddled against his arm. "I've missed you," she said plaintively.

"You knew I was busy. You knew about Dr. Enns . . ."

"Oh sure, I knew. But I still missed you."

Red sighed. He leaned forward and cut a slice of cheese. When he sat back, his right arm went around C'ele's shoulder, but it was an impersonal gesture. It meant nothing, except that he was there, big, and warm—and Red.

She rubbed her head against his shoulder, and he let her. No more. He was eating that piece of cheese.

C'ele sat erect and turned to look into his face. In the light of the lamp beside him his short hair was really blond. It grew to a little point on his forehead; her hand touched his cheek, and his eyes slid her way.

"Why, Red?" she asked plaintively. "Why aren't you in love with me?"

"Oh, C'ele . . . " He was laughing at her.

"No," she insisted. "I'm serious. This means a lot to me. You and I—we've known each other for over a year. We have fun together—why *can't* we love the people we ought to? You and I—our life together would be good. If you—"

She sat back and shook her head. "But as things are—" she said morosely.

Red's arm drew her back against his shoulder. His hand stroked her smooth, dark hair. And he sat thoughtful, not speaking at all. Probably not thinking about what C'ele had said either.

Well, she would wait. She was used to that with Red. If

he wanted to sit relaxed on her couch, and would let her sit close beside him—why, that was what C'ele wanted too.

She was even getting a little drowsy when finally he stirred. "You got your wish, didn't you, C'ele?" he asked.

"What wish?"

He laughed shortly. "My shadow, as you call him, is gone."

"I don't know what you are talking about, Red."

"I am talking about Dr. Enns. You have always claimed—"

"Oh, that!"

"Yes, that!"

"He won't be laid up permanently, will he? And while he is, aren't there other doctors to tell you what and how to do?"

Red nodded. "Yes," he agreed. "Yes, there sure are!"

He set the glass on the table; he stood up. He went over to the chair, took his coat, and thrust his arms into it. "Thanks for the beer, C'ele," he said. "I'll be seeing you."

And he went out, disappointed in the evening. He had hoped that Vince would be right. That C'ele might be able to—well, do something for him.

And C'ele sat on the couch, watching the bubbles die in her beer glass. Of all the flops . . .

Often she had made a good evening on much less. But not tonight. Not tonight.

4 ❀❀❀❀❀❀❀❀❀❀❀❀❀❀❀❀❀❀❀❀❀❀❀❀❀❀❀

BUT perhaps the break in the hospital routine, perhaps the hour with C'ele, did help. For from then on Dr. Cahill visibly relaxed his tension on the floor. He had always worked hard and expected others to do the same. He had always been absorbed in each patient, anxious about them, expending every ounce of his knowledge, his willingness to study and work, upon them.

But now, for the first time in two weeks, he was again ready to joke with them and about them to the other doctors. Red was coming round, Polly told Dr. Enns, who was improving to the point where he could be told about the spin into which his senior resident had gone.

"He shouldn't depend that much on me!" cried Bill.

"He does. He has."

"Then I have failed in what I was supposed to be teaching him."

"You couldn't fail in anything."

Bill smiled at her. "I am glad I have you fooled, Polly. But maybe I should talk to Cahill."

"I wouldn't now. He seems to be getting back on his feet. He has even agreed to go to Dr. Sebaja's party Sunday afternoon."

44

"What party is that?"

"I guess it will be gay. It's a wedding—on the Hill."

Dr. Enns laughed. "It will be gay, all right." He tugged impatiently at the traction apparatus which overhung his bed. "If Ebenloh would ever let me get out of this torture rack," he fumed, "I'd go to that wedding myself."

"You'll make the next one."

"Those things . . . Ever been to one, Polly?"

"Not me."

So Bill told her—about the food, the wine, the music and the dancing, the tricks that were played. The family hired a hall, he said, or engaged a restaurant. "If you don't get drunk within an hour, you aren't trying."

On Sunday it was all there, just as the Chief had described it. Dr. Cahill left the hospital at four, still doubtful about taking as much as twelve hours. Enns said less than twelve wouldn't do him a bit of good.

Red laughed and agreed. He picked up C'ele and kissed her when he got into the car beside her.

"You're feeling better," she told him.

"I've been told to enjoy myself."

She nodded. They both could take a bit of that. This past month had been rugged!

The celebration was going full blast when they arrived at the restaurant. As they opened the outer doors, the noise of it hit them.

"It's going to be good," said Red happily.

It was good. The place was filled with happy people in their best clothes. Vince's cousin, the bride, was radiant, the bridegroom flushed and triumphant. There was a small and lively orchestra. At the end of the room food and drink were set out abundantly. Laughter rang out freely;

45

talk was varied, intimate talk at twosome tables up on the balcony, argumentative talk, gay talk, rowdy talk around the big table which extended the length of the hall.

One could get drunk on gaiety quite as soon and as deeply as one did on wine. Red danced with the bride; he danced with C'ele, and with half the other women present, young and old. The polka, the waltz, the mashed potato, and the frug—it was all one to him.

"He never does anything by halves," said Sylvia Sebaja admiringly.

"He and C'ele are certainly a couple of wild ones," pronounced Dr. Iserman reprovingly.

"Oh, they're just young and having fun!" Sylvia protested.

"It's pretty wild fun," pointed out a woman farther down the table. "I didn't know it before, but C'ele can be as wild as Red."

"Yes, she goes along with whatever he does. Outside of his profession, I mean, of course."

Vince Sebaja got up to fetch a new bottle of wine. "C'ele backs Red up in his job, too," he said, filling glasses. "And of course in that, as well, the man does everything intensely."

Out on the floor Red whirled C'ele away, caught her, lifted her. . . .

The party went on for hours. Even Red finally got tired and a little drunk. Dr. Iserman got very drunk and was miserable. He was quarrelsome, too, and became a nuisance to Red and C'ele who had retreated to a small table up on the balcony to "get strength enough to go home."

Red took a little of the small man's pestering, but when Iserman persisted, the big man stood up, lifted the little doctor by his elbows, leaned over the balcony rail, and set him down. His friends at the big table, laughing, tenderly laid Iserman prone upon the floor, then rolled him in the length of red carpet which was there. They left him, bundled snugly, near the door and snoring mightily.

"I won't want to be you tomorrow," Vince warned Red, "when he tells you what he thinks of you."

"Tomorrow even Iserman won't have the strength to say much of anything."

"Think we ought to go home?" asked C'ele.

Red squinted at his watch. "I think I have two more hours. *Then* I think I ought to go home!"

The next day, of course, Dr. Cahill had a head. "A bloomer," he told Polly Ferris. "I must be badly out of practice."

Polly fetched him a glass of tomato juice, and he drank it, grimacing. "The only thing good for my kind of head," he told the anesthetist, "is not to go to Hunky wedding parties."

"I heard about Dr. Iserman."

Red chuckled. "I never saw him looking as good as he did with his head and feet sticking out of the ends of that hall carpet."

"He says you humiliated him in public."

Red laughed. "Oh, he helped. Come on, Polly, let's get to work."

"You're able?"

"Sure I'm able. In fact, I'll be brilliant."

"But not modest."

"You can't have everything."

Smiling, Polly followed him. She would never, she told herself, ask more of life than to have her son, Joe, grow

47

into a man like Red Cahill. Or that her daughter should marry such a man.

The morning's work went well, and Polly and the resident surgeon came out of recovery ready to congratulate each other, or themselves individually if that should be necessary. They both wanted coffee, and Red was now in the mood for food if any was available.

"Special Diets can always turn up toast," Polly suggested.

"Let's pay them a visit," said Red, starting down the hall.

But they had not taken ten steps when Polly's head lifted. "That's my page," she said, a frown between her eyes. Who would be paging her?

"It must be home," she said anxiously to Red who had followed her to the desk. "But I've told them—" She picked up the phone, and Red saw the color drain from her cheeks. He took the telephone out of her shaking hand.

"This is Dr. Cahill," he said crisply. "Will you please repeat your message for Dr. Ferris?"

He felt as if he might be going a little white himself. The speaker at the other end of the line was also a doctor. He had been called to the Ferris home at eight o'clock, he said. Sturm Ferris, Polly's husband, had had a stroke. Yes, it was severe . . .

"Dr. Ferris will be home at once," said Dr. Cahill. "Can you stay?"

He sent a nurse with Dr. Ferris while she changed. He summoned an intern and told him to go home with Polly. "I can't get away, but you stay with her, Doctor. I'll come when I can or get in touch with you."

The intern put a coat on over his whites and was ready

48

when Polly came out in her street clothes, her eyes big, and her poise reclaimed.

Red went with them to the elevator, then he walked down the hall again to tell Bill what had happened.

Dr. Enns would have heard Polly's page; these days he was straining at the leash, wanting to be back in the full stream of affairs on N.S. And, of course, he would have to be told soon, anyway. So better make it now, and quick.

Red told it, and he made it quick. A sentence or two only sufficed; Polly Ferris's husband had suffered a stroke of some kind. The local doctor had phoned. Red had sent her home—with Damron, the intern.

Bill Enns went white too. Even his injured hand clenched upon the folded sheet. "Is there a chance he will die?" he asked gruffly.

"I don't know, sir. There was just this message. We'd come out of o.r., and this hit us."

"D'you know the man?"

"Ferris? No, sir. Do you?"

"Never met him. He's fifty—and no good, Red. No good!"

"Yes, sir."

"While Polly—" Bill Enns sighed. "I guess we'd better bring him here."

"Yes, sir," said Red. Yes, they should do that. A cerebral accident—a hemorrhage, a clot in the brain—it might be operable. . . .

He made the arrangements; he went to Recovery and looked at the morning's surgicals. It was while he was there that the call came from Emergency Admissions.

The call was urgent, but as he slipped quickly down the stairs, turned, ran down again, and again, Red's first thought was that while he was downstairs, he could get himself some food. He wondered how Polly was making it and if Damron was proving to be a help.

The nurse behind the desk of Admissions pointed to the proper cubicle, and Red ducked his head as he pushed the canvas curtain to one side and entered. An intern was in charge. The patient was a child.

Without speaking, the intern lifted the shrouding blanket and displayed a bundle of horror. Red winced and turned his head away.

The intern made a sound of agreement. Red went to the table and bent over it. One of the child's eyes was black and swollen; his cheek— "Boy?" asked Dr. Cahill.

"Boy," said the intern. He pulled the blanket clear away. Blue and ugly bruises stood out on the tender skin of the arms and chest; one leg hung twisted and limp. Red leaned closer. A burn, the size of a cigarette end, was beginning to heal on the child's stomach.

A woman, probably the little boy's mother, was standing at the far side of the table, twisting her hands into the folds of her coat. She was nervous, seemingly in a state of stupor which could be shock. Red questioned her but got no satisfactory answers about any of the injuries except the broken leg which, she said, had happened when Ronald fell out of bed.

"I called you because of the injury at the temple, Doctor," the intern told Red.

The N.S. resident nodded. The intern knew, as did Dr. Cahill, though neither wanted to admit it, that the child's condition almost certainly was not the result of one recent accident.

The doctors began to examine the child thoroughly, to chart all of his injuries; it was soon apparent that possibly for the entire four years of his life this little boy had been the victim of sudden violence.

Finally Red bathed the swollen eye and put ointment on the puffed, dry lips. He read through the chart which he and the intern had made.

"Take him to X-ray," he decided, speaking gruffly, "then bring him up to N.S. His reflexes—"

"What about his leg, Doctor?" asked the intern.

"We can get a man up from Ortho to handle that." He turned to the mother."

"Is the child's father available?" he asked.

It took rephrasing to get the question through to her, but eventually she said yes, that "he" was outside; he didn't want to see no blood.

Only slightly below his breath Red said something profane.

The intern and the assisting orderly looked up at him in surprise. Red shrugged and lifted the curtain so that they could take the child out.

"Come with me, please," he said to the mother.

They found the father talking to a couple of other men who were waiting in the lobby of Emergency Admissions. These days Emergency was big business—a large segment of the hospital personnel had to be assigned to the service.

The little boy's father was a burly man, dressed in corduroy trousers, a plaid shirt, and a jacket of fleece-lined imitation leather.

"Jim," said the mother breathlessly, "this is the doctor. He says he's got to talk to us about Ronald."

Jim came forward readily, his hand outstretched to Dr. Cahill. "Kid broke his leg, huh?" he asked.

"It's broken," Red confirmed. "Will you come down here, please?" Red pointed to a corner of the room where there was a bench. He got a chart board from the desk and sat down beside the parents.

He asked the usual questions—name, age, address, religion.

"You gonna keep the kid here, Doc?" asked Jim Scholle.

Red glanced up. "Oh, yes," he said firmly. "He has been badly injured."

"Once you put that leg in a cast, m'wife can handle him."

"I don't think so, Mr. Scholle," said Red crisply. "I am fairly sure the X-rays will show a skull fracture. He's lost a couple of teeth."

"Yeah. Got quite a fall. But if you think his head's busted—"

"I am sure it is fractured."

"You are, huh? You the head doctor?" Jim Scholle laughed at his own joke. "I meant—you're only the intern, ain't you?"

"I am the resident, Dr. Cahill." Red spoke stiffly.

"That still ain't tops, is it?"

"No. Dr. Enns is my superior."

"Good! Well, he prob'ly knows from experience that kids fall, maybe break a leg, but—"

Red tucked the chart board under his arm; he looked hard at the burly man who could have used a shave and a clean shirt. He looked hard at the woman who cowered in the shadow of this—this brutish father.

"Mr. Scholle," the young doctor said sharply, "I don't think your boy had any kind of fall. I think he was struck. I think he has been struck many times. What's more, I think you struck him. Maybe this morning, maybe last night, you slapped him across the room, and—"

"Oh, now, look, Doc—"

"*You* look! If you had been caught kicking a dog—or a horse—the authorities would step in. Well, I think someone is going to have to step in and protect your boy."

Jim Scholle got to his feet. "See here, Doc," he said, blustering, "I have my rights, and I know 'em. I brought the kid here to have his busted leg set, but you nor nobody else is going to keep him here if I don't want him to stay. Kids get hurt, sure. But—"

"You don't beat him?"

"Sure, I whack him when he needs it. Didn't your dad whack you?"

"He certainly did not break my leg or black my eye."

"And you say I did? Well, it's your word against mine, Doc. And the way I see it, that ain't very good odds for you. I'm takin' my kid home."

Red stood up. "I think you are mistaken about that, Mr. Scholle," he said coldly.

"Oh, you want to play it that way, do you, Doc?" cried the big man. "Shut up, Darleen! I'm handlin' this. Well, two can play at that game, Doc. And you'll soon find what a parents' rights are. Maybe the hospital should teach you that. But if it hasn't, I stand ready to do it for 'em. Now tell me where my kid is, and I'll go get him."

"He is in X-ray."

"You set his leg yet?"

"No. I'm down here because of his fractured skull."

"Aw, he ain't got no fractured skull."

"I don't agree."

"We don't agree on nothin', do we, Doc?"

"I'm afraid not. Now, I have other things to attend to. If you'll wait here, someone will bring you word about Ronald."

"Damn right they will," Jim Scholle was saying as Red

walked fast toward the elevator. He had a busy day ahead of him. That angioma, this skull fracture, Sturm Ferris, his post-operatives. . . . Yes, and he had forgotten to eat too.

Though the sight of that beaten child had taken the edge from his hunger. Now he could wait until the noon break.

He went upstairs, he checked on his patients in Recovery; he told the supervisor that there would be a child admitted to the ward with a possible skull fracture. "Not a pretty sight, Miss Greenberg."

"We don't usually run a beauty parade, Doctor."

"No, we don't, do we? And Mr. Ferris is coming in. I want to know immediately when each of these cases comes up."

"Yes, doctor."

Red got a bite of lunch—a sandwich and a malt at the snack bar. He was upstairs again and ready when Sturm Ferris was brought in, Polly with him. She was close to the breaking point, and Red talked to her while her husband was being put to bed.

"I never thought of anything like this happening," she told Red. "I should have—I just didn't." She was distraught, clasping and unclasping her hands.

"Did he have any symptoms?" Red thought that this sort of professional talk might steady Polly more than sympathy.

"Oh—yes. A quick temper. He drank too much—not an alcoholic, though. His blood pressure was too high." Distracted, Polly looked around Dr. Enns's office, where Red had taken her. "I thought everything was going so well . . ." she murmured.

"It still may be," Red told her. "I'll go see now."

"I can go with you?"

"Not while I make my examination. There you'd be just one of the family, my dear."

Polly managed a weak smile. "He's paralyzed," she said faintly. "And he can't talk—"

"I'll see. Wouldn't you want to go down and get something to eat?"

Polly shook her head. "No," she said firmly, "I wouldn't."

"All right. I'll send in a cup of coffee."

He did this. Then he went down the hall to see Sturm Ferris.

He was not prepared to like the man; recognizing this feeling, he sternly put it aside. Here was a patient. He had had a cerebral accident. Dr. Cahill was the neurosurgeon on the case.

Sturm Ferris, he found, was a big man—tall. Probably six feet. Fifty years old. Handsome. Very handsome, even today, with his face flushed and swollen and his eyes wild. Fear lay in those tortured eyes and in the clutching fingers of his left hand.

This was a terrible thing that had happened to so young a man, to any man. A terrible thing for the man's wife as well.

Finished with his examination, Red flexed his shoulders and glanced at the nurses, at the intern. "What a day!" he said softly to himself.

A day it had been, but he was not yet at the end of it.

Because, before he was finished with Polly's husband, Miss Greenberg came in and said that Dr. Enns wanted to see him at once.

Red frowned. "Did you tell him . . . ?"

"I told him, Doctor. He said *at once!* In fact, he said

55

'*Stat!*' He—he is terribly upset about something, Doctor."

Miss Greenberg had said that Enns was upset. That was, at first glance, an evident understatement. He was in a state! Red found him sitting straight up in bed, his blue eyes flashing fire!

"Dr. Cahill!" he roared, the minute Red stepped through the door.

"Yes, Doctor?" Red stood where he was, his head up, his face quiet.

"What in hell do you think you have been doing?" shouted Dr. Enns.

Red was surprised. "Why, I've been examining Mr. Ferris. I—"

"Did you also examine a *child* today?" shouted Dr. Enns.

Red nodded. "Yes, sir, I did. Down in Admissions. He's been brought up here by now, I'd think, and I'll look after him next."

Dr. Enns's face was like marble. He was a handsome man, his thick hair iron gray and precisely combed. His eyes were turquoise blue. Red, in proper white coat and trousers, did not begin to look the doctor that Enns did, propped up there in bed, and wearing a hospital shirt with the name of the medical center stenciled across the chest. "Tell me about that child," he said icily.

"Well, Doctor—"

"Clinically, please."

"Yes, sir. I was called to Emergency Admissions around ten-thirty. I found the child—boy of four—with a broken leg, body bruises—some recent, some days old—a burn on the abdomen to the right of the navel—it looked like a cigarette burn. There was an enlarged elbow joint, right, a badly bruised face—mouth swollen, two teeth out, cuts, discoloration, eye swollen shut. Contact examination indicates a depressed skull fracture at the temple. I would conclude that the boy was beaten, sir."

"The Administrator has been up to see me."

Red looked surprised. "Has he, sir?"

Dr. Enns felt of the cast on his right wrist. "Tell me this, Doctor," he said coldly. "*Did* you chew out the parents?"

"I—yes, sir, I did."

"Did you curse them?"

"I don't—well, maybe a word or two did slip out."

"But you don't know specifically? Well, tell me this: Did you call the police?"

"No, sir, I did not! However, I might have promised to. You see, they—"

"I see only that you have asked for a damage suit against yourself and the hospital. This family, whom you abused, quickly found themselves a lawyer, Dr. Cahill, and went to the Administrator."

Red opened his mouth to speak and closed it again. He could not think of a word to say. He was completely stunned. Those ignorant—those— But they had been smarter than he. Because Red had not been "smart" at all. He knew—he should have known . . . The thing that shocked him most was the belated realization that if Enns had been on hand, this situation would not have developed. Red shouldn't need the Chief for such a matter, but evidently he did need him. And the boy's father had known that he did.

"Is there someone over you?" the father had asked. . . .

"What can I say, sir?" cried the anguished young doctor.

"That you lost your head. That you got mad—and—"

"No, sir. If I was—it was righteous indignation, sir. That child—"

"*That child* was brought to our hospital for medical attention."

"He got it."

"Yes, and he will get it."

"But the parents, sir . . . "

"But the parents *brought* the child in, Dr. Cahill."

"I know. But they said—the father did—"

"And you threatened him, antagonized him. Didn't you?"

Red sighed. "Yes, sir. I suppose I did."

"The thing we have to remember, Doctor," said the Chief, relaxing against his pillows, "is that when we are confronted by a battered child, we have presented to us two medical problems, that of healing the sick parents as well as the injured child. This always is and should be the objective of the physician, social agencies, and law-enforcement officials. The process *should* start with the examining physician."

Red gulped. "Yes, sir. So—I have nothing to say, have I?"

Dr. Enns nodded. "Just at the minute I think the less said the better. Now, tell me about Sturm Ferris—and Polly."

Red told him, glad to speak of other things. Ferris, he said, had had a massive stroke. He was mortally ill, apprehensive, and overly aware of all that went on. No, Dr. Cahill could not yet say positively whether surgery might help. He had ordered sedation and observation. Oh, yes, there could be another stroke. B.P. fluctuated. . . .

As for Polly, she was upset, of course. Shocked. But she would get hold of herself, not that she was hysterical now or anything like that. Just shocked.

At nine o'clock that night Vince Sebaja came over from P.N. for a visit with his friend, and found Red sprawled out on his bed, sound asleep, dead to the world.

"You sleep like a fourth-year med student," said Vince when Red opened his eyes and looked at his visitor.

Red sat up and shook his head. "I feel like one," he admitted. He went over to the basin and splashed cold water on his face. "Whooosh!" he gasped. "What a day I have had!"

"And after last night, too," murmured Dr. Sebaja.

Over the towel one of Red's eyes peered at him. "Last night? Oh, the wedding! Was that only last night?"

Vince laughed and produced two apples. Red took one and lay down on the bed again, but now he was wide awake.

"What's all this about a malpractice suit?" Vince asked, biting noisily into the red apple.

"Oh," said Red, his mouth full, "they can't. They couldn't."

"Ah-huh," said Vince. "But what if they *do?*"

Red finished his apple and threw the core at the wastebasket. "Yes," he agreed morosely, "what if they do? Mine would be the shortest medical career on record, I guess."

Vince made no comment, and after a gloomy minute Red looked across at his friend. "Who told you?" he asked.

"Iserman told everyone in the cafeteria at dinner break tonight."

"Iserman?" cried Red. "How did *he* know?"

"He has his little ways."

"Yeah," said Red. "Little."

The next day, and the next, Dr. Redding Cahill was assigned to duty in Emergency Admissions. He considered

59

this no coincidence. He was angry that he should be so disciplined without a hearing and even angrier when, on the second afternoon, he was told to attend a residents' meeting at three o'clock.

"You're on the agenda," Dr. Iserman told him cheerfully when he came down for a patient.

How in hell do you know? Red silently asked. He would not give Iserman the satisfaction of a quarrel.

He had come on Emergency duty with the stern vow to keep his nose clean. He was still bruised and bleeding about the Scholle child.

It had not helped Red's pride one speck, on examination of the boy, to have to rule out neurological damage and to transfer Ronald first to Ortho, with plastic surgery to follow. There was a fracture of the ramus and body of the mandible. And the boy was responding to routine treatment. Cold packs for twenty-four hours had decreased the metabolism at the site of the facial injury; now hot packs and medication were reducing the edema and resolving the extravasated blood.

At noon today Red had found that the jaw fracture had been reduced and fixed with a Winter-type arch. Dr. Cahill's first diagnosis of "battered child syndrome" remained on the chart.

Red had gone back to work, telling himself that he was glad that Ronald was being cared for, really grateful that he had not had to perform brain or skull surgery, and sincerely hoping that Dr. Cahill would not soon again meet up with such a case.

But he did.

At seventeen minutes before three—within seventeen minutes of Red's release from this duty, seventeen minutes before the residents' meeting—the police brought in a child. D.O.A.

Dead on arrival. A little girl of three.

The mother came with the child, and a policeman stood sternly by.

Dr. Cahill said the child was dead.

"We know that, Doc," said the policeman. "But we had to bring her in."

"Yes. Yes, of course." *Keep your mouth shut,* Red warned himself. *This child has been abused—but keep still.*

He asked the child's name. Thelma Mary Favaza.

He got the parents' names and their address. The child was three, one of five children.

"What happened?" asked the big doctor quietly.

"Tell him," said the policeman to the mother. "Tell him what happened."

The mother had wept a little. Now she lifted her head. "You gotta teach kids!" she cried. "I didn't think—"

"Just tell the doctor what happened," said the policeman. "He's busy. He ain't got time—"

Red glanced at his wrist. It was now eleven minutes before three.

The mother was beginning to talk, still defensively. She had a baby, see? Nine months old. And this Thelma, she always was taking the baby's bottle—"I told her, and I *told* her!" But today she again had taken the bottle. So, to punish her, the mother—twenty-eight years old, mother of five —screwed off the top of the pepper shaker and told Thelma to hold her head back.

"I had to do it! That kid *never* minds!"

So the mother had held the child's head back and had poured black pepper down her throat. . . .

Dr. Cahill's face was sternly impassive, though the nurse gasped in horror. "What happened?" asked the big man.

"She turned white as a ghost, Doctor," said the mother, "and her lips were like purple. She went all limp. I never seen nothing like it. I yelled for the lady who lives next door. She's the one that got the police into it."

Red wrote something on the chart.

"Tell her, Doctor!" said the policeman. "Tell her what she *did!*"

Red glanced at the man in uniform. "You've already arrested her?"

"I sure have."

"Then you don't need me to say a word!" The doctor looked down at the chart. Again he had written there: "Battered child." This time he had added: "D.O.A."

He gave the chart to the nurse. "I have a meeting," he said, and walked out of the room.

The meeting was a sizable one and held in the Center's Board Room. When Red came in, the Administrator was present, and the Chief of Medical Services. Red had not yet found a place when Dr. Enns arrived, an orderly pushing the wheel chair. Quickly Red went to him and guided the chair up to the end of the room without saying much of anything to his Chief. Iserman was right. Red Cahill would certainly be on the agenda.

There was no chair close by, and Red went around the table to a seat beside Vince Sebaja.

"Hear you've been on Emergency," murmured that doctor.

"I have," said Red. "And got another battered child too."

"Oh, oh!"

"This *was* one. The mother admitted it."

The Chief of Services rapped for silence, and Red sat back in his chair. He glanced around the room, which was a large one, almost completely filled with the huge oval table and the chairs that were set about it. At the far end of the room were windows, curtained in thick white silk, hung into folds. Twelve folds to a window; Red counted them. The lighting came softly from circular openings in the ceiling. There was a large black-glass ash tray between every other place. The room was soundproof, and . . .

"Thank you for coming, gentlemen," said Dr. Baird, the Chief of Medical Services. A smile tugged at Red's lips; he restrained it. Kenneth Iserman was sitting directly across, and he at least was watching Dr Cahill. The pompous little squirt!

Vince's knee touched Red's, reminding him to pay attention. Red nodded.

"One of your number," the Medical Chief was saying, "has lately exposed himself to a malpractice suit. Since Dr. Cahill is due to learn much from this experience, the staff thinks that the learning opportunity should be spread out to all of you. I am aware that you have attended lectures on this subject, but, regrettably, experience firsthand is often needed to supplement one's academic knowledge."

Red folded his arms across his chest and listened to what Dr. Baird was saying about malpractice suits—their incidence, their increasing frequency, their undesirability. "The best thing to do about them," he said pleasantly, "is to avoid them entirely, to so conduct oneself professionally that you never deserve one!"

He had a few words to say about undeserved suits, but he was of the opinion that always some lapse on the doctor's part triggered the action. He cited as example personality, attitude, unconsidered comment, facial expression. "Of course these things do not hurt a patient! But the important thing to us is whether the patient *thinks* he is

63

hurt! What I am getting at, gentlemen, is strongly to urge you to watch yourselves! It is of as intense importance that a physician should routinely remind himself of basic malpractice prophylaxis as it is for him to keep abreast of the new drugs!

"Whatever you do, whatever you feel—stop and think before expressing yourself. If there is any doubt, ever, in your mind about your behavior, professional or ethical, wait! Which is what Dr. Cahill failed to do this past week. Isn't that true, Dr. Cahill?"

"It seems to be true, Doctor," said Red quietly.

"Ah, yes. Now, would you care to discuss this case here before this group and tell what you did or thought you did?"

Red sighed, and stood up. "There should be a stack of reports on the boy, sir," he began.

"I am interested in what happened the day the boy was brought into Admissions, what you did and said then."

"Yes, sir." Red glanced at Dr. Enns, who was watching him anxiously.

"The child came in," he said. "I was sent for, came down, and found him on the table. Four years old, leg broken—dangling—and his face a pulpy mass of bruises." He went into technical detail. He mentioned old bruises and injuries and got in a word that the X-rays had borne out his diagnosis of them. "He was a battered child, sir," said Dr. Cahill earnestly. "I am sure that any work done on this case by social workers, or the juvenile court, will bear me out."

"And you told the parents that?"

"No, sir. The father wanted to take the boy home after his leg fracture was set, and I said we wouldn't permit it."

64

"We," murmured the Chief.

"I don't know that I used *that* term, sir." Red's face was flushed now, and the skin glistened. "But I was certain that this boy's worst enemy was his parents."

"Did you threaten them?"

"I may have mentioned the police."

"Which might not seem too great a danger to you, Dr. Cahill. I don't have your record here before me . . ."

There was a ripple of low laughter around the table. Dr. Baird frowned. "The threat of police action is more terrifying to other stratas of our society."

Don't say "stratas," thought Red peevishly. He jerked his attention back to the question, to the situation, in hand. And on his strata, danger was definitely present.

"I—" he said slowly. "I am ready to admit that I got excited. But, sir, both down on Admissions and up on N.S. we see so many children who appear to be victims of abuse."

"I know you do," said the Medical Chief.

"Isn't the incidence increasing?" Red asked.

The Medical Chief was not one to reply offhand. He rubbed his hand across the back of his neck; he pursed his lips; he looked up at the ceiling. "I would need statistics down in black and white," he said slowly, "to answer that positively, Doctor. I would say that there is a question as to whether child abuse itself is on the rise or whether the greater concern over the problem is largely the result of increased professional awareness of it."

"Yes, sir," said Red respectfully. "I am aware of that rising concern within myself."

Dr. Enns said something which Dr. Baird leaned down to hear. "Yes!" he said, straightening and facing his audience again. "The Chief of Neurological Services tells me that

65

there are no available figures on child abuse."

Enns would have inquired. Red sighed, and waited. He would answer questions as they came but try to avoid voluntary contributions. Though he had plenty that he could say!

One of the residents wanted to ask a question. He was on Pediatrics services, and Red looked at him with interest.

"Is there some code or diagnostic symbol for these cases?" the man asked. "To identify them?"

Softly Red cracked one fist into his other palm. He knew there was not.

But he let Dr. Baird answer the man. "No," said that gentleman. "Physicians have only lately come to see child abuse as part of a larger pattern of social behavior, and hospitals have not as yet begun to file such cases under a special code."

"Is the incidence great?" asked someone.

"No," said Dr. Baird. "In our own hospital, during the last year, we have had five cases definitely diagnosed as 'Battered Child Syndrome.' Dr. Cahill's boy would be one of those."

"I believe," said Dr. Enns, to whom the Administrator had been whispering, "and I think this belief would be shared by physicians concerned by the syndrome, that a considerable number of inflicted injuries in children are being treated as 'accidents' and going unrecognized by doctors not aware of the problem."

"If the parents don't admit they have abused the child . . . " said Red quickly.

"That's our trouble," Dr. Enns agreed. "Of course many injuries come in to us looking like accidents. Yours happened to be a dramatic case."

"Which you would have done better to call an accident,

maybe," said the Administrator.

Red frowned and shook his head. "There was no chance it was an accident, sir!" he cried. "And I felt that I had to do what I did."

The Administrator shrugged. "I trust you won't have that compulsion soon again, Doctor."

"I probably will if I get another boy so terribly hurt," said Red. He looked around the room. "You should, every one of you, go up and look at him!" he cried. "He's being cared for now. His parents have *not* taken him home. I don't know how this was managed, but surely there is some law that would hold such a case in hospital?"

"He was held and could be held on the basis of his injuries, Doctor," said Dr. Baird, "not because of the methods of their occurrence. You would have to be able to prove abuse—with witnesses or confession."

Red stood shaking his head. "These kids should have protection," he said sadly.

"Thank you, Dr. Cahill," said the Medical Chief in a certain tone. Red sat down. But *he* was not finished. Though when the Chief asked the meeting if there were questions or further discussion wanted, he did manage to keep still.

Others—Iserman, for one—did not.

Iserman thought it should be said in Dr. Cahill's behalf that "the doctor was not feeling well the day the boy was brought in." Vince touched Red's arm warningly, but Red sat there like a rock, gazing at the little doctor across from him.

"I understand," said Iserman pompously, "that he made a mistaken diagnosis of skull fracture. Perhaps his other opinions were—well, unreliable, due to his condition."

Even the Chief of Medical Services looked annoyed.

Every resident present was disgusted with Iserman, and their faces showed it. But the Administrator courteously asked Red if he had anything to say on Dr. Iserman's point?

"No, sir," said Red quietly. *Next time,* he told himself, *I'll roll Iserman up and set him down six flights! On his head!* "Fortunately we found that there was no neurological injury, and skull surgery was not required."

As he spoke, he glanced at Dr. Enns and was rewarded by a flash of relieved approval in his Chief's eyes.

This made it easier to take Dr. Baird's concluding words which he announced as directed to all the residents but which, of course, were pointed specifically at Dr. Cahill.

Red was to be "let off," stated the Chief of Services, with a warning, which was explicit and to be heeded. He was *not* to do the same thing again in a similar case. He was to follow medical procedure by the book! All doctors must so proceed or, the Chief warned, he would promise instant action to separate the offending doctor from service at this medical center. Did he make himself clear?

"Dr. Cahill," he concluded, his face and voice softening, "is entirely too good a doctor in many ways to allow himself to be lax in some! Gentlemen, you are excused. Return to your assigned duties at once!"

Before anyone could talk to him, and not wanting anyone to talk to him, Red was out of his chair and around the table to assist Dr. Enns.

Dr. Enns did not talk. He was, he said, tired. "Get me to bed," he said as they came out of the elevator up on N.S.

Red performed this. The schedule said he would go on duty at five. This gave him an hour, and he used some of it to go downstairs to look at Ronald Scholle. Visiting hours were over; he would not run into the parents.

Yes, the boy was definitely better. Edema was reduced,

ecchymosis was rapidly dissipating. Red would inquire as to the medication which had accomplished this. The child seemed comfortable; he could see with his right eye. To Red's question, Ronald said he was fine and glad he could see.

Red was still beside the child's crib when Vince Sebaja came on the ward. Red talked to him a little about the boy. Improvement was tremendous, Red assured the other doctor, who had winced at first sight of the child's face. "If that isn't battered . . . " he had murmured.

"Ah, ah!" Red warned. "Mustn't say the dirty word!"

"What do you suppose . . . ?"

"Ronald says his father threw him into the corner." The two tall doctors walked at a steady pace out of the ward and along the corridor.

"A corner full of table edges and chairs?" asked Vince.

"I believe there was a stove," said Red softly.

Vince pressed the elevator button. "What else do you know about the kid?" he asked. "And his family?"

"I know Ronald was badly hurt." Red's jaw was stubborn.

"D'you know *why* he was hurt? After you, Doctor."

But Red stood where he was and stared at Dr. Sebaja. Vince put his foot on the sill to keep the elevator door open.

"You'd better find out, pal," Vince told him as they went into the steel cage. "You'd better find out."

The elevator sighed to a stop at Vince's floor. "P.N.'s," said Red as his friend stepped out.

He went up to his floor and signed in, took a chart out of its slot, and then answered the telephone. The nurses were down the hall talking to three patients in wheel chairs. Red spoke tersely and hung up. He leaned back against the edge of the desk and read the first chart. He took a second one—he had been off the floor for two days, and things had happened.

He was scowling over the third chart, and answering the phone again, when Polly Ferris came down the hall. She was wearing a blouse and skirt, but not her white coat. She smiled at Red; she looked tired.

"Hello, Polly," said Red, going around the desk to write something on the supe's memo pad. "Get me a frilly cap and call me nursie," he growled.

"On you it will look lovely," said Polly brightly.

Red growled again. "Don't be cheerful on my account," he said. "*I* am in a mood."

"Yes, you are, aren't you?"

"With reason. I've had a day."

"I know, Red," she said warmly. "I heard about it. I mean, about your trouble over that child. But don't let one case get you." Her hazel eyes were steady, her face serene.

"Do you want to talk about it, Red?" she asked. "I am certainly interested."

He managed a wry smile and he touched her shoulder. "I know you are interested," he agreed. "And sometime I will talk about it to you. But for now—you have troubles of your own, and plenty of them."

Polly looked back toward the room where her husband lay helpless, his face frozen into a meaningless smile. Sturm Ferris could not speak or move his right hand, his right leg, but it did not seem that he would die.

"Yes, I have problems," said that man's wife calmly.

"What do you plan?" Red asked her.

Polly shrugged. "Everything is being planned for me, Red. After another week or so here I'll take Sturm home and care for him. There seems to be nothing to do for him except nurse him. He'll probably be up in a wheel chair —perhaps therapy will help him. We hope it will. The kids will help."

"Yes. That's Sturm. But what about you?"

She looked at Red in genuine surprise. "What do you mean?" she asked. "What *about* me?"

"Are you planning to nurse him yourself? Or—as I hope —will you stay on here and work? Of course you can't do both."

"I'll have to do both."

"Polly—"

"It is a matter of money, Red. I have to keep on working to pay our daily living expenses. The kids must stay in school too. These years will not return for them. So we'll arrange our hours. Of course it is not going to be easy, but—" She shrugged.

Red could only stand and gaze at her. And he thought he had troubles! "I'm sorry," he said inadequately.

"Yes," said Polly. "Everybody's sorry."

"Dr. Enns," Red began, and noticed the way Polly's head snapped up and her hands clenched.

"Dr. Enns," he repeated, "came down to a residents' meeting this afternoon. In a wheel chair."

"But that's wonderful," said Polly quickly. Little round spots of color burned in her cheeks. "He's going to be all right, Red.'

"I sure hope so," said Red. "He should be. He's a very swell guy."

Polly made no comment. She turned away and went back to her husband's room.

Red finished his charts; he made a quick tour of the floor, then he told the nurse in charge that he was going down to the cafeteria for his dinner.

"Chicken pie," she told him. "Pretty good."

"I'll make my own diagnosis," he said. "If you need me—"

Miss Cleveland nodded. "I've been nursing longer than you've been doctoring," she reminded the young man. She was checking the medicine list, but when Red walked away, her eyes followed him to the elevator. By then the whole hospital knew about his session on the carpet. Personally Miss Cleveland thought good doctors should be encouraged, rather than not.

5 ❋❋❋❋❋❋❋❋❋❋❋❋❋❋❋❋❋❋❋❋❋❋❋❋❋

FOR the next few days Red knew that he was not being the man he had accustomed himself and others to identify as Redding Cahill, though he sometimes made a conscious effort to throw off the cloak which had been thrown smotheringly about his face.

His friends watched him, and his efforts, with concern. What had happened to old Red? they asked.

They answered themselves in various ways, Dr. Gutzell, his junior resident, Dr. Sebaja, Jumper, the orderly, Miss Cleveland and Miss Greenberg, the supervisors . . .

"A lacing down in public would get to any man," Gutzell told Damron, the intern.

"Dr. Cahill is a good doctor."

"Everyone—even the Chief—recognizes that, Damron. Red himself knows it. He knows he doesn't often make a mistake. That's why he is taking this one so hard. He isn't ready to settle for second-best doctoring, even in himself."

"How did he ever come to do such a thing?"

"He's asking that question of himself. And I don't think he has found an answer."

"I can't get through to him," Polly told Dr. Enns. "I tried to tell him to forget it and go on—"

"How is he working?"

"Oh, he works fine. It's at other times—in the hall, at the coffee breaks he doesn't take, the little joking get-togethers he doesn't have with anyone any more. He makes rounds, he does his surgery, then he goes to his room and closes the door. He reads—he brings loads of books up from the library and spends his free hours down there too."

"He'll come out of it, Polly. A reprimand shouldn't—"

Polly gazed at the handsome, gray-haired doctor in his wheel chair, and she shook her head. "It isn't the reprimand," she said. "Red is fretting over the near-bobble he made."

"Learning can sometimes be painful."

"I know, but he is questioning himself—his behavior, his feelings—"

"And his theories," said Bill Enns.

"Was he so wrong, Bill?"

"He was as wrong as hell, Polly. No doctor chews out a patient's family. Under any circumstance."

"But—"

"There were other and better ways to protect that child. And if you ask me, Red knows that and he is being angry at the way he handled the matter."

"Ye-es. The little boy is recovering."

"He is. What's more, the Scholles have withdrawn their complaint against the hospital and Dr. Cahill."

Polly clasped her hands together in joy. Bill watched her, his face wistful. She had wrapped him in a blanket and, bundled into her own coat, she had taken him out on the terrace beyond the solarium for a breath of winter air and sunshine.

74

"There's to be no malpractice suit?" she cried. "How was one avoided?"

"Oh, the insurance company had no difficulty finding neighbors who might have testified that the Scholles did abuse Ronald."

"Will the child be taken from them?"

Dr. Enns smiled at her. "Suppose we leave that to Social Services. Which is where Red should have left it to begin with."

Polly stood thoughtful, the wind blowing her thick hair. "There will be some trauma. For the child, I mean."

"Oh, surely."

"And Red certainly has suffered one."

"He's jumpy, all right."

"Oh, he is! He fights to conceal it, and the effort makes him seem to be very grouchy."

"Seem to be? I understand he *is* grouchy!"

Polly laughed. "Red will be all right. Don't you think so?"

"If I didn't, we'd quickly have a new senior resident on this floor."

Polly said nothing, but her face again was troubled.

All of Red's friends were troubled; except for Iserman, no one felt that he had done such a horrendous thing, nor had his session on the carpet been so severe as to warrant the depth of Dr. Cahill's present mood.

Red was well aware of this concern, and he renewed his efforts to take his mind elsewhere. He paid meticulous attention to the work he did, the charts he checked, the directions he wrote, the consultations he attended, his rounds, his surgery. But against his will there were times when his mind would slip away to his own affairs.

C'ele said . . . Was C'ele right? *Was* he—had he been —too completely in the shadow of Dr. Enns? It was only when Enns was disabled that Dr. Cahill had notably stubbed his toe. Even that stupid Scholle had said that an older doctor would have proceeded differently.

But Red was no green intern! He had been a doctor, an M.D., for six years! He should be able to stand on his own, make his own decisions, not needing the presence of his Chief to guide him and watch him to the extent of insuring that he would do the right thing!

He began to check on himself, on his decisions; he even wrote out his diagnoses, his decisions on treatment, before he talked those matters over with Dr. Enns. On paper his average of being right appeared to be pretty good, and his spirits began to rise.

Then one morning, unexpectedly, a phrase popped into his head. Enns had said, way back at the beginning of the Ronald Scholle thing, that Red had let himself become "too involved with a patient's problem."

Now Red wondered about *that* charge. While he worked, while he followed his surgical schedule, while he scrubbed—*one thousand and ten, one thousand and eleven,* elbows, forearms, between the fingers—while he diagnosed and observed his patients, he thought about it. What did Enns mean? Where did the degree of involvement cease to be objective and desirable interest and become emotional involvement? "Too involved with a patient's problem."

The phrase stayed with him like the thread of a song. Over and over Red made an effort to escape from it. He should know the answer, just as he knew all aspects of his profession. If he was ready to be a doctor on his own, he should be able to define such degrees of judgment.

Once he had a flash of asking himself if all residents had

76

these bridelike tremors and doubts? Could he ask Vince?

Later he wished he had asked him. But he did not. All he came up with was a decision that, if he was ready to be on his own, he would be doing something about the battered-child problem. They kept coming at him, those children.

That girl, Thelma, whose mother had poured pepper into her mouth. Ronald Scholle, of course, and before him the little girl, Caroline, whom he'd seen at C'ele's. More recently, just three days ago, a child had come up to N.S. with a back injury; supposedly he had fallen out of a moving car. But his bruises . . .

There were many suspect cases, and things should be done for those children. It well could be that Red Cahill might find something to do. He would study the problem. Even with protocol, there were things he could do on his own. Perhaps Enns was waiting for a show of such initiative. So Red could and would do things for the battered child.

He would study the matter; he would search the record files and go down to Social Services and hunt out cases. . . .

Within days of this resolution and Red's acting upon it, the hospital authorities became aware of what Dr. Cahill was doing. Once alerted, they set up a stern watch on him, waiting, but watchful. Finally the hospital Administrator spoke of the matter to Dr. Enns.

"We don't want any more trouble, Dr. Enns."

"Certainly not. I'll see what I can do, Mr. Ovian."

Then Dr. Enns watched Red carefully, checking his duty hours and his free time. He mentioned his concern to Dr. Sebaja, Red's friend. "What's the chap up to?" he asked.

Vince made his own inquiry, and with Dr. Enns's approval he went to C'ele. "Get on to Red," he urged the

77

girl. "He's gone Galahad on us. He's set himself up as a one-man committee to rescue the battered child. So stop him, will you, C'ele?"

"Doesn't the battered child need someone . . . ?" she asked.

"It doesn't need Red at this stage of his career. He's still a resident in this hospital. He should and must obey the rules set down for him. He's on the wrong track, C'ele, and I wish you'd help me get him back.

"How would I be able to help?"

"By persuasion, a diversion of his interests. Maybe get him to talk to you about it and prettily disagree with him, coax him to—" Vince stopped and looked at her.

"C'ele?" he asked.

Because she was firmly shaking her head, her face serenely stubborn. "I wouldn't say a word," she told Red's friend. "What Red wants to do he will do."

"But you—"

She continued to shake her head. "I wouldn't say one word to change him, Vince."

Vince sighed. "I only hope then that Red will come to his senses by himself and before it is too late."

"He will, Vince," said C'ele serenely. "If that is what he should do."

"All right," agreed Vince. "All right." He started to walk away, then he came back to C'ele. "Do you think Sylvia has such faith in me?" he asked curiously.

"I hope so, Vince," said C'ele. "It would be very nice for her."

During the next ten days, Polly took Sturm Ferris home, and Dr. Enns regularly enlivened things on N.S. by his arguments with Orthopedics. Enns liked to adjust his own traction; Dr. Ebenloh said that he should stick to the brain and leave the bones to him.

Dr. Ebenloh told Red that he would be glad to have Enns back at work. By then Red could laugh and say he hoped things would improve all over.

"You've done a good job, he tells me."

"He hasn't breathed a word like that to me," said Dr. Cahill.

"And he probably won't. But he feels that way."

Which was a tremendous relief.

As it always did, immediately before Christmas, work slacked off a little. On a surgical floor the scheduled operations that could wait were held off until after the holiday so that patient and personnel alike could be at home around the family tree.

Emergencies came in, of course, and more of them because of traffic hazards and other risks attendant upon the festivities. Patients already in hospital must be attended.

But wreaths hung behind every nurses' station, small Christmas trees were set up in the wards, and a larger one brightened the solarium. Down in the gymnasium-auditorium of the medical school there was always a Christmas Eve party for personnel on duty. The different services arranged for each of its people to get down to this affair for a couple of hours.

Dr. Enns asked Red, at four-thirty on Christmas Eve, if he had made such arrangements on N.S.

"Yes, sir. We've figured out for our people to be off in two shifts."

"That's good. Which are you taking?"

Red looked over his shoulder. He had been showing his Chief some X-ray films of a supposed back case. The plates were indicating a circulatory disturbance that Red was fearful might be an aneurism, in which case . . .

Now he frowned and with a visible effort brought his attention away from the plates to the question posed by the man in the wheel chair.

"I'm not going downstairs," he said, as if this was a truth which need not have been stated. "Now, sir, do you think . . . ?"

"We'll get a heart man up here and ask him what *he* thinks," said Dr. Enns impatiently. "But why, Cahill, aren't you going to the party?"

Red snapped off the light and walked toward the wall phone. "Because I think I should remain on the floor, sir."

"Wait a minute, Red," said Dr. Enns. "Let's handle one thing at a time. You can call Cardiology later. Five minutes later. But now will you tell me why this party is arranged for personnel on duty?"

Red frowned. "Well, it's Christmas—they can't go home or anything like that. It's supposed to cheer 'em up."

"Ah-huh!" said Dr. Enns. "Did you go to the party last year?"

"Yes, sir, I did."

"Have fun?"

Red laughed. "I was lame for a month. We danced the limbo. That's a dance, sir, where—"

"I know what the limbo is," said Dr. Enns. "Remember, I've been watching TV for the past six weeks, solid. I am well up on life as it is being lived!"

Red's hand went toward the wall phone.

"You're to go down to that party tonight, Doctor," said the Chief firmly.

"Oh, sir—"

"Don't argue with me!" Dr. Enns's blue eyes sparked. "I

may be tied to this confounded chair, but I still am Chief of this service, and as such the welfare of my personnel is one of my responsibilities. I am worried about you, Dr. Cahill. You have been putting in too long hours on duty! And your name may not be Jack, but it is making you a very dull boy. Which isn't any help!"

Red stood defenseless under this attack. "I'm sorry, sir," he said stiffly.

"Humpf! If you *are* sorry, you will go to that shindig without any further argument. Haven't you asked a girl?"

"Well, there was a sort of understanding, but I was going to call her after we handled this aneurism thing—"

"And tell her that the hospital would go out of business if, tonight, Dr. Cahill took two hours off for fun and games? Is that it?"

"No, sir, but—"

"Well, then go get your girl and go to that party. You're to have a good time at it too. That's an order! I've already reminded you that I am Chief of Service up here. I'm better right along, and I plan to be back at work the first of the year." He caught the alarm in Red's eyes. "Well," he amended, "I'll be back, anyway."

"Yes, sir."

"All right. *Now* call your heart man."

Red went to the party, determined to do as the Chief had ordered, with no retrospective or introspective thoughts about it. He picked up C'ele, told her that she looked like a million dollars—she was pretty in a white wool dress with a narrow gold belt and pointed gold slippers—and they had a very wild evening. Perhaps too wild, and this somewhat worried C'ele. Red's mood lately had been so directly opposite. . . .

The party was the same party held every year. Some of the people there had dressed up; some were in their duty whites. Some were on call, and some were called.

The food was the same as always—bowls of punch, cheese dips surrounded by crackers and potato chips, plates of fruit cake, a coffee urn and cups, dishes of candy.

There was a Christmas tree.

"It's pretty, isn't it?" a nurse asked Dr. Cahill.

He turned to look at the tall green tree, spangled with lights and colored balls. He shrugged. "It looks like all Christmas trees."

"And what's wrong with all Christmas trees?" asked the redheaded nurse. People close by waited for Red's answer. He seemed to be in form.

"It has no oomph," said Red, dipping out some punch.

"No?" gasped the nurse. "But—are you crazy, Doctor? Christmas trees don't have oomph! They aren't supposed to have."

Red shrugged and drank some of the punch. It was cold and wet. Now a circle, two people deep, surrounded him and the redhead. C'ele saw the group and stopped dancing with Dr. Damron.

"Christmas trees could have oomph," Red was saying.

"How?" challenged someone.

Red put the cup down on the table. "I'll show you," he offered.

"How will you show us?" the nurse demanded. "You got an oomphy Christmas tree in your pocket?"

Red grinned. "I don't have and I don't need one in my pocket. But look around. There's Christmas trees all over here."

"Oh, sure," said a man's voice. "On Baptist punch already he sees Christmas trees all over."

"I see 'em, my friend," said Red firmly, "because they are here. You're one. You're a tall one, and there are some low, fat ones, and—" His gaze circled the group of people. By then nearly everyone had drawn close. "Iserman's a spindly one," Red continued, "and he doesn't have any decorations."

Little Dr. Iserman stood undecided whether to be pleased at being singled out by name or suspicious of Cahill's idea of what was funny.

Somebody put a folded red napkin on Iserman's head. He shook it off.

"No," said Red, "he doesn't make much of a Christmas tree, does he? But, let's see . . ."

He turned full about, surveying the room. "Six of you men," he directed, "line up against that wall." He pointed to the white brick wall. "Move those chairs out of the way. I want six good stout men. You, Schonwald, and other men about that height and weight. Adams, you'd be good."

He got his six men. Two doctors, a male nurse, an orderly, an ambulance driver, and a security officer in uniform. Red liked this last one. "You're beautiful!" he said warmly, polishing the man's badge with his coat sleeve.

He had his six men stand at arm's length apart from each other. Then he selected five men to stand on the shoulders of the original six, four to pyramid on their shoulders. The "tree" was beginning to grow. Three men were boosted and lifted up, then two, and finally only one was needed. There was no choice. Little Iserman was the candidate! Hands were stretched down for him. Red stood ready to help him mount.

Iserman was in a turmoil. He did not want to get up there on Cahill's damned Christmas tree, and still he didn't want to be left out, either. He wanted people to like

83

him. . . .

Finally he kicked off his shoes. Vince Sebaja in the third row had discovered that shoes were a hazard. And the little man scrambled up and up . . .

Red went out to the middle of the floor and surveyed the results. "An angel would be better on top," he murmured.

"What we need is decorations," said C'ele, taking off her gold belt and looping it from Dr. Schonwald's shoulder to Dr. Adams's. The other girls caught the idea. Bright scarves were contributed, and jewelry. Bright necklaces were the best ornaments, and the big glittery pins some of the girls wore on their shoulders.

"It looks swell!" cried Dr. Cahill. "Now, all we need—"

He went up the climbing bars like a cat. "Here, Iserman," he called. "Catch! But don't fall—you'll kick someone in the eye." And he tossed his pencil flashlight to the doctor at the top of the "tree." Iserman just did catch it, everyone holding his breath.

"You're a star, Iserman," Red shouted. He was down on the floor again. "Let's see you *twinkle!*"

This made a plump man on the third row giggle. For agonizing minutes it seemed that the whole structure would collapse. There were shouts, laughter, held breaths, and finally equilibrium was restored. Then someone began to sing "Tannenbaum," and the chorus swelled mightily. It was a good party.

Though almost at once little Iserman seemed to be in trouble. His face worked; he was gasping. "I have to get down!" he cried. "I have to—" He clung to the wall, and evidently he did need to—

"*Please?*" he begged.

The men directly below him began to yell. They wanted down! Some of the girls squealed.

84

And then, in a moment of truth, Iserman sneezed. Mightily, for so little a man. He opened his mouth; he shouted "Agggh!" and then he sneezed. Wetly and explosively. Under the blast the Christmas tree collapsed, the upper "branches" sliding down the lower ones, and everyone laughed. And laughed. They roared.

"That little *mouse!*" gasped Red Cahill. "And *such* a sneeze!"

C'ele had never seen him laugh so hard. She began to be afraid. She tucked her arm through his. "Let's go home, sweetheart," she said. "It's time Ben Casey went beddy-by."

Red stiffened; he drew himself to his full height. "Don't call me *that!*" he said tightly.

C'ele laughed at him. "You don't want to be the medical legend?" she said pertly. "The Paul Bunyan of the white coat and stethoscope?"

Red was not amused, and he showed that he was not. This tremendously bothered C'ele. Usually she was able to go along with his mood, whatever it turned out to be, but not tonight. For weeks she had been worried about Red, and tonight she showed that she was worried. She even said that she was worried. This one time she was ready to cross Red, to . . .

He didn't take it. He continued to stand stiffly while she told him how worried she was. She wanted to leave the party, so they could talk.

When she had said her little speech—it was not long—he looked down at her. His eyes were cold; his face was set into rigid lines. His tone was ugly. "Will you please leave me alone?" he said tightly. "I came here—I brought you here—so we could have some fun. Now it looks like the fun is over. So I'll go back to work. And a good night to you, Miss Davidson, and all your goony friends!"

He turned on his heel and walked across the floor. He kicked a wad of paper out of his path.

C'ele would have followed him. But Vince Sebaja grabbed her arm. "Let him go," he said firmly, as he walked her away from those who had stood near, who had heard. "I'll take you home," he promised. "And put Red's car into the garage."

C'ele stood looking down at her golden slippers. "The man's sick," she said, and she brushed a tear from her cheek.

"Ugh-ugh," said Vince. "Not sick. Just suffering mightily from growing pains."

C'ele looked up at him; her mascara was smudged. "At his age?" she asked.

Vince held the door for her; she got her coat and they went along the hall, down the ramp, and over to Red's car. The keys had to be kept in it when it was on the lot.

"Red takes his growing pains pretty hard," Vince said then to C'ele. He pulled out into the street. "But as far as his age goes, as a doctor, you know, C'ele, Cahill is still in the playpen." He glanced down at her. His eyes were nice.

C'ele liked Vince Sebaja. She had to like him. She wished she had no reason to fear him. Had he ever talked to Red about her? Maybe Vince didn't know that C'ele had lied to Red about her family.

Oh, she did wish that all was clear and clean between her and Red. She should tell him that she had lied, and she would, some day. If now she ever got the chance.

"Is Red mad at me?" she asked Vince when he unlocked her apartment door.

He shook his head. "He's mad at everyone these days, honey. Especially himself. He'll get over it. You just be patient. And have a Merry Christmas. Are you going

86

home?"

C'ele nodded. She might as well. "Thank you, Vince."

On the day after Christmas, as she might have known he would, Red made a chance to go down to the records room and apologize to C'ele.

He did this by asking her to find something for him in the files and following her to the room with its narrow aisles between ceiling-high rows and rows of shelves.

Red glanced around. No one was very close. "I'm sorry I acted like a louse the other night, C'ele," he said gruffly.

C'ele was sitting on her heels, searching through the files on the lowest shelf. "It's all right," she murmured. "I guess." She stood up, a manila folder in her hand. "Is this what you want, Doctor?"

Red took the folder, opened it, pretended to read. "I think this is it. Wait a minute, you can have it back." He stepped closer to C'ele. "I don't know what got into me," he said gruffly.

"I do."

He glanced up. "You do?"

"Yes. Your Chief is laid up, and you are working too hard."

Red straightened the papers and handed the folder to C'ele. "I hope that's the answer," he said. "If it is, I'll soon show improvement. Because Enns is back on the floor this morning."

"He is?" C'ele was surprised. "Able to work?"

"Well, no, not to work. But he's taken over his office, and he's up and down the hall in his chair."

"Well, that's fine." She returned the folder to its place. "Anything else, Doctor?"

"No," said Red. "But thank you very much." His voice

dropped. "I'll be seeing you, C'ele."

She nodded and preceded him to the door.

Dr. Cahill spent an hour in Pathology, then came upstairs in time to get in on an impromptu lecture from the Chief on the battered child. About the time Red was talking to C'ele in the file room, a case had come up from Emergency Admissions and had been examined. There was found to be a head injury and evidence of earlier and repeated abuse.

In the hall outside of the children's ward Dr. Enns had Dr. Gutzell, two interns, a med student, the o.r. team, and Miss Greenberg for an audience. The Chief saw Red join the group, but he did not falter. Evidently he had been reminding his staff of the need for care in diagnosing a child as "battered."

Such a notation had come up on the chart from Admissions, but even then, said the Chief, one must be very careful.

"Dr. Martin," he said to one of the interns, "did the history you took from the mother include any recent or repeated injuries?"

"No, sir, not as taken."

"A-hum. Such injuries are often conveniently forgotten or suppressed. And if the immediate symptoms today had not been severe, this episode, too, might have been considered too trivial to mention. We think we have a subdural hematoma, Dr. Cahill," he threw out. "Rather large. Child of two."

Red nodded. "Yes sir."

"These situations can be very difficult," Dr. Enns continued blandly. "One parent may try to protect the other whose hand has been too heavy. Sometimes one of the parents is afraid to tell the other about an injury that has resulted from rage or carelessness. A sitter—a grandmother in

88

charge—may be reluctant to report an injury to a parent for fear of being called negligent.

"I think our child in yonder is supposed to have been injured by an older brother in the course of play, and of course that can happen. Bone trauma can be caused by a baby's leg being caught in the crib slats. Grabbing a child out of the path of danger may cause a lesion at the shoulder. So what do we conclude?"

"That histories aren't much help," offered Dr. Gutzell.

"Well," agreed Enns, "they can be misleading, and in the case of deliberate injury they can be entirely untrue."

What was he getting at? Red asked himself.

"We were lucky this morning," the Chief was saying, "that our little boy—his name is Peter, Dr. Cahill—that our little Peter was brought to the hospital. There are too many skeletal injuries that are not recognized or treated."

"And remain with the parents," said Red quietly.

Dr. Enns nodded. "And left in the parents' ungentle custody where other injuries can be expected. We hope not fatal ones. Now, I have some questions to ask. Speak up if you know the answer.

"Tell me: Who can prove that an injured infant was thrown and not dropped?" He waited.

"You can't tell, sir," said Dr. Damron, "unless the child testifies."

"Our Peter is only two, Damron."

"Yes, sir, but if he'd seem afraid of someone . . ."

"That would increase our suspicions, yes. Now here's another point. We get an injured child. What is our first question?"

"How was he hurt?"

"That's right. How was he hurt? Then we go on—was it a car accident? Did he fall out of a window? Only where the evidence is clear-cut do we begin to ask if there was personal violence to blame. We don't think of that first, though there are various and important clues. Can any of you suggest some? Dr. Gutzell?"

"Well, of course, if comprehensive X-rays show healed or healing fractures in other parts of the body . . ."

"Good! Dr. Cahill?"

Red clenched one fist. "If you have a subdural hematoma, you might—on a child like Peter—you might also take X-rays of the long bones immediately after hospitalization and again in ten or fourteen days."

"Yes. What about bruises?"

"Yes, sir," said Red. "Ecchymosis, broken nose . . ."

"General abuse shows up," said the nurse supervisor, "in a child who seems to be chronically underweight."

"Peter's a bundle of nobbly sticks," said one of the o.r. girls.

Dr. Enns nodded. "Yes, he is. So, all of you, please remember these clues whenever you examine an injured child. Keep in mind the possibility of deliberate injury when you question the parents.

"However"—he did not look at Red—"remember, too," he continued, "that severe injuries *can* occur by accident. And there is always a chance you may overwhelm innocent parents with undeserved guilt feelings."

Not Ronald's parents!

Red's hands thrust hard into the pockets of his trousers, and he jiggled impatiently, his weight on one foot.

"You don't want to risk doing this," Dr. Enns was saying, "any more than you want to miss the deliberately battered child. I point out that you can be cautious with the family even while detecting your clues. It won't hurt a thing to explain that you understand that it may be necessary to inflict minor injury in order to prevent a major one. A parent may violently grab an arm in order to prevent a serious fall."

Red sniffed. Audibly.

Dr. Enns's voice went on smoothly. But his eyes had hardened. "I'd hope any of you would want to allay any possible guilt feelings in an innocent parent by explaining to them that children's bones are often and easily injured and the trouble usually follows a benign course. Don't forget *that* yourselves."

"But we still must remember to look for clues?" said Dr. Gutzell.

"Oh, definitely. You must always watch, too, for the possibility of injury to the internal organs—brain, spleen, liver, and kidney."

"But not mention it," said Red Cahill delicately.

Dr. Enns's lips thinned. "When you know you have reason to suspect that the child was injured deliberately, you should make a report to someone in authority. Here in the hospital that authority is clearly defined to you. When you get into private practice, report such a situation to a child's protective organization or directly to the police. You—"

An orderly had come up to Red with a whispered message. The resident walked away down the hall, Dr. Enns's voice fading behind him. Dr. Cahill answered the phone; he agreed to go down to the kitchens where a worker had fallen on the tile floor—there might or might not be a head injury.

While downstairs, always locating himself to the floor desk on N.S., Red ate his lunch. Though the big dining room was crowded with people who would have talked to him, he sat and thought about Enns's lecture. It might not have been aimed at him—he was not around when the

91

thing began—but still he thought there had been a special message for him about the newly admitted child.

Which, incidentally, he had not yet seen. He must look at the boy, of course. And soon!

Hurriedly he finished his bread pudding and went upstairs.

"Dr. Cahill," said Miss Greenberg at the desk, "Dr. Enns would like you to come to his office at your convenience."

"Does he want to see me right away?"

Miss Greenberg turned over a sheet of paper. "He said at your convenience, Doctor."

Red hesitated. "Yes. Well, I'll go look at the boy who came in this morning, and then . . ."

He examined the injured child. He too thought the boy was a battered one. He read the chart, he studied the lab reports; he agreed with Gutzell that surgery must be done, and soon. He would go right out and schedule it.

Thinking about this, he opened the door of Dr. Enns's office and was three steps inside before he saw . . . what he did see. Polly Ferris kneeling beside Dr. Enns's chair, her head on his shoulder, his arms about her. She was weeping. Hard, difficult sobs shook her, and the gray-haired doctor was talking to her earnestly. Neither saw Red Cahill, as big as he was, with his white garments standing out like a lighted candle against the dark wood paneling.

"You do not have to martyr yourself!" Bill Enns was saying to the woman who clung to him so desperately. "There is no virtue in destroying your life and mine!"

Red took a cautious step backward.

"I love you, Polly, and—"

Polly fumbled in her pocket for a tissue. "I—love you, Bill," she said. "But—"

"But you still think you must give up the man you love

to nurse the husband you no longer love." Dr. Enns's tone was anguished.

Red's hand found the door latch; he opened the door soundlessly and eased himself out into the hall.

Whew! He stood for a minute, shaken by the pain which he had just seen. He sighed and shook his head, then walked down the hall to the nurses' station.

He looked at the schedule. He hunted and found Dr. Gutzell, and together they went back to look at Peter and to talk to the mother. She "guessed" surgery would be all right, if the doctors thought . . .

Red scheduled the job for five o'clock. "I'll tell the Chief," he said to his junior resident. "He wants to see me about something."

He crossed the hall again and put up his hand to knock. Though he never did knock on this door, and doing it would show that he had come in on them ten minutes ago. Red stood for a second, undecided. Then he put his hand on the latch, and as he pushed the door open, he called across to Greenberg to be sure the X-ray plates were all in o.r. by four-thirty.

He turned and walked into Dr. Enns's office. "Did you want to see me, Dr. Enns?" he asked briskly.

Bill Enns sat behind his desk, alone. He was looking tired.

"You have put in a long enough day, maybe," said Red, going over to the couch and sitting down.

"Not at two P.M.," said the Chief.

"You're looking pale around the gills. Maybe if you'd go back to bed for an hour—"

"Dr. Cahill!" snapped the Chief. "I have been shut away from the wind and the sunshine for six weeks. I am thin. My hip hurts like hell, and my wrist is stiff. If I look pale or any

93

other way, I have a real excuse for looking as I do and acting as I do, which is cross."

Red looked down at a yellow stain on his right thumb. Enns had a real excuse, but he had not mentioned it and would not.

"Now," Dr. Enns was rasping, "can you give me any excuse at all for the way *you* have behaved lately?"

Red looked up in surprise. Then he frowned. For the minute he could not think of a thing to say. "Did you have me come here . . . ?" he began.

"I did. I called you in to talk about the way *you* look, the way *you* act, and to say that I am ordering a week's rest for you, Dr. Cahill."

Red's jaw dropped. "But, why?" he asked in honest inquiry.

Dr. Enns flapped his hand. "Don't you know?" he asked. "Really, don't you?"

Red shook his head. He was genuinely puzzled.

"Well, then, Doctor. I will tell you what I am talking about! I am saying that for the past six weeks you have been damn hard to live with."

Red drew his lips thin. "I think I have done my work, sir," he said stiffly.

"You have done your work and mine as well. Yes. That is, you have done the mechanics of your work. But you are like a thin wire drawn too tight, Red, and before you break I am passing out this order."

Red stood up. "But a *week*, sir!" he protested. "*Now?*"

"Right now!"

"I've scheduled that hematoma for five this evening—"

"Gutzell can do it."

Gutzell could. But, "What am I supposed to do with a week off?"

94

"The saints defend us!" cried Bill Enns. "If at your age and state of health you do not know what to do with a week's vacation, Dr. Cahill, you need one more than I realized."

"I'm afraid I don't understand, sir."

"No, I am afraid you do not. So I shall tell you what I have in mind. First, we'll see what we have on hand, what we have to work on. We'll take, in a manner of speaking, a case history of Red Cahill, M.D. And what goes down on the chart? Name: Redding Cahill. Age: thirty-two—thirty-one?"

"Yes, sir."

"Yes. American. Male. White. Height six foot two, or thereabouts. Weight, two hundred, give or take ten pounds. Profession, medicine. Surgery. Other interests: none."

Enns's blue eyes looked piercingly at his senior resident.

"Sir . . ." Red attempted.

"*Other interests: none,*" Dr. Enns repeated. "And so here we have a man who is only half a man. He has never heard, he has never learned, the truism that medicine is not, cannot be, should not be, the whole of any man's life!

"Oh, there are men who think it is! We have such zombies right here in this complex. Men, stoop-shouldered and nearsighted from peering into microscopes, desiccated doctors who look at their patients and see only the endocrine system."

Red was able to identify both instances.

"Medicine is not the whole of my life!" he said stiffly. "I know how to have fun. And I have it too."

Dr. Enns gingerly leaned back in his desk chair. "So I've heard," he said dryly. "But I still say, take a week off, and do the best you can with it. And, for Pete's sake, Red, come back feeling and acting something like your old self. Able to forget a minor mistake, able to look at your patients objectively and to deal with them as a well-trained doctor. Able to get along with your co-workers, able—Oh, the devil with it! Get out of here, Red! And don't let me see hide nor hair of you for a week!"

6

❋ ❋

MORE than anything else, Red was angry. He was
tempted to do exactly, precisely, what Enns had ordered.
Walk out. But he did not. He spent the afternoon assigning
surgery for the next five days, getting his "housekeeping"
records in order, talking to Gutzell and to Miss Greenberg.
"I am going to be away for a week, so—"

He made careful rounds of the entire floor; he tidied his
room and packed a bag. Sometime during his busyness he
got in touch with C'ele, and at six o'clock he presented
himself at her front door. In the street behind him stood his
car, the top up, his bag in the trunk. It was raining—a cold,
steady rain.

In the crook of his arm was a large paper bag which
contained two steaks, a bottle of wine, and a loaf of French
bread.

C'ele welcomed him with quiet pleasure. It had been too
long since Red had come to see her in this way. "Are you
off duty?" she asked, going to the kitchen to unpack the
groceries.

"Yep." He hung his raincoat on the corner of a picture.

"Take it to the shower rail in the bathroom, Red," she

97

called. "If it's wet, it will smudge the wall." She turned on the broiler.

Red put his raincoat where she had directed. He came back to the living room and turned on the TV; he watched the half-hour newscast, conscious of C'ele's moving about. She was wearing an orange sweater and muddy-brown slacks. On her they looked good.

The steaks and the bread smelled delicious. C'ele was whipping up a salad. She brought it to the table, the coffee-pot, the steaks. "Come and get it!" she called to Red.

He snapped off the TV. He came to the table and held C'ele's chair. "Looks good," he told her. "Smells good."

"Taste it and see."

"It tastes good, too," he said, grinning.

C'ele all but held her breath. What had brought about this change in Red? Would he tell her? If he did not, she would just know her luck and enjoy the evening.

"You're not even on call?" she ventured to ask.

He shook his head and broke off a chunk of bread. "I'm off tonight—and all this next week."

C'ele put down her knife and fork. "Red!" she cried. "What . . . ?"

"Enns told me to take a week off and said that he hoped I'd know what to do with it."

C'ele brushed her hand across her eyes. "I never heard of such a thing," she said. "What happened? Why should he . . . ?"

Red ate his bread. "He says I'm cranky, hard to live with—"

"Well, you are," C'ele agreed, picking up her fork. If *that* was what was behind this order . . .

Red laughed. "Yes," he agreed, "I am."

"And have been," said C'ele calmly.

"I guess you and Enns are both right," Red said thoughtfully. "My disposition has gone sour lately. I know I have been ugly to you, C'ele. And I'm sorry." He was looking at her.

C'ele shrugged. "It's all right, Red," she said, smiling at him.

"It is not all right!" he cried. "And don't you take my ugliness, C'ele! Don't take ugliness from any man!" His voice lifted. "You should have more spunk!"

C'ele leaned back in her chair and watched him, still smiling. Then she reached out her hand and touched his. "Let's get married, Red," she said softly.

"*Agggh!*" He cut his steak. "Eat your dinner, and don't go soft on me."

C'ele looked down at her plate. She shouldn't have said that; she should never push things with Red. She was sorry she had done such a thing, because it seemed that he was really upset about the vacation order. He evidently was shocked to realize how far he had lost control of himself.

She waited, as quietly as she could, for Red to make the next move. If he was worrying about Enns's implied criticism of his work . . .

Red was worrying about just that.

"I keep thinking," he said aloud, speaking slowly, "that all has not been said and done about that trouble I got into right after Enns was hurt. You know—that child who was injured, and his parents I chewed out? Some ways I look at it that doesn't seem to be such an important thing. And at other times it appears to be just about the most important thing I ever did."

"You think about it too much, maybe," said C'ele. She filled his coffee cup.

"Yes," Red agreed. "I could be doing that too. Anyway,

99

I have gone sour at a very crucial time for me."

"What means *crucial?*" asked C'ele, using an idiom which had, on previous occasions, made him laugh. But not tonight.

He was dead serious. "Well," he pointed out, "here I stand with six months to go on my residency."

"Yes."

"I have always thought I could—and might—renew. Do another year, you see. But now I don't know if such an opportunity is still in the picture, should I want to renew."

C'ele got up to change the plates. She moved with deftness in the small space. She opened the refrigerator and took out small glass bowls that contained scoops of orange sherbet and chocolate ice cream; she put these on glass plates that already held two crisp cookies. She set Red's dessert before him. "Don't you want to renew?" she asked.

He had been watching her as she moved about, a slender girl, young, capable. A good listener. She knew just enough about his profession to make her understand the terms of his present problem. He liked C'ele. . . .

He scrubbed his knuckles through his short hair. "I don't know what I want," he cried. "Lately I have worried about myself. Here I've put in ten—almost eleven—years studying medicine. And during all that time I've been sure of myself. Now, in what could be my last year of training—and not until now—I begin to wonder if I am fit to be in brain surgery."

"You're very good at it, Red," said C'ele firmly. "The whole hospital says you are."

"Maybe the whole hospital doesn't know what it is talking about. Maybe I am not good at a service which takes—which demands—a particularly stable personality. It does not take a man who can blow his stack the way I've been blowing mine lately. I know that!

"Why, do you know, C'ele, I've got into such a state about battered children that I cannot consider any child without trying to prove it a police case? And that ain't good, darling. That ain't good!"

"I won't believe you're that bad," said C'ele confidently.

Red shrugged. "I'm bad enough. And Enns recognizes it if you don't. He knows I'm in a constant dither. And the main reason is, C'ele, I literally do not know what I want to do next with my medical life.

"And that, for a guy who has been as one-personed as I have always been, is a terrible feeling." He sounded angry, indeed furious, at finding himself caught in such a trap.

"Perhaps I was too confident," he said. "Too sure of myself. I certainly thought I had life nailed down. I would finish my residency, pass the boards, go into staff work, have my own office—diagnosis, consultations, treatment, teaching. A busy surgeon, and a successful one . . .

"It's quite a thing, my dear, to have a balloon of that color and size blow up in your face."

Could she tell him that nothing really had blown up and probably was not apt to? Now she was pretty sure that Enns had given Red a week to think out his problems. But she decided to say nothing.

Except to suggest that they move into the living room.

He sat down on the couch. She brought his coffee cup, filled her own, and curled up in the big chair, where she could look at Red.

Red stirred his coffee. He used neither cream nor sugar, but he always stirred a fresh cup of coffee, around and around. "I guess my first tremors came," he said thoughtfully, "when you kept fussing about my being always in Enns's shadow."

C'ele made a soft, moaning sound of regret.

"When Enns was hurt," Red continued, "I had to think you were right, because I sure as hell missed him. Right off I made that terrific boo-boo with the beaten child."

C'ele leaned forward. "It was not a boo-boo, Red!" she cried. "The child *had* been beaten. Social Services proved it."

"You don't see where the boo-boo came, dear," he said patiently. "I should have known that Social Services would handle the matter and that I didn't *need* to threaten the parents. I should not have had to stand up before a crowd of my peers and listen to myself being lectured on the subject.

"And now—" He leaned forward to put his cup on the low table. "*Now* I get this suspension."

He made a growling sound.

"Dr. Enns," said C'ele earnestly, "just thinks you have worked too hard while he was laid up. You should be happy to have this chance to get away."

"And do what?" Red regarded her fishily.

"Well, you could take a trip, couldn't you? Go to see your mother, maybe. Or there's Florida. I read where the whole southeastern coast is crowded with girls on their Christmas vacations."

Red lifted an eyebrow. "That's an idea. Would you trust me?"

C'ele shook her head. "Frankly, no."

He laughed.

"That's better," said C'ele. "Now, tell me where you will go."

He nodded. "I'll go to a motel or something. For the night. Tomorrow—well, there's this hospital upstate. About a hundred and twenty-five miles north of here. It's a big shiny new teaching hospital connected to a new medical school. The university up there has instituted a four-year medical course. Enns told me—two weeks ago—about an opening there. It seems they want a resident neurosurgeon."

"A *resident?*"

Red brushed the air between them with his flattened hand. "Oh, not generically a resident!" he corrected C'ele. "Not in the sense that I am a resident here. I'd be a staff doctor there, a part of the organization. But I would not have a private practice and an office outside the hospital."

"I see."

"Dr. Enns thought I might go up and look at the place, talk about the position to those in charge, see their setup, find out roughly how much N.S. work they get—things like that."

C'ele laughed. "And spend your beautiful vacation in a hospital that will look and smell just like the one you're leaving."

"It won't take all week!"

"Yes, you might find time to see some other hospitals. But go on, Red. If that's what you like. Are you going to take me with you?"

"Do you think we could keep such a trip a secret?"

"Oh, my," said C'ele. "That wouldn't be any fun."

Red stood up. "No, it wouldn't be. So—let's wash the dishes."

The next morning when Red started his drive north, the rain was reduced to a fine mist. Fog was thick along the river as he crossed the bridge at Glen Owen. That was the town where he and Polly had come the morning after Enns's accident. Red looked around to see if he could locate the hospital, and he wondered how Dr. La Fleur was doing.

On the far side of the bridge rain began to fall more heavily. It was a miserable day. He turned on the car radio. The news was not especially good, and the weather report was even worse. Rain, the temperature dropping, the barometer . . .

Red drove steadily along, the windshield wipers going rhythmically. Now the rain made a sharp, hissing sound as it fell.

He wondered how things were going back on N.S. Had the Wilkins child been dismissed? How had Gutzell made out with his hematoma? Gutzell was a capable surgeon, but he did not like being put in charge of decisions and in spots where he could be blamed for an error of judgment. Well, look who was thinking *that* about Gutzell!

Red frowned. The wiper was pushing small platelets of thin ice across the glass. He watched for a road sign. Yes, he still had sixty miles to go.

Yesterday Red had taken a minute to look in on Ronald Scholle. The kid was doing fine. They would be moving him out of the hospital during this coming week. He was to go to a foster home.

Another weather report came on the radio. The temperature, said the announcer, was plummeting. It was now at the freezing point and due to drop.

Even as he listened, Red felt his tires slip. He had a long downhill grade before him; he had come into hilly country. The freezing rain now pelted the car like fine shot. He edged gingerly across a small bridge. It was getting really slick; the farther north he got, the icier it would get. He could still turn back . . .

Or stop some place. If he saw a place. Along here the

towns were small and the distances between them great. The wooded hills were probably beautiful, but the two-lane road built up and down around their slopes was pure murder!

Cautiously he slowed to read an upcoming sign. It said that he was approaching the town of Old Pardee and the Northland Motel—Modern. TV. Air-Conditioned.

That last Red could spare on this chill day. But anything reasonably modern—if he ever got to the top of this long and winding hill road. Easy does it, he told himself. Keep strictly away from the brakes. Go with the skid. . . .

He made it. Of course now he faced the long downhill grade, but before that, and here, right at his hand, beautiful in gaudy neon lights, was the Northland Motel. In, presumably, the town of Old Pardee.

There was no sign of a *town*. That Red could see. Maybe everyone lived in tree houses, for the wooded hills pressed close. But why quibble? There was this-here-now modern motel, with TV and air conditioning. There was a restaurant, a filling station, and the place looked clean. If he found a NO VACANCY sign, he would cry like a baby.

Fortunately he found no such thing. A sign said that the manager's office was in the restaurant, and he went there, shaking the rain from his hair, and slapping it off his coat sleeve as he came inside. The place was bright, steamy. There were tables with cheery red tops and red-padded benches. There was a counter complete with shiny urns and a half-dozen customers, a girl; the fragrance of hot coffee and pastry was warmly welcome. Two or three people greeted him and agreed that the weather was not fit for man or beast.

"Goin' to be good for hog butcherin', though, if it keeps up," said one man. He wore bib overalls and a sheepskin coat, redolent in the heat of the restaurant.

The girl on the counter stool winked at Red. "It takes all kinds," she said, her eyes round above the rim of her coffee cup. He nodded and walked across to the desk which proclaimed itself as the domain of the *Manager*. There an eyeglassed man, thin, in his fifties, was rustling papers. He had already looked Red over.

"I'm driving north," Red told him. "But in this weather . . . Could you put me up overnight?"

"Certainly can, sir. It is bad out there."

"That's one word for it," Red agreed. "I was happy to see your sign. But where's the town?"

"Old Pardee, you mean?"

"That was advertised."

"Yes, sir." The manager was not a humorous person. "Well, Old Pardee is on top of the next rise. It's about two mile."

Red took the offered pen and signed his name. After a moment's thought he wrote his car license. "How big a town is it?" he asked.

"Three thousand. It's considered right pretty."

"Yes. I like hills and woods when they aren't ice-covered."

"Yes, sir. Hunting's good, and we have a couple of lakes with fishing."

"Not tonight, thank you," said Red. "Does your town have a hospital?"

"Yes, sir, it does. It's small, of course. But real good. It's owned by two doctors, Dr. Graham and Doc Robinson."

Red's ear caught the difference in the men's titles. "Proprietary, hmm?" he commented.

"What's that, sir?"

"Oh, I just meant it was a privately owned hospital."

"Yes, sir, it is. Now I'll tell you who can give you information about the hospital. The office manager of it is sitting right over there now, drinking coffee and eating a hamburger."

Red turned to look at this manager, aware that the man behind the counter had turned the register around so that he could read Red's name and address.

The hospital manager—it had to be the one!—was the girl in the tight beige skirt and the very high heels. Her hair was combed into a great round dome; her make-up was heavy. This was the girl who had winked at Red, and she had to be the hospital manager because she was the only one who was eating a hamburger. She was not looking at Red now, but she obviously was conscious of him and that he was looking at her.

Red wished it were C'ele sitting there. The little nut, she would make an adventure out of this interlude. Even the hog butchering would intrigue her.

He went out to his car and drove it to the space adjoining his motel room. He put his suitcase inside, then he returned to the restaurant. Out in the open there was ice. He hung his raincoat on a hook and went over to the counter, straddling the stool next to the young woman who was still eating her hamburger.

"Nasty day," he told her.

"It surely is nasty," said his neighbor. Her voice was high, clear, a little louder than was necessary. She wore a very tight beige sweater under her suit jacket; some magnificent engineering had lifted her bosom. . . .

Red coughed and said "Thank you" for the coffee. He took up the spoon and stirred the steaming contents of the cup.

The girl—she must be thirty, but no matter—smiled at Red.

"You are very intelligent," she said warmly, "to decide to remain here for the duration of this storm."

"I'm a coward," Red told her.

She laughed trillingly. "You would not want to destroy your fine car, either," she told him.

"It isn't very fine when it goes sideways. Besides, I saw you through the window."

"Oh . . ." She gasped; she laughed; she drew her shoulders up to her ears. But, no, she did not blush.

Red grinned and tasted his coffee. *Any port in a storm*, he told himself, ashamed of the thought. He should be able to do better than *that!*

"I understand you are a physician," said the girl. The manager must have spread the word while he was out of the restaurant.

"Yes, I am. I'm a surgical resident down at Lincoln."

"Oh yes. That's a sort of intern, isn't it? I know about those things, you see."

"Yes. The manager—" He nodded his head toward the cash register.

"His name is Dean, William E. Dean."

"Thank you. He said you were the administrator of the hospital in Old Pardee."

"I am," admitted his companion. "My name is Smith, Maurita Smith."

"Mrs.?"

"Oh, goodness, no!" She looked coy. "I've had the opportunity presented—"

"Of course." Red listened to her and watched her, fascinated. She was a monument of exaggeration—and volubility. She was certain that she could impress this doctor, and she was more than ready to try.

"Tell me about yourself," he urged, nodding to the waitress to fill their coffee cups.

"Well . . ." she bridled. Red had met that word in books. Now he saw it in action. This woman *bridled*. She tossed her top-heavy head; she made chirruping sounds; she flipped her hands.

"Do you live in the vicinity?" he asked aloud. Privately he wondered what the hospital manager, or administrator, was doing on the afternoon of such a day two miles from her desk.

She told him that she lived in Old Pardee. "In a big old house. Some persons would consider it a mansion, but it is just home to me. There's only my mother and me there now, and a servant, of course. Our family is an old one, you see. Gracious, I am related to half the residents of this county! I love Old Pardee. When I went away—to school, you know, and then to college—well, I tried managing an office for an advertising firm in the city, but it just wasn't *home!* I presume I am sentimental, but anyway, I am happiest at home! I began helping Dr. Graham—and of course hospital work is very worth while. Now he cannot do without me, and I wouldn't want to ask him to. He's such a dear. But with no idea of business. You know?"

She flapped her heavily weighted eyelashes at Red. She was, almost certainly, a liar, he decided. She probably sat at the front desk, answered the telephone, and made out the bills at the hospital. She probably was the clerk.

"How will you get back to town?" Red asked, lighting her cigarette. He would bet her make-up was an eighth of an inch thick.

"I am a very good driver. And I stopped here to have chains put on."

109

Red snorted. "I could drive, too, with chains," he told her.

"Well, you don't have to, but I do," she pointed out. "And I must get back to the hospital. You see, on a night like this is going to be we will have accidents come in, and arrangements will need to be made."

She hadn't yet explained why she had found herself two miles from town on such an afternoon, and it probably did not matter. Red's guess was that she worked split-shift. In the morning, and for a couple of hours after four o'clock.

"Tell me about the hospital," he said. "How big—the doctors—all about it. I was going on to Bridgeton to see about a possible opening there, but I may just decide to stay in Old Pardee. It seems to have attractions."

She laughed, hard, and heads turned to look at her. Dr. Cahill, she told all concerned, was a real joker.

The men in the room were, off and on, listening to Maurita talk to the stranger—a city doctor he was, they told each other.

The hospital where she worked, Maurita told the big young doctor, wasn't so big, of course, but it always got an A-rating. "You know? We've got a sprinkler system, fire doors—things like that—tissue meetings . . ."

Two doctors owned and ran the hospital. "They are very good, too," she assured Dr. Cahill. "Just because they work in a small hospital here in the hills, don't think—"

"I don't," Red assured her. "I admire any man doing a job I know would be beyond me."

"Oh, you'll learn," Maurita comforted him.

"Do they do surgery?" Red asked.

"Of course we perform surgery! All sorts. Dr. Graham is the surgeon, and Dr. Robinson assists; he is the physician, you understand?"

"How old are they—these men?"

"Oh, age never signifies too much to me. Dr. Graham, I should estimate, is in his fifties. He is a large man—tall. He has been blond, but his hair is very gray now. He is not very loquacious but friendly, if you comprehend me? People trust him. Now Dr. Robinson is a small man, and I estimate him to be ten years younger than Dr. Graham. He is dark, wears rather thick-lensed glasses, and, well, Dr. Graham is the best of the two. He comes from a very old family, you know. There are Grahams all over this county. Now Dr. Robinson is all right, but he is the cranky sort. You know?"

Red nodded. "I'm that kind myself," he told Maurita. She laughed at him, and said she really must go.

Red helped her into a hooded coat; she put her high-heeled slippers into the pockets and thrust her feet into red boots. She took up her huge purse and went out to the red car which, rear wheels now bound in chains, stood under the portico of the filling station. The attendant talked to her for five minutes, then she drove away, having no trouble.

The rain still came down, freezing as it fell.

Red bought a magazine and took it to one of the booths. Now and then the manager or one of the customers would stop and talk to him. He read and listened to the radio. . . .

At five o'clock he decided to go to his room, watch the TV news reports. No earlier than seven he would eat dinner, get himself a good night's sleep, and tomorrow . . .

He had been sitting where he could not watch the road, and when he stepped out of the restaurant door, he stopped in amazement. The whole world was frosted white with ice. Even in the dusk the light that came from the illuminated motel and its service buildings showed Red a hillside forest of crystal. Each small twig was fringed with icicles. The power lines and telephone lines looped down in incredible, glistening arcs.

Red shook his head. Such a world was both beautiful and terrifying. He walked gingerly over to the filling station and looked in on the attendant. "What happens if one of those wires out there should break?"

The man chuckled. "We'd be in a hell of a mess," he said cheerfully.

"What would you do?"

"Well, I guess we'd wait till the service truck came around. They always do in time. Dean keeps some candles handy over at the motel, but of course if you don't have juice you don't have no heat or light."

"Do these storms come often?"

"No, sir, they don't. Ain't had one this bad in ten year, I'd figure. Here comes the wrecker."

Red stood with the attendant and watched the wrecker inch up the hill toward them. Its double-wheeled tires carried chains; the driver was being careful. He came to a full stop when a lighter car attempted to make the downgrade, skidding, straightening, and skidding again.

Red shook his head. "I wouldn't have that man's nerve," he said. "I wonder if Miss Smith made it. Perhaps I should have gone with her. In this weather she might have needed a doctor close by."

"She'd 'a liked that fine," said his companion. "But I reckon Maurita made it. If not, she could walk for help." He went back into the warm, bright office, exaggeratedly swiveling his hips in a good imitation of the way Maurita walked. Red laughed and went toward his room.

The branches of the trees across the road clashed and rattled in the light wind. He unlocked his cabin door and went into the warm, pleasant room. He wondered if he had a flashlight in the car; he had not brought his medical bag which would have contained one.

He hung his raincoat and suit jacket away, turned on the TV, and lay down on the couch bed. The TV newscast came on with a road report. Superfluously, to Dr. Cahill, it told that the roads in mid-state were "impassable" because of freezing rain, falling wires, and downed trees. Outside his window Red could hear a car whine along one of the roads listed as impassable. He shook his head. Preventive road warnings, like preventive medicine, did nothing for the individual who would not listen and co-operate.

He yawned and again decided to go to bed early—right after he ate some dinner. This was his vacation, and on this night at least he would get in some sack time. He should spend the whole week catching up on his sleep—that was what a doctor's vacation was for.

Though Red probably would not know how or what to do with the opportunity. He was used to working long, long hours and snatching sleep as he could. He was used to having the problems of a floorful of patients to think about.

Now, in this isolated room, he had only himself and his problems, if any, on his mind. But where did he start? As any physician started? With a case history. Who are you? What seems to be your trouble?

Ah, yes. What seems to be your trouble? Was it organic, functional, psychosomatic? When did it start?

With the first battered child? Red could use that as a starting point and from there try to trace down his problems, get them sorted and spread out in the open—write a list of them down on a sheet of motel stationery—and then attempt to solve them, at least by plan.

Some could be solved. A doctor could work toward laws that would protect a misused child; he could talk on the subject to the proper people. . . .

7 ❋❋❋❋❋❋❋❋❋❋❋❋❋❋❋❋❋❋❋❋❋❋❋❋❋❋

AT exactly seven o'clock Red went back to the restaurant, sat down at a table, and ordered his dinner—a steak, French fries, a vegetable, and pie. The choice was not great. Nearly everyone else ordered the plate dinner which, that night, was stew. Not that there were many others.

The manager, the waitress, and presumably a cook; two men seated at the counter, two others and Red at the tables. There was talk about cars in the ditch along the highway.

An hour later, when Red went back to his room, it was still raining and freezing. A nasty night.

At nine o'clock, restless, unable to do the thinking which he had determined to do, bored with the TV program, Red put on his coat and went outside. He would get some cigarettes and walk as far as the ice would let him.

The driveway of the motel and restaurant had been salted heavily, but it still was a-slush and slippery.

Watching his step, Red walked for a way along the road shoulder. This was a strange world where he found himself. To either side of the road there were sagging, white-glistening trees. They were like a hundred, a thousand, silver-sprayed Christmas trees, without colored lights or ornaments. The wind whispered and clashed faintly among the branches. The power lines looped heavily toward the ground, incredible tinsel garlands for his Christmas scene. Up at the top of the next "rise" there was a glow of light. That would be Old Pardee. Even a moderate illumination would glow pink against tonight's low-hanging clouds.

Red turned back to the motel. Two miles in this rain, on this ice, was not for him. He would go to bed.

His own footsteps crackled as he walked. There was no other sound; the world was eerily silent. Not a voice, no sound of cars—nothing! No car engine labored up the hill, no horn sounded. He was as alone as he would ever get. He shook the rain from his hair and walked more rapidly toward the green and red lights of the motel.

And then, while he was still two hundred feet away, a sound shattered the silence. It was a car, driven fast. Now he could see the lights of it coming up the hill.

He shouted in the lonely night, with no one to hear him—certainly no one in that car which came over the hill, driven much too fast . . .

Red stopped dead where he was, watching in fascination as the car topped the ascent, skidded to one side of the road and then across, spinning clear around.

The car came on sideways, sideways. It was righted and skidded again. The seconds all this took seemed like an hour. The car must crash!

It did crash.

Fifty feet away from it, Red sprang for the ditch, but the car skidded again and struck the gas island of the filling station, then came to a stop against the pump. . . .

And Red Cahill ran. As in a dream, he ran, his weighted

feet going up and down, getting him nowhere. He ran slowly, heavily, laboring. But he must reach the car!

On impact a woman—a girl—had been thrown clear. A man was crumpled behind the wheel. Red shouted and shouted again. The driver *must* be pulled free—away from the gasoline!

Now others joined him, running, shouting men, stretching their hands to tug at the driver of the car. The manager of the motel was there, and the cook in his white apron. Their eyes showed that they knew the danger. With Red, they managed to pull the driver out of the car, free of it, and then to carry him far enough away . . .

He was dead.

Red knelt over him. Fire licked upward from the gasoline pump, incredibly bright against the shadows, reflected in a million points from the icy glitter.

There was no silence now. The fire roared angrily, and men were shouting. "Get back!" they screamed. "*Get back!*"

There was the brightness and the dark. There was the noise—the shouting, the roar of the flames, and the car's horn blowing. The scream of it was a maddening accompaniment to hell!

Red went to the girl who had been thrown free of the car and crouched beside her. She lay crumpled at the far edge of the wide driveway.

She was safe enough from the flames, and the flames gave the doctor the light which he needed to make his examination.

Carefully, feeling for injuries, he straightened the slight body and drew her coat about her. She was a slender girl— a mere handful of girlhood—young and lovely.

117

His hands felt of her head, her neck. He rotated the head gently, and he rolled back an eyelid. There was a purity in the line of her cheek, her eye, her ear and throat. Her hair was the color of burnished copper, cut short, thick and soft upon her head. Her eyelashes were bronze and lay thickly against her cheek.

Red lifted the small hand—as delicate as a shell—and let it drop, limply. He stroked the bright hair back from the forehead, and his touch was tender. It was as if—almost as if—he had long known this girl, as if she had long been loved by him.

The flames shot up higher and brighter; their heat could be felt. The monotonous blat of the horn pressed on one's nerves. Red straightened enough to unbutton his coat, and doing it, he looked curiously at his hand. There was blood on it, thick and sticky. He turned the girl's head again. Yes, there was a wound and slowly oozing blood, dark and thick. He found his folded handkerchief and pressed it firmly in place, held it. He turned and shouted, hoarsely, loudly.

"Send for an ambulance!" he roared. "And make it fast!"

Squatting again on his heels, he gently handled the girl; aware of someone standing close, he asked that someone to fetch a blanket.

The man moved away, and Red heard him—or someone —say he was a doctor. He heard the voices; he saw the monstrous shadows cast by the fire, but he saw clearly, and was keenly aware of, only the girl. The lovely young girl, badly hurt—her skull, probably her spine, maybe other fractures.

The fire truck came in, roaring. It carried foam, and the blaze dropped around the pump and the burning car. The horn moaned still, a pleading death cry.

Yes, said one of the black-slickered men, the ambulance was on the way. The roads were murder, but it would be along.

And it did come—really, Red supposed, help arrived quite quickly. It was just— He wanted to gather this girl into his arms and run with her to where he could help her.

The ambulance men tumbled out and went first to the dead man.

Red stood up and swore at them hotly. "It's the girl, you blithering idiots!" he shouted. "*She's* your concern! She must be taken to the hospital at once! Bring the stretcher, and I'll tell you exactly how to handle her."

"Who are you, mister?" asked the ambulance driver, a big man in a heavy overcoat and a felt hat. His helper was young and wore a light raincoat.

"What difference . . . ?" Red began hotly, then stopped. Of course it made a difference. He fumbled for his wallet. "I'm a doctor," he said more quietly. "A surgeon. I put up here overnight and this wreck came to me. I—that man yonder is dead. But this girl—I think her back is hurt, and there must be a concussion. We'll take it very slowly."

Very slowly indeed the girl was lifted to the stretcher, wheeled to the big ambulance, then lifted. "Don't jar her!" cautioned Dr. Cahill. "The least thing—"

The girl's eyes now were open; they were a deep violet-blue. Red spoke to her, but she did not answer. His fingers felt of her head injury, and he winced.

The stretcher locked in place, he got into the ambulance with it.

"Let's get going!" he called down to the driver. "You can come back for the dead man later. Now we must get to the hospital as quickly—and as safely, of course—as is possible! Ask someone to phone ahead."

The authority in his voice, in his eyes and his face, directed those who needed direction. The heavy doors slammed shut; the driver and his young assistant got into the wide front seat. Red looked at his patient and strapped himself into the jump seat beside her. The slow drive began. The ambulance backed out to the road, straightened, and started down the hill, moving with care and agonizing slowness.

The girl was alive, which was the first thing. Her reflexes were not the best; she was only semiconscious, and probably not in pain, though once or twice she moaned softly. Red watched her closely. There was oxygen if it was needed. So far it was not.

His hand on the girl's wrist, the doctor sat and gazed, almost unseeing, out at the ice-coated branches of the trees which arched across the road. Some of the trees were bent to the ground.

Eventually they came to houses, widely separated, then closer together, and closer. Once, ahead of them, the wires arced in a flash of blue flame and shooting sparks, and suddenly the house windows were not there any more; the street lights were gone.

The heavy car moved on, gingerly negotiated a curve, and moved on again. Red wished they could hurry; he knew they could not. That they were moving at all was a miracle. He should settle for that.

But—how much farther to this hospital? And what was that hospital going to be like? He tried to remember what the Smith woman had told him, and then he cautiously divided that memory by two. Her "wonderful" must be—had better be—considered as "adequate." Well, adequacy would suffice and be better than the kitchen table which Red might have had to use.

Maurita's "genius of a surgeon" would more likely be a capable man. Which was not bad, either. Red could be thankful for that much.

8

THEY had gone down a hill, and up one, and now they were into town streets. Paved. Lined with stores, with houses, and finally—at last—standing behind tall trees, the wide lawn littered tonight with broken branches, a lighted sign bloomed over the columned entrance. A driveway went up and around the building . . .

They had reached the hospital.

The heavy ambulance turned slowly, slowly, between the gateposts into the drive, started up, hesitated, then went on, under a porte-cochere, and around the building to the rear.

And there on the lighted doorstep stood a man in a white coat, waiting.

Red sighed. At long last, the hospital, and the doctor—a big man, bigger than Red Cahill. His shoulders were stooped a little—he would be fifty—and his hair was graying blond. His face, as he waited, was calm and alert.

The ambulance stopped; the helper came around and opened the doors. Red jumped down. He went swiftly over to the waiting doctor. "I have a head and spine case, Doctor," he said crisply. "Critical. We should get it to your emergency room as quickly as possible."

He turned to watch the men take the stretcher out and down. The hospital doctor opened the door for it to pass through. He glanced at Red. "I'm Graham," he said quietly. "We don't have much of an e.r., I'm afraid." He stood aside for Red to precede him.

Red's hand rubbed moisture from his hair. "I'm Cahill," he said. "M.D. How do you manage without— At our Center we have an emergency room bigger than the whole hospital."

"Yes," said Dr. Graham, his manner calm and unhurried. His eyes were on the nurse and the orderly who were taking charge of the stretcher. "Big e.r.'s," he said, "are the present trend."

Red stepped over to the stretcher with a word of caution —there must be no jars; the girl must be lifted on the blanket.

Dr. Graham nodded confirmation to his people, and Red went back to him.

"How do you serve your big e.r.?" politely asked the hospital owner. "Rotate your service?"

The two doctors were marking time. Walking slowly along behind the stretcher, watching it, talking to one another.

"We rotate the interns on duty," said Dr. Cahill. "And staff it with salaried men. A surgeon, an internist, a pediatrician. Residents are assigned duty in e.r. as need arises."

The stretcher negotiated the door into the hospital corridor. There was a nurses' station, a double swinging door into the front lobby. A nurse passed and looked curiously at Red.

Dr. Graham was considering what Red had said about the Center's emergency service. The doctors were feeling each other out, like dogs, Red thought. Circling, sniffing, watching—wary, yet ready to be friendly.

"Salaried staff, eh?" said Dr. Graham. He wore white ducks, a knitted white shirt, and a long white coat. "There's a trend to that, too, I believe. Do you do e.r. service?"

Red shucked out of his raincoat. "I'm still fairly young at the game, Doctor. Just now I'm a resident at Lincoln, and—yes, I do my turn in e.r. when assigned."

Dr. Graham nodded. He was a slow-speaking man. A slight gesture of his hand stopped the stretcher. The ambulance driver still guided it by its chrome handle. A blanket had been spread over the girl, and it had begun to slip. The nurse straightened it. They had reached the elevator; there was a surprisingly modern steel door. The nurse pressed a button; the door slid back. The cage was lighted and large enough for the stretcher and two attendants.

"We'll use the stairs, Doctor," said Dr. Graham, leading the way back along the hall and through the swinging doors, then up a curving stairway. The hospital originally had been a large house—a mansion. The ceilings were high; the carved woodwork and the chandeliers were noble.

The second floor was a replica of the first—two corridors stretching away from the nurses' station. The nurse on duty had gone with the stretcher to the small emergency room. It indeed was "not much," and after a glance at Red, Dr. Graham said to take the patient straight to o.r.

He had quickly explored the girl's head injury, felt gently of her limbs, and listened to her heart and lungs. "I'm afraid she is badly hurt, Doctor," he told Red.

"Yes, she is."

"I'll get you some whites."

Red nodded, and seeing the stretcher go into the operating room, he followed his host to the scrub room at the end

124

of the corridor. Graham produced a scrub suit and cap, and Red changed quickly, thinking about the case. Dr. Graham had gone out of the room, but he was back again by the time Red was dressed in the baggy garments.

He could feel tension in his every muscle; his brain tingled with it. If he had this case back at the Center, with Gutzell standing by to assist, and his own familiar o.r. team, he might have managed calm and clear thinking rather than feeling—

But here—with the copper-haired young girl at the mercy of this hospital, on such a night . . .

Red nodded to Dr. Graham's suggestion that they now might go on to o.r. "We want to know what we have," said that doctor.

The girl was on the table, and the nurses were busy with her, one on each side of the table. They had cut her clothing away, and . . .

Red glanced at Dr. Graham and stood back. This was the other man's o.r.

Dr. Graham asked for more light and moved to the table, Red at his shoulder. The girl moaned softly—a nurse was gently sponging her face and trying as best she could to clean the clotted blood from her hair.

"Let it go for now, Rosie," said Dr. Graham softly.

Red winced at the name, though the girl, the nurse, was professional in a green wrap-around; she wore a cap and mask. Her hands had known what they were doing.

Red watched Dr. Graham, who seemed to know what he was doing too. His hands were swift and sure. He examined the limbs—one leg, the other. He lifted each hand and let it drop; he felt of the arms. He examined the eyes, counted the pulse and respiration with a frown of absorption. He used his stethoscope and then put both palms flat against

125

the girl's cheeks and rotated the head. He turned it one way, then the other; with a flashlight he examined the wound on the back of her head.

"What did she strike, Doctor?" he asked. "Do you know?"

"Yes. I saw the whole thing. She was thrown from the car—it had crashed into the filling station gas pump—at a high rate of speed. The girl was thrown out on impact—thrown several feet—to the ground. She first struck a sort of platform—an island, I think it is called—then slid. She fell on her back and head, hard."

"Mhmmmnnn," said the doctor. He turned the girl's head again, his finger tips upon the spine. He lifted the hair. Next he examined the reflexes, lifting the hands, dropping them, stroking the tube of his flashlight against the bottom of her feet, testing the knee reflex.

He stepped back from the table. "There's a probable subdural hematoma, Dr. Cahill," he said gravely. "And a probable spine fracture as well."

Briefly Red closed his eyes; he had not hoped . . . "And we should operate at once," he said firmly.

Dr. Graham lifted an eyebrow. "Let's get out of Rosie's way," he suggested, starting toward the scrub room.

Red did not want to go. He wanted things settled here and now, then— "What's her temperature?" he asked the nurse.

She—Rosie—looked around him to Dr. Graham. He nodded and smiled. "This is Dr. Cahill, Miss Steckman," he said in a fatherly tone. "He's a resident doctor at Lincoln Medical Center."

The nurse acknowledged the introduction and gave Red the information he wanted. Red thanked her and followed Dr. Graham.

That doctor had gone to the hall doorway and was asking the charge nurse if she thought she could find him some coffee.

He turned back to Red. "I am not one for doing things in a hurry, Doctor," he said in his deliberate way.

"But—"

"If we have spine and skull fracture, yes. By delay we may lose the hematoma. There's the risk of shock as well, damage to the soft tissues, infection . . ."

The nurse brought the coffee in two brown mugs. Dr. Graham thanked her and said to be sure they got a blood match.

"I would like to start a transfusion if possible," he told Red, giving him one mug.

"See here, Doctor," Red attempted.

Dr. Graham nodded. "You feel we should do some midnight surgery."

Red shook off the term. "If there is compression of the spine, as well as subdural effusion of blood—"

"A hematoma, yes," said Dr. Graham quietly.

"I think we should correct at once!" cried Dr. Cahill.

"If we have spinal compression," said Dr. Graham. "Yes."

"Don't you think we do?"

"I am pretty sure we do, but what about anesthesia?"

"What about it?" Red was getting angry. And frightened.

"I find it wiser to wait a bit for the patient to be evaluated as a surgical and anesthetic risk. You see, Dr. Cahill . . ."

Red did his best to be patient and courteous. Dr. Graham seemed to have a "thing" about what he called midnight surgery. He declared that he was in no way fascinated by the excitement and glamour of such surgery.

Red drank his coffee and hoped the man soon would talk himself out. He respected Dr. Graham—he had decided that this quaint old building housed a good hospital. Such personnel as he had seen were quiet and efficient.

Graham was very probably a good doctor, even a good surgeon, though probably not on the brain or nerves, but . . .

Was he holding back on that account?

Red put his mug down on the shelf above the waste can.

"Doctor," he said firmly, "you agree with me that if there is compression, you should do immediate surgery?"

Dr. Graham regarded the ruddy-skinned young man, his muscular arms and strong wrists. "Surgery on the spine?" he asked mildly. "I couldn't do such a job."

Red rubbed his hands together. "If such a job is needed," he said, "I can do it."

He turned and pushed back into the operating room, knowing that Dr. Graham was following him. He could not be patient any longer, not when the life of that lovely girl . . . He shook his head. The life of *any* girl, he corrected himself. *Any patient!*

"Perhaps I neglected to tell you," he said, still courteously, "that I am a resident—the *senior* resident—in Neurosurgery at Lincoln."

Dr. Graham was impressed. But, "You couldn't operate here," he said.

Red bent over the table. The girl had gone into convulsion. He glanced at the nurse. "Has she . . . ?" he asked.

"For a minute or so, yes, Doctor."

Red nodded and straightened. "We have to save this girl," he told Dr. Graham. "Look at her. How lovely she is! Her eyelashes would sweep a bird from the bough."

Dr. Graham gazed quizzically at the young doctor. "You don't sound too much like a big-hospital-center medic," he said dryly.

Red flushed and watched their patient relax again. "How old do you think she is?" he asked. "Fifteen? Sixteen?"

Dr. Graham shrugged. "Don't you know who she is? You brought her in."

"Yes, I did, but—look, I only happened to be at the motel. I was out for a breath of air when this car came barreling up the hill and skidded out of control. The girl was thrown out. She's just a kid. We got the driver out before the car burned—he was young too. Twenty, maybe. He wore jeans—and he was killed instantly. His neck was broken on impact. Perhaps he had identification on him."

He was watching the girl; she was in and out of consciousness. Once her wavering hand caught Red's and clung to it. He bent over her, soothing her with his voice. Wanting to help her, *wanting* to . . .

He recognized his emotion, and indeed, he had never felt quite this way about a patient before. Protective, hurt that she was hurt, anxious that she could be helped to live and go on being lovely . . .

Graham was talking. "She probably is from some farm family close by," he was saying. "And the boy too. From your description of him. These girls date young. Her clothes indicate decency, respectability, but no great amount of money, at least not spent—"

Agggh! What difference did all that make? Red spoke brusquely. "Whoever she is, we must operate immediately," he cried. "These convulsions—look at her eyes—they are sure signs of spinal injury. Compression. And this *is* one time for your midnight surgery, sir." He looked at the nurse. "Could you get me a stethoscope, please?" he asked.

"Yes, Doctor. Of course."

Dr. Graham was shaking his head—not at the nurse. "I don't have to remind you, Doctor," he said quietly, "that we cannot do any kind of surgery until we have located the girl's family and secured permission. But I agree—time is an item. So I'll start inquiries."

He walked out of the room. Red took the stethoscope from "Rosie," smiled as he thanked her, and then did not smile as he used it.

By the time Dr. Graham returned, he was again impatient. "We have to operate at once, Doctor!" he said urgently. "She is failing." He gestured toward the chart. "The bleeding is continuing, and we have to start at once! Surgery like this takes hours! I don't know if our girl has the three hours it could take to halt the cerebral hemorrhage from a ruptured blood vessel. Doctor . . ."

Dr. Graham stepped to the table. Now the girl lay limply, deep blue shadows on her temples, her hair startling against her milk-white forehead; she looked frail and very young. He lifted an eyelid. Nothing. She was in coma.

"We must not operate without permission," he said firmly.

Red's face was stern. "We have to operate!"

Across the operating table they faced each other, their eyes steady, their faces masks for any emotion they might be feeling. Even as Dr. Graham prepared to speak further, the lights in the room flickered, dimmed, and went out, then came on again.

Red spoke his alarm. "What if . . . ?" he cried.

But Dr. Graham was being quite calm. He went to a

shelf and from it took down, in turn, three Coleman lanterns. He lit each one and hung it on an I.V. rack which stood against the wall; he pushed the racks to exactly the right positions about the operating table. It was as if he had done this thing many times before.

"I keep these lanterns on hand," he told Red. "I have them all over the hospital." He adjusted a flame. "I regularly inspect them to see that they are clean and filled."

Red put his hands to his head. All of this was incredible! A nightmare!

"We could not afford an auxiliary power plant," Dr. Graham was explaining. "But we also could not afford to find ourselves in the dark at a critical time."

"This is a critical time all right," Red said gruffly. He was by then coldly determined to save the young girl's life, no matter what the hazards and objections. "I feel responsible for this patient," he said urgently. "She was hurt right in front of my eyes; I brought her here for help. I've told you that I will do the surgery, that I can. You could identify me and check on my ability by a call to the city, which I urge you to make at once!"

Now his anger was coming through; it rasped in his voice, flared red in his cheeks, and gleamed icy-blue in his eyes.

Against his passion Dr. Graham stood and spoke quietly. "I know you are what you say you are, Doctor," he said. "The minute a man steps into my hospital and tells me that he is a doctor, I find clues to the sort of doctor he is. By now I have you well pegged. But there still is a matter of ethics—and law."

"If you found someone—anyone—at your feet, Doctor, hurt to any degree, would you deny help to that person?"

"Well, now, help is one thing. . . . How well up are you, Doctor, on the good-Samaritan laws?"

Red shook his head impatiently. Then he took his stethoscope and bent over his patient.

"In Japan, you know," Dr. Graham told him, "if a man is hurt, any Samaritan trying to help him can be held as a criminal who must account for any further injury to him."

"This is not Japan!"

"Isn't it?" asked Dr. Graham quietly.

Red straightened. The electricity again was failing, and the lantern light threw his shadow enormously against the wall and ceiling of the operating room. Sleet rattled against the skylight.

"Dr. Graham," Red demanded, "would you let this young girl *die?* For a matter of *ethics?* Whatever the law says, would your conscience let you do *that?*"

"I am making every effort to identify this child, and I shall make any effort in my power to locate her family. No one here seems to know her, but we'll keep trying. This is an icy night, Doctor. The phones are out, their wires down. The police have had no report, but we will keep trying. Though until we do locate someone responsible—"

Red nodded. "You'll let her die. You'll let her blood seep into her brain tissues; you'll let paralysis grip her limbs. Well, *I'll* not let her! *I* am the Samaritan, Doctor! The choice is mine. This girl lay on the roadway at my feet. Now it is *my* job. And I'll take it on. Any risk will be mine. I'll put that in writing for you, if you like . . ."

Dr. Graham gazed at him and smiled faintly. "I should be envying you your training, Dr. Cahill. I should envy your ability to go into the brain and the spine. But what I really envy you tonight is your bravery. Your guts."

132

Red shook that off too. "You wouldn't let her die," he told the older man. "You would not, Doctor!"

Dr. Graham sighed. "I am glad I don't have to find out," he answered.

9 ❀❀❀❀❀❀❀❀❀❀❀❀❀❀❀❀❀❀❀❀❀❀❀❀❀

THINGS moved faster then—a little faster. At least Red knew that he was going to operate.

Dr. Graham said that he would increase his efforts to locate the girl's family. "I'll send for Maurita," he told himself, speaking aloud of his plans. "That girl—" He glanced over his shoulder at Red. "You'll have to use this room, Doctor. Can you?"

Red looked around the o.r. White-tiled walls, the table and lights, the sloping window and skylight, the instrument cabinets and an autoclave. He went over to the anesthesia tanks.

"I'll send for the anesthetist, too," said Dr. Graham. "She's a nurse whom I've had trained. Maurita will bring her. If you can manage . . ."

"Of course I can manage," said Red. "I'll have to. We couldn't possibly move our girl."

"Not clear to the city, no. And—well, this is as good as you'll find under fifty-sixty miles. What about instruments? If you have a bag at the motel . . ."

Red laughed and shook his head. "I don't have, and anyway, it wouldn't contain what I'll need. I'll see what you have and make do."

"I'll show you. Just a minute, please." Dr. Graham went to the phone on the wall and talked into it, his voice crisp with authority. He concluded with, "Now, be careful. I noticed that you had chains, Maurita, but—"

Maurita.

Red went over to the instrument cases, and Dr. Graham joined him. There was a good supply. In fact, the amount of instruments surprised Red in their abundance. They were good ones, too, sharp and well cared for. Not everything that Red would have had back on the seventh floor of Lincoln, but he would manage.

"I have a good drill," Dr. Graham told him. "I do a lot of hip pinning, you know."

"I can imagine, if you have many of these ice storms."

Red talked to Rosie about the instruments, their layout. He talked to the nurse who came in to prep the patient. He didn't especially want to see that shining hair cut away, but—

He examined the lights more closely. They were good, if they would hold.

Red stepped into the hall to ask a question and met the nurse-anesthetist, with Maurita Smith, at the head of the stairs. They were both breathless from their rushed trip.

Maurita greeted Red effusively. "Little did I suspicion, Doctor," she cried in her peacock voice, "that we would encounter one another on such an occasion!"

Dr. Graham told her to go in and look at the patient, see if she might know the girl.

Meanwhile Red talked to the anesthetist who was a thin young woman with a weathered skin and wiry arms—he'd believe her tale of pulling half of a maple tree out of the way so that they might reach the hospital. Yes, she understood his orders. No, she had never done just this job. Dr. Graham had trained her, and he didn't . . . But if Dr. Cahill would give his orders loud and clear . . .

Red patted her shoulder. "You'll do fine," he assured the nurse. "What's your name?"

She told him. Eunice Math.

"Like in arithmetic!" cried Maurita, coming out of the o.r. She laughed at her own joke and urged Eunice not to fall too hard for Dr. Cahill. "I saw him first!" she said archly.

Red went into scrub in search of Dr. Graham. He supposed the doctor would assist him. Dr. Graham was at the telephone; he turned from it to ask, "Did Maurita . . . ?"

Red shook his head. "She has a vague idea—she's going to phone around."

Dr. Graham nodded. "I'm talking to my partner," he explained.

"We won't need him," said Red. "I'd like to have you assist me, and the anesthetist seems to know her job."

"She does. But I called Dr. Robinson. He is a partner in this hospital, and—" He spoke again into the phone.

Red nodded and leaned against the counter, listening to the one side of the conversation, trying to fill in the unheard part of it, trying to picture the other doctor.

That afternoon Maurita had spoken of him. He should have listened and remembered, because now he was curious about this second doctor, and interested. This two-man hospital was proving itself to be fascinating, at least. He wondered how many of the slick specialists back at Lincoln could take on such a job. And evidently do it well. Enns might—and some of the others. Could Dr. Cahill? Probably not; he was too temperish. Vince Sebaja could. . . .

"Dr. Robinson wants to know," Dr. Graham was asking

Red, "if you will release us from responsibility should you operate before we locate the family?"

"Well, of course," said Red. "I told you that."

Dr. Graham turned back to the phone. "He is a young man," he said, and his tone was wistful.

He said a little more, then hung up.

"I'll sign that release," Red began.

"Weren't you waiting to take the patient to X-ray?"

Red had indeed been waiting.

"We'll go right down," said Dr. Graham.

Maurita followed them to the basement with a report for Dr. Graham. Red watched her and listened as he helped slide his patient to the table; he was grateful to find out that the machine was a good one.

As she went out of the lead-lined room, Maurita brushed against him, and he looked after her with annoyance. "I wish she would stay on the job," he growled.

Without comment, Dr. Graham manipulated the X-ray machine; he also developed the film, in a small darkroom. Then he and Red again went upstairs. The plates showed what Red had feared—a spinal compression. There was a broken wrist, but that certainly offered no urgency. The spine did, Red felt, as well as the hematoma.

The girl's condition was deteriorating, and all speed was indicated. As soon as the o.r. girls could get things ready . . .

He went into scrub and examined the manipulation of the faucets, then he began to scrub, looking at his face in the mirror, but not really seeing himself. One corner of his mind counted, but he was thinking of the task ahead and how he would proceed. He heard someone in o.r. say that the telephone was out.

Red's hands stopped their rhythmic scrub-scrub-scrub.

Dr. Graham stepped up to the second sink. "They'll give us priority on telephone service," he told the younger man. "In minutes someone will be out here tying things they call Westinghouse knots."

Red had never given much thought to telephone service to hospitals. But, yes, they should have priority. Only tonight he was beginning to guess at some of the complexities of his profession. He had trained and worked in a huge center where someone else took the responsibility of maintaining service.

He switched hands, and even as he did so the lights went out. Dr. Graham alertly told someone to turn up the lantern. Sure enough, there was a Coleman here in scrub. It had no reflector as did those in o.r.

"You have the lanterns all over," Red told Dr. Graham admiringly.

"Well, not really. Not in the wards or in the patients' rooms. There we rely on flashlights. But we do have lanterns wherever they will be needed. We have drills in their use and care, you know. Weekly drills. Same as fire and evacuation drills."

The Center had fire and evacuation drills too. But not weekly.

Dr. Graham was telling about the filling of the lanterns when a man came in from the hall. A small man, in an overlarge trench coat. He exuded a fine fragrance of cigar; he wore thick-lensed glasses. . . .

Iserman! thought Red, panic brushing him. But of course it was not Iserman. Just the same type of man, small, and with the psychic pugnaciousness, the defensiveness of such a small man.

Dr. Graham made the introductions. Red acknowledged them. Dr. Robinson just grunted.

Bad manners as well. That also was like Iserman.

Now the bristling little man was demanding to know if "this thing" couldn't wait.

Red turned back to his scrub. "No," he said quietly, "it cannot wait. Where there is compression—"

"You'll get our hospital into a hell of a mess if the family should happen to oppose surgery," said Dr. Robinson.

"We'll hope not," said Dr. Cahill.

"I can't take the case to the city," he explained, "as I would, frankly, prefer to do. But with the icy roads and the risk, the trip would take hours, and we do not have that kind of time. So I must do with what I have here, and I must do it *now!*" He bit off the final word, remembering in a flash all that Dr. Graham has said earlier about midnight emergencies, the risks, the matter of anesthesia, the—

"You can't possibly wait?" Dr. Robinson asked again.

"Not any longer. No, Doctor. The girl is convulsive; her temperature is elevated. The spine condition is such that pressure must be relieved. At once!"

"Have you found out who the girl is?" Dr. Robinson asked his partner.

"No," said Dr. Graham. "Everyone in the house has had a look at her. Maurita is trying to find out, and she will make a noble effort because she has a great crush on Dr. Cahill."

Dr. Robinson snorted. Red raised an eyebrow to his mirrored face. Iserman would have snorted too.

His knee kicked off the water, and the pipes chattered. "There seems to be just one question," he said impatiently, "and it is a simple one. Can we give this unknown girl a chance to live? Or should we stand by and let her die?"

Dr. Graham nodded agreement.

"You're going to help?" Dr. Robinson asked his partner.

"I am going to help. Yes."

"Well, I'd say let Cahill do this on his own. It's enough to lend him the operating room. Our hospital does not do spine and brain work, Graham, and you know it!"

Rosie brought gloves to Red, and he thrust his hand into one with a snap. "I am on my own," he agreed, speaking quietly, but the words shouted in his mind.

He was on his own—out of the shadow. . . .

IO ❀❀❀❀❀❀❀❀❀❀❀❀❀❀❀❀❀❀❀❀❀❀

THE nurse tied Red's gown and his mask. His eyes smiled at her, then he went out to the operating room. He spoke softly to the anesthetist.

His girl was slipping ever deeper into a coma; her temperature was a scorching 105; the blood pressure now was rising rapidly, guaranteeing the intracranial pressure which Red had identified without benefit of the angiograms he prayerfully wished he could have. The reflexes were limited and had been from the first—the Babinski reflex particularly; the big toe had jerked straight up! This told the surgeon that the fragile brain stem deep within the skull was being squeezed.

Red had secured only fair skull X-rays, but he did not think there was a fracture. An angiogram would have shown him what he had, and that sort of X-ray would have clearly shown the skull arteries. Now the surgeon could only guess that the arteries of the left occipital quadrant were displaced and that massive bleeding was present.

The blow which the girl had received had jarred and twisted the thin stalk which supported the brain, and probably hundreds of tiny veins were ruptured.

Red's fingers sought the pulse in the patient's throat. The girl's life was seeping away. He—

The lights went out. Someone adjusted the lanterns and asked him questions about them. He replied.

But he was not thinking of lanterns or of anything except the work ready for his hands. He had decided against drilling burr holes to drain the blood away. Because of the delay, Dr. Cahill suspected clots, both at the site and in the center of the brain. If he was right, burr holes would be fatally ineffective.

No. He must do radical surgery—a craniotomy.

His hand was steady and purposeful as he made his first cut. Even under his handicap he worked steadily.

About him the room was shadowed; the lantern light centered upon the field was pink instead of the cold-white fluorescence to which he was accustomed. People moved about him; rain rattled against the skylight above his head.

The anesthetist was not Polly Ferris, but she was trying valiantly to please. What needed to be done she did, crisply telling off the numbers—pulse, blood pressure, respiration. Red missed the *beep* and *ping* of the oscilloscope, the recorder of the pulse, but he could be grateful for a good scrub nurse, and Graham was an excellent assistant. He knew exactly what to do, where, and when. There was a lack of instruments, but Red was, in a cleansing surge of awareness, sure that he was doing a good, neat job.

The incision was a long one—it had to be—around the ear and down. The huge flap of scalp and bone was laid forward, and the fibrous dura—the hard brain covering—was delicately slit and pulled over the top of the skull.

The opening—about the size of the surgeon's hand—revealed a scene of bloody wreckage. Dr. Graham gasped a

142

little, and the circulating nurse pulled the gauze free of his lips.

Red nodded and said something below his breath. Two blood vessels were still spurting—he cauterized them. Dr. Graham began to remove the clots. Gently Red washed the crinkly brain surface with saline solution and peeled the clots away with swabs. Then he asked for the suction, put his mouth to the tube, and sucked one deep clot up and out. The brain, relieved of pressure, became quite slack, but— there was— His hand faltered.

Graham looked up at him. Dr. Cahill nodded. He still was sure of himself. He was here, at this time and in this place, to help the lovely young girl as he could—as he already had done.

So he worked on. He must remove all the injured tissues, the tiny bone chips. He worked painstakingly. He had not thought of the possibility that the optic nerve would be injured. He should have thought of it . . . He still must get out all the clots and tissue.

For a second his eyes blurred, and he shook his head impatiently. The nurse patted his brow with a square of gauze.

Red was thinking of his patient as he had seen her first, the curve of her cheek, her slightly tilted eyes, the glorious hair . . . He gulped and resumed surgery. Though doomed to blindness, he still must save this life.

The lights surged on, and he scarcely noticed. He was heartsick.

He closed up, bandaged, and walked out of the operating room. His head down, he tore off his mask, stripped off the gloves, then went out into the hall and followed the cart along the corridor to the assigned room. He took the chart from Miss Math and wrote his orders. The temperature was down to 103, and he ordered ice packs placed all along the girl's body. At Lincoln he would have had a rubber mattress which could have been filled with ice. Here . . . He spoke his orders to the nurse who would attend the girl: Ice. Urea concentrate given by I.V.

The nurse must never leave the patient, and that meant *never!* He himself stayed with her for an hour, until the blood pressure had stabilized and the breathing improved.

He stood beside the bed and gazed at his patient. Beneath the swathing bandages there was again the purely beautiful young face, the lashes curled against the soft round cheek.

He would stay close, he promised the nurse, and he walked out of the room. Out in the hall he found Dr. Robinson talking to Graham, the little man's manner urgent, his voice a harsh whisper.

"But just answer me this one thing!" he demanded. And he probably had said it many times before. "Did that Dr. Cahill *do* it?"

Dr. Graham may not have seen the tall man in the green robe who approached from the far end of the hall.

"I am sure," he answered firmly, "that Dr. Cahill did the best job anyone could have done. Without him, our patient would not have had any chance at all to live. I was, and would have been, far too much of a coward to attempt such surgery. He had the courage . . ."

By then Red was close to them. He looked up at the clock above the nurses' station. It was five o'clock.

"Has the rain stopped?" he asked as he passed the two doctors. They may have answered. Not hearing, he went past them to scrub and took off the borrowed green robe. For a second he stood looking at the heap of it on a chair. Robinson's question . . .

Did he do it? Had his knife slipped? His finger? A clamp? The question had startled him. He was devastated to think that he might, indeed, have "done it." Destroyed the optic nerve was what Robinson had meant. *Had* Red done that? He had not suspected optic injury. When he first bent over her, out on that icy tarvia driveway of the filling station, he was sure that the girl had looked at him. Her eyes were a deep violet-blue, and she had *looked* at him. Seen him. Later, of course, a clot, or the shock of moving her—even the process of surgery—

He bit his lip and beat his fist into his other hand. Had he guessed that the girl was blind, had he suspected that she would be, would he have . . . ?

"Yes!" he said aloud.

Yes, he would have proceeded. He had done such surgery before—he had done it many times. He remembered a slum child . . .

II ❀❀❀❀❀❀❀❀❀❀❀❀❀❀❀❀❀❀❀❀❀❀❀

IT had stopped raining. Red ate breakfast with Dr. Graham and Dr. Robinson. He talked of the storm and of the damage done by it. He talked as little as possible about his patient. It would take a day or two to know. Yes, he would stay around. He happened to be on a week's vacation.

"You could go on up to Bridgeton," said Dr. Graham, "about the position there. If it is something you want."

Red shrugged. "It isn't," he said. "For a while it seemed to offer a solution for a problem I thought I had."

That noontime Maurita offered to get his "things" from the motel. Red mentioned his car. He would ride with her, he planned, and bring it back to the hospital. Pay his bill and collect his clothes.

This he did, Maurita volubly impressed by his car. Red laughed about this to Dr. Graham. "Don't disillusion her by telling her what a resident gets paid, sir."

"Not if you'll tell *me* how you financed such a jalopy."

Red laughed at the term and told about his mother. "She married a second time and married rich. I get some side benefits."

146

"Did she pick out the car, or did you?"

"Oh, I did. But she liked the color."

By then their patient was almost positively identified. This was done through the dead boy. As soon as the car cooled, the registration was available, and the boy's family said, by phone, that they thought he had had a date with Carrie Lockette last night. Redheaded? Yes, that would be the girl.

It was proving more difficult to get through to the Lockettes who lived several miles into the "back country." The rural telephone lines had broken down under the storm's assault. But an attempt would be made by radio.

"Trouble is, those people listen only to the stock and weather reports," said Dr. Graham. "The State Patrol is swamped. I may have to drive down there myself."

"Do you know them?"

"Not really. The man—the father—is a county-court judge, I think."

That news cheered Red. A lawyer, he thought, would be understanding of the need for surgery.

Maurita invited Dr. Cahill to stay at her home; she and her mother, she said, would be "most happy." Dr. Graham said that he would take the doctor home with him, when Red thought he could leave Carrie.

The name fitted the girl, and everyone immediately used it. She was doing all right, except for some difficulty in breathing. During the night the nurse became worried and woke Dr. Cahill, who was using a bed in the next room.

The unconscious patient could not swallow or cough up the normal secretions of saliva and mucus.

"I'm not having any luck with the suction, Doctor," the worried nurse told Red. "I hated to disturb you—you need some sleep."

147

The hospital, as a unit, had decided that they liked Dr. Cahill. He was friendly, courteous, and capable. "Cute," said the younger women. A "dream," said Maurita Smith.

Now this paragon patted the nurse's shoulder and said she had done right to call him. He bent over Carrie and tried the suction. No, it was not doing the job. And at this stage he was not about to let the girl drown in her own body fluids.

"I'll talk to Dr. Graham," he said. "We'll fix things up."

Dr. Graham said that Carrie was Cahill's case. "You're not going to get me out of my bed just to watch you do a tracheotomy, are you?"

This time no mention was made of a surgical release. So Red took Carrie back to the operating room and inserted a tube directly through the throat into the trachea. Immediately she began to breathe more easily.

Red went back to bed, and when he roused at six and went to look at his patient, he found Dr. Graham in the room. The girl, he said happily, was doing real well!

"I hope we reach her family today," said Red.

"We will. I'll send someone out there. Now look, Red, I've got my orders. Miss Rachel says I'm to bring you out for breakfast. And you will find out, young man, that what my wife says must be done *is* done!"

"All right," Red agreed. "But will you let me shave first?"

"Oh yes. Make yourself as pretty as possible. Meanwhile I'll take a look around."

At seven Red got into Dr. Graham's durable sedan, finding himself eager for this diversion. He had been holding himself tense for so long about Carrie, but she really was doing fine. She'd soon be conscious again; her parents would come to the hospital. Red would stay until the end of the week, then confidently hand the case over to Graham. Now he could enjoy his visit to the good doctor's home and the breakfast which the doctor's wife would have ready for them.

"This is historic country round about, you know," Dr. Graham was telling him as they drove through the streets at the edge of Old Pardee. "The house where I was born, reared, and still live is a hundred and twenty years old. Slaves laid the rock foundation and raised its homemade brick walls to the skyscraper height of two stories." The doctor was smiling at his own extravagance.

"But that's wonderful," said Red, matching his tone.

"It's singular," corrected Dr. Graham. "Nowadays folks want new houses. Picture windows and air conditioning. Rachel and I, we like the orchards round about us, our thick walls, and the four fireplaces. Of course we have a furnace now, but we use the fireplaces too. I keep my shoulders and arms in shape by chopping wood and sawing it. We lost some apple trees in this storm, which we regret, but they'll make us sweet firewood for next winter."

He drove steadily along, and within ten minutes they came to a mailbox largely lettered GRAHAM. The gate was open, and Dr. Graham drove through, up along a rutted lane toward the house which stood serenely beneath tall trees.

It was an oblong block of pale-pink brick; the windows and doors were white-framed in stone. There was little adornment, but the lines of the house had dignity and pride.

Dr. Graham pointed out the barn and the packing shed. "We have always made a business of apples," he explained.

They went up to the door and in the hall were greeted by Mrs. Graham, a tall, strong-looking woman with a twinkle in her eyes. She was glad to meet Dr. Cahill, she said. She had heard quite a lot about him. Breakfast was ready. Were the men?

The planks of the hall floor were wide, pegged into place, and rubbed into a fine golden gloss. To one side Red had a glimpse of a parlor with a white-paneled fireplace wall, pretty wallpaper, and a primitive portrait hung above a mahogany square piano.

The dining table was covered with a red homespun cloth, and through an open door Red could see a sitting room with two more portraits and a shell cupboard in the corner.

Dr. Graham, seeing his guest's interest, promised him a tour of the house after breakfast. "But if Dora's biscuits are ready, we had better eat now."

Grace was said and the food brought in by the smiling cook who was proud, she said, to welcome Dr. Cahill. There were biscuits and sweet butter, honey, and a compote of red cherry preserves. There were slices of country ham swimming in red-eye gravy; there were eggs on a platter sprigged with blue and pink daisies. There was hominy, and more gravy, and a baked apple in a blue saucedish, good coffee with cream as thick as whipped butter.

Red ate enormously and enjoyed the good talk. Dr. Graham discussed the countryside, the apple business, and invited Red to come back the next day for the hog killing.

Mrs. Graham laughed at the expression on the young man's face. "I don't believe city folks appreciate some of our rural diversions," she told her husband.

"Do you cure your own hams?" Red asked.

"But of course!" said the Grahams in unison.

"I've never eaten meat like this," Red assured them. And indeed he had not; the ham was more sweet than salt, and its flavor lingered deliciously on the tongue.

"I don't know why you ever go back to the hospital," he told Dr. Graham. "You have everything out here a man could want."

"Well, there's Doc back there," said Mrs. Graham in a certain tone. Red quickly glanced up at her, his eyes narrowing.

"Did I strike a nerve?" she asked.

"No." Red laughed. "But I was remembering—you know, the day I got here, I stopped at the motel for the night because of the ice, and Maurita Smith was at the lunch counter. She told me about the Pardee hospital, and I noticed that she called the staff men *Doctor* Graham and *Doc* Robinson."

The Grahams were nodding. "Everyone does that," said Dr. Graham. "Though Doc really is an able physician, Red."

"I'm sure he is. We have a man at the Center who is very like him. I've decided that there is psychology attached to a small man. He seems to need to assert himself, to make his presence known."

"That sounds like Maurita, too," said Mrs. Graham, laughing gently.

Red agreed. "She's quite a girl," he murmured.

"Don't say things like that, boy!" cried Dr. Graham. "Unless you are prepared to have Maurita take it as a declaration of your intentions."

"Huh?" Red was startled. "But I only said—I meant—"

"We know what you meant," teased his host. "But Maurita—now that's a different thing. The years are creeping up on her, and now she is declaring that she always did intend to marry a doctor! She goes on and on—she *does* like a crew cut! She *does* like a really *big* man! And of course she was the one to discover you. *She* is behind your bringing Carrie to our hospital. . . ."

Red's cheeks were blazing. "Oh, come off, now!" he cried.

"She's a determined young woman," said Mrs. Graham, enjoying the fun they were having.

"Well, I can be determined in my turn," Red assured them. "And since I already have a girl—"

"Oh, do you, Red?" cried Rachel. "Tell us."

And to his own surprise Red found himself telling them about C'ele. How she looked, her smooth, dark hair—"She'll go swimming without a cap, and when she dresses, her hair looks just fine." She was slender and neat . . . "I've never seen her fussing with lipstick and stuff."

"She doesn't sound much like Maurita," decided Mrs. Graham. Then, impatiently, she glanced around, for the telephone had rung and her husband was on his feet.

"I hope it isn't anything more than a neighbor wanting to help with the butchering," she told Red.

But Dr. Graham came back only to the dining-room door. His finger beckoned to Red. "The Lockettes are at the hospital," he said. "I left word they were not to see Carrie without you and me on hand. So we'll have to go, boy." He kissed his wife's cheek; Red thanked her for the meal and the talk.

"May I come back to see the house?" he asked.

"Any time. You may sleep here too. If the doctor will let you."

Dr. Graham drove swiftly back to the hospital, fuming about Maurita's doubted ability to hold Lockette away from Carrie's room. He had left word to be called if the girl roused or the family showed up.

"I reckon they heard the radio message," he decided.

"If the man's a lawyer," said Red, "an educated man—"

Dr. Graham snorted and swung the car into the hospital drive. "He's not your kind of lawyer," he said gruffly. "These people . . . You thought my house was old and quaint. Wait till you run up against some of our citizens."

Red followed Graham up to the hospital's back door. "But, Doctor—"

Dr. Graham lifted his hand. "Let's not borrow trouble," he advised. "For all I know, everything will be fine. Now, look, Red. You go upstairs the back way and put on a lab coat. I'll talk to these folks in the parlor, then bring 'em up. You be in Carrie's room."

For a minute Red stood looking at Dr. Graham. Then he sighed and nodded. It was going to be a job telling the girl's parents that Carrie was blind . . . He supposed that Dr. Graham should be the one to do it. When the parents came upstairs, he could add his own technical explanation.

He put on the prescribed lab coat; he went to Carrie's room and looked at her chart. He examined the girl—she was restless that morning; consciousness was imminent. Her condition was good. He could be glad of that.

It was a long fifteen minutes before the Lockettes came upstairs. Red could hear them approaching; he could hear Dr. Graham's low, deep voice and a woman's—shrill, harsh —then a man's, loud. *He* called Dr. Graham *Doc*.

Red stood in the corner of Carrie's room, next to the window, and waited. He had excused the nurse "for a few minutes."

Dr. Graham came into the room first, followed by a tall, rangy man and a little birdlike woman who looked frightened. They did not seem to see the second doctor. They went straight to the bed, exclaiming over their girl, their baby. The tracheal tube disturbed them the most, and Dr. Graham, in the kindest possible way, explained the necessity for such measures with unconscious patients. It would, he said, be taken out as soon as Carrie could handle things herself. No, it would not leave much of a scar. No, it in no way resembled the voice box which a friend of Mrs. Lockette's wore.

Red stood quietly and studied Carrie's parents. They were older than he would have guessed—both were surely into the fifties. The man talked a jargon of bad grammar and profanity. The mother had a nervous, shrill laugh; her hair was frizzed. How in the name of Darwin had these two spawned a girl like Carrie?

Finally Dr. Graham found an opening in which to introduce Dr. Cahill.

Red bowed and said something about knowing that Mr. and Mrs. Lockette must have been worried about their daughter.

"Well, not exactly, Doc," said Mr. Lockette. He unzipped the quilted jacket which he wore. "You see, she and the Trigg boy had gone to this fun party. When the roads got bad, we decided they just had stayed with some folks. Our phone lines was down so they couldn't-a called us. Last night one of the neighbors stopped by to say they'd heard on the radio that Carrie'd been hurt. We decided to wait till mawnin' to come in. Doc here says she was real bad hurt, and she sure as hell looks it, all those tubes and things. . . ."

Red nodded and wiped the palms of his hands against his coat. "Yes, Mr. Lockette," he began. "You see—"

"Name's Judge, Doc," Lockette corrected. "'m magistrate of our township." He turned to Dr. Graham. "You know that, Doc."

Dr. Graham nodded. "Yes, I do know it, Judge. I remember meeting you at political rallies."

"You sure have! I'm a damn good party man!"

Dr. Graham kindly brought Mrs. Lockette into the conversation. "I don't think I've had the pleasure of meeting your family before . . ." he said gallantly.

"No, sir, you have not. Gener'lly my women folk stay close to home."

"Do you have other children?" Red asked.

"A few," said the judge. "All grown except Carrie. She come along fifteen year late. And I reckon we've spoiled her. Like lettin' her go to a dancin' party with the Trigg boy."

"Now, Judge," said his wife. "You don't know they was dancin' at that party."

"No, I don't. But I do know the Trigg boy got hisself killed, and Carrie damn near got her head knocked off, goin' to it!"

There was no disputing that. Mrs. Lockette withdrew from the lists. She stood at the foot of the bed, smoothing the spread and smiling wanly at her unconscious daughter.

Judge Lockette turned to Red. "How come you to operate?" he asked sternly.

"Well," said Red, "I happened to be here. You know, I saw the accident. I was staying at the motel. Your daughter was thrown free of the car, and when I saw that she was badly hurt, I had her brought here to the hospital. It was a good thing I was on hand, for brain surgery is my specialty."

"So you took it on yourself to—"

"Judge Lockette, under the circumstances of the storm and the location, I could do nothing but care for your daughter."

Judge Lockette's eyes bulged and his chin jutted. "Nobody ast you!" he cried angrily. "Nobody told you to cut on her! What right you got decidin' you're the one to doctor her and to cut!"

He said more. Much more. Red stood, his hands balled into fists at his side, his face stern and white. He was angry, and he was shocked. Once he opened his mouth to tell this ignorant—this—this—

But he closed his mouth again and waited.

". . . I sure as hell didn't give my consent for you to operate!" Judge Lockette was crying. "Don't you know, accordin' to the law, you ain't got the right even to examine a minor without proper consent from that minor's parent or legal gard-een? Much less to operate on her!"

"We couldn't get your permission, sir," Red attempted. "We didn't know who she was. This was an emergency; the injury caused bleeding into the brain. There was pressure on her spine. The optic nerve was crushed. We could not correct that. She will be blind, but we saved her life."

There was no shock. Red decided that Dr. Graham must have told the Lockettes of Carrie's blindness earlier. Stubbornly the judge said that the doctor should not have "cut," and all of Red's explanations did no good. The parents departed, promising to return.

Red spoke of his concern to Dr. Graham. That calm man only shrugged. "I knew we ran this risk by operating," he said.

"And you told me—"

"We had to operate."

"Yes," said Red soberly, "we did." He stood thoughtful. "They seem to trust you. But they don't trust me. That seems to be the main trouble."

"They don't know you. Also—if I had been the one to operate on Carrie, they might have had it in for me."

"Had he let me, I would have explained to them in greater detail . . ."

"I know. But Lockette wasn't being receptive to logic or intelligence, Red. He was frightened, he felt guilty—"

"Ha!"

"He *did!* Without acknowledging it, of course. So he blamed his wife for letting Carrie go to the party; he blamed you for the bandages and suction tubes which, in his ignorance, frighten him."

This was good reasoning, but Red was troubled for his patient and for his host-doctor whom he had grown to admire tremendously. "I think the best course for all concerned," he said, "would be for me to clear out. I only complicate the situation."

"You'll not leave until you are six hours from going on duty at Lincoln," Dr. Graham told him firmly. "Doctors cannot be governed by the reactions of a man like Lockette."

"Judge Lockette," said Red thoughtfully.

"Yes! A symbol of his office. A little office in a tiny town—less than two hundred people—literally into the backwoods, Red. He has very little genuine learning or education. What law he has he learned by 'reading law' in the office of a man just like himself. He's into politics, because that is what backwoods lawyers do. They round up a hundred votes; they get thrown scraps of political favor. They aren't powerful, but they can be a considerable nuisance."

"Amen!" said Red fervently.

"Such a man," Dr. Graham continued, "resents people like you, Doctor. You are educated. This type of rural character feels bound to prove he can outsmart you city slickers."

"He's welcome to try," Red said. "I want no part of him."

"More than you already have, no. Well, now let's go have another look at Carrie."

Over the period of the next three days Carrie regained full consciousness. Red had bandaged her eyes rather than let the shock of her blindness slow her first recovery. She was doing very well, and he was happy about that. After meeting her parents, he had awaited, almost fearfully, the sound of her voice. It turned out to be sweet and childish; she spoke gently. Often she used the backwoods idiom, but there was none of the harsh, earthy quality of her father or the nasal drawl of her mother. Red was glad.

By his last morning in Old Pardee all the tubes were gone; the head of Carrie's bed was elevated, and Red came into her room to take off the eye bandages. He had already prepared the girl for his departure.

"I was just passing through, the night you were hurt."

"And Johnny Trigg got hisself kilt."

"Yes."

"I didn't so much like Johnny, but I didn't want him kilt."

"No, of course not."

"What do *you* look like, Dr. Cahill?" She lengthened the first syllable of his name, the vowel as soft as fur.

"Me? Oh, I'm pretty big—and if I stayed around here eating biscuits, I'd get bigger."

Carrie laughed softly. "I hear folks call you 'Red.' Is your hair . . . ?"

"No, it's not red. Just sort of old-straw colored."

"And your eyes . . . ?"

"They're blue"

"You're young. I can tell by your voice. Are you married?"

Red had answered a hundred questions like this, about himself, his family, about the city.

And this last morning he was prepared for still another barrage. He came into the room, announcing himself with a cheery, "Good morning, Carrie!"

"Good mawnin', Dr. Cahill. Is the sun shinin'?"

"Yes, it is. But it is cold outside." He used his stethoscope. She put her fingers on his hand. "Is today . . . ?"

"The day I leave? Yes."

She stroked his hand and arm. "I don't want you to go."

"Well, as a matter of fact, I don't want to go, either."

Her fingers tightened on his wrist. "What about me?" she asked tensely. "Will *I* be all right?"

Red stood close to the bed and took her small hand between both of his big ones. "I think that is going to be up to you, Carrie," he said quietly. "How all right you are."

Then, still holding her hand, he spoke gently to her. "You were badly hurt, my dear," he said. "When you were thrown from the car, the back of your head struck very hard against the edge of the concrete island at the filling station."

"And I broke my wrist." She held up the cast of her injured arm.

"Yes, you broke your wrist. But mainly you hurt your head, dear. Back where your spine—your backbone, you know—comes up into the head. We had to operate—"

"On my head?"

"Yes, and on your upper spine—to relieve the pressure

caused by the blow. And when we did operate, Carrie, we found that some of the nerves were injured. Now nerves are things like the roots of a tree. If you cut them off, they won't grow back."

"No," she agreed. "I could have died, couldn't I?"

"Yes, you could have died. Or you could have been paralyzed—not able to walk, or move your arms, or talk."

"I can talk."

"Yes, and you are not paralyzed. But, Carrie, you won't be able to see."

At first she didn't grasp what he had said. Then for a long, stunned minute she lay stiffened on the bed. Her hand clutched at his, dragged upon it. Her small white teeth bit at her lips. "I can't believe—" she whispered. "Not ever —see—nuthin' again?"

She wept, and then she cried out in panic. She couldn't be blind, she protested. She wouldn't be! He must do something!

He held her and comforted her as best he could. Once she tore at the bandages, and he cut them away. Her violet eyes were as lovely as ever, the lashes as thick . . . Red bit his own lip. If only he could have saved them too.

Carrie turned away from him in hurt and disappointment. He stood back and waited for that protest to end. He had known this session would not be easy, but he had steadfastly insisted on telling Carrie himself.

Finally the girl broke down and wept piteously. "Help me," she begged. "Help me!"

"We'll all help you, Carrie. But—"

"I know. That's what you meant. I'll have to help myself."

"Yes. You will."

"And you are going to leave."

160

"I must leave. Yes."

She reached for his hand. "Will you kiss me?" she asked.

"Of course." And he did kiss her. First on her cheek, then on her soft lips. Her fingers stroked his face.

He left then. He had to leave. He would come back and see Carrie on his next free day. He had talked to Graham about her care.

He said good-by swiftly and drove his car out of the hospital grounds, to the highway. He was anxious to get back to the Center, to the work which he did there.

It was New Year's Day, and when Red walked out of the elevator on N.S., he was ready to point out to those who greeted him that it was a good thing he *was* back! He seemed to be the only one on duty without a head.

His friends refused to believe that the night before he had gone to bed before ten. Yes, of course they were glad to see him. Who wanted to do his work?

Red checked with the floor supe; he looked up Gutzell and said "Hi!" He put the contents of his bag away in his room and changed into a white coat, then he went up the hall again and knocked on the door of the Chief's office.

"Come!" said that familiar voice.

Red opened the door and went in. Dr. Enns looked surprised, then pleased. "Well, *Red!*" he cried. "Come in, come in! You're looking fit."

"I am fit."

"Have some coffee."

Red filled two mugs from the carafe on the hot plate and handed one of them to Dr. Enns. "How're you doing?" he asked.

"Fine. Walk a little. Hurts like the devil—and my posture isn't good."

Red sat down and considered the Chief. He was, he decided, an exceptionally handsome man. "You don't seem too busy . . ."

"We've had a few emergencies. Tomorrow will show up a busy schedule."

"Yes, I saw the list."

Dr. Enns was watching him critically. "Glad to be back?"

"Yes, sir."

"No matter what?"

Red stirred his coffee, around and around. "No matter what," he agreed.

"Good! Then fit yourself into that schedule."

Red nodded. "I say no matter what," he explained, "because anything you might turn up could not possibly beat what I've been through this past week. Let me tell you . . ."

He leaned forward in his chair, and he did tell—all of it. He spoke with animation, his voice and his face revealing the impact of his experience.

He mentioned his intent of going to Bridgeton; he vividly described the weather and his decision to stop at the motel.

"I thought it would be safer." Then he smiled wryly and told about the accident and his taking the girl to the hospital.

"Was it a good one?" asked Dr. Enns.

Red considered his answer. "It wasn't the Center," he said. "It was small—thirty beds—put into a big, remodeled house. But, yes, sir, it was a good hospital."

"Proprietary?"

"Yes, it was. Owned and operated by two doctors, Graham and Robinson. Graham is the surgeon and an excellent one. They get a first-class rating—"

Dr. Enns's eyebrows went up. "Oh? Audits and all?"

"Audits, fire protection, the works. A really well-run place. Graham, as I said, is an excellent surgeon. I am sure he could work anywhere with distinction."

"Did he operate on the injured girl?"

"No, sir. I did." Red went on to detail the surgery he had performed. When he reached the matter of the optic nerve, Dr. Enns winced.

"Bad luck," he said, in the manner of a trained doctor accepting, though regretting, the situation as it stood. "Was the nerve crushed on impact?"

Red hesitated. "I could say, of course, that it was. And it may have been. But I really don't know. I am sure I did not cut it."

"Well, I would hope not!" said Dr. Enns sharply.

"I didn't. There were bone chips—and injured tissue . . ." He continued his technical report.

When he had finished, Dr. Enns pursed his lips and nodded. "It sounds as if you saved that girl's life, Red."

"I—I guess I did, sir. Graham said he could not have gone into the skull. There was no way or time to take her elsewhere. She was convulsive and failing. So—yes, I saved her life. But . . . Well, she is a lovely thing—glorious red hair—she's not quite sixteen—and now she is blind."

"Too bad, certainly. But at that age she will adjust."

"I hope so. I truly hope so. But just the same, I do wish it had not happened."

"Of course. However, had you not been at the side of that road she would now be dead."

"Yes," said Red. "You'll probably say again that I'm letting myself be emotionally involved with a patient, sir. But I mean to do what I can to help Carrie."

163

"If you save a life, you're responsible?"

"Not that. No, sir. But this case seems a little special."

Dr. Enns laughed. "I am glad it does. And now I am glad you are back, ready to go to work."

When Red was assigned to duty, he found that he could eat his dinner and still have an hour free. In that hour he decided that he would go to see C'ele.

Putting his topcoat over his whites, he drove over to her apartment and was welcomed happily by that girl. She was, she said, about to wash her hair. "I didn't have any idea you were home!"

"You knew I'd be gone a week."

"Who knows anything about what you'll do? The telephone might as well never have been invented."

Red patted her head and went on into the living room. Curiously he looked about him. It was the same as it had been—last week, last month—yet it looked different to him. The bookshelves, the twisted ceramic of an impressionistic horse, the little brass bowl, the tall vase of smoky glass . . .

"This past week," he told C'ele, throwing his topcoat on a chair, "I was in and out of a house that I wish you could see sometime."

"What kind of house was it, Red? The last word I had, you were going to look at another hospital."

"I never made it," said Red, sitting down on the couch and patting the cushion beside him. "Cuddle close, sweetie," he said, "and watch my time. I'm on duty as of eight."

C'ele nodded. "Then talk fast."

"Will do. Want to hear about the house?"

"Anything you say." She tucked her feet under her and

sat warmly close to him.

So he told her about the Graham house at Old Pardee—the apple orchards . . . He mentioned Dr. Graham's dog —a white setter, with legs as *long* . . . The house, he said, was of pink brick.

"Whose house was this?"

"It belonged to the surgeon of the Old Pardee Hospital."

"Ah-*ha!*"

Red smiled faintly. "I didn't plan to stop there," he said. "But I did. And while I stayed around, the Grahams invited me out to their home."

"And you liked it."

"I liked it. Some day I'll own an old house, and I hope I can have in it the peace and the serenity there was in that home. When I think that if there had not been an ice storm—"

"What ice storm?"

"The one last week. Didn't it rain and freeze here?"

"It rained."

"Well, a hundred miles north of here that same rain froze into solid ice. That's why I never got to Bridgeton. I stopped off at this motel—for fear I'd smash the car and me. And then, right in front of the motel, these kids did smash themselves up. They were hurt, C'ele. One was killed, and I helped take care of them."

He didn't mention Carrie specifically, and he could not have said why.

"That's how you got to your hospital," said C'ele.

"Yes, that's how. I wish you could have seen it, too, C'ele. It had originally been a fine, big home. The ceilings were twelve feet high. There was this double-curving staircase, with modern heavy-glass fire doors on the landings."

"Did they have an operating room? Things like that?"

165

"They had a good operating room. Bigger than was necessary, but the floors and walls were tiled. They had apparatus and instruments—and I must tell you about the lanterns."

"In the operating room?"

"Lanterns all over. Do you know what a Coleman lantern is, C'ele? It's a very efficient gasoline lantern with a mantel—it's protected from the wind—and in this hospital they had them everywhere a light might be needed in case the power went off, which it sure did that night. While I was operating, as a matter of fact."

"Could you see?"

"Of course I could see. They had reflectors on the lanterns in o.r."

C'ele regarded him with smiling wonder. "I never know what you'll like," she marveled.

"Oh, you girls all have that trouble," Red told her pompously.

"Girls?" asked C'ele, wide-eyed. "*What* girls?"

"You think they don't have girls in Old Pardee?" asked Red, his blue eyes shining and his cheeks deep-creased.

C'ele recognized the signs, and she settled contentedly against the cushions of the couch.

"Let me tell you about one they had up there," Red continued. "Her name was Maurita. And *she* was quite a dame!" He shot a glance at C'ele.

"Go on. I can always learn."

Red chuckled. "She could teach you plenty," he agreed. "She was—well, she called herself the hospital manager. And she was somewhat in charge of things in the office."

"Pretty?"

Red pursed his lips. "All made up, cinched in, and dressed high. Her pancake make-up was thick, her eye shadow and mascara and pencil—"

"In the *hospital?*"

"I don't think the doctors even see it. Nor her figure, for all her work. She wears very high spike heels, and she stumps around on them, shaking the floor when she walks." Red got to his feet, puffed out his chest, pushed out his hips, and he teetered across the floor, swiveling his hips as he walked.

C'ele laughed and wiped her eyes. "I can see you were impressed."

Red flopped down on the couch again and glanced at his wrist. He had ten minutes. "Maurita could see I was, too!" he admitted. "In fact, she told everybody in the hospital that she had caught herself a big fish."

"You?"

"Me. She looked at my car and decided I was rich."

C'ele made a face and shook her head. "She sounds awful, Red."

Red stretched his legs before him. "Well, I guess she was awful," he said. "She was vulgar—she used some pretty plain language at times. I heard her telling off a patient who was questioning a bill."

He lifted his voice. "If you don't think you received service for what you are requested to pay, Mr. Miller, you could *try* taking it up with Dr. Robinson. But I can inform you . . ." He took a deep breath and resumed his normal tone.

"The worst thing about Maurita," he said, "was her phoniness. She was a liar in everything she did and said. And I *hate* that!"

C'ele was no longer laughing. She watched Red with sober eyes, her face a little pale. *He hated liars.*

She knew that.

He got to his feet and went across the room for his coat. "I'd better get cracking," he said. "See you, C'ele."

She followed him to the door. "Oh yes, sure," she agreed. "And I'm glad you're back, Red. You seem to be your old self again."

He buttoned his coat. "Is that good?" he asked.

She smiled. "It suits me fine."

12 ❀❀❀❀❀❀❀❀❀❀❀❀❀❀❀❀❀❀❀❀❀❀❀❀❀❀

HAPPILY intent, Red went back to work on the floor and in Surgery, glad to know that it was good work and that there was plenty of it. For the next month he was alertly aware of himself as a surgeon.

Three times during that month he called Dr. Graham to inquire about Carrie. He still hoped to go up there, though evidently she was progressing nicely.

And Red was busy. . . .

One night he took C'ele bowling, and twice, when on call, he bought her pizza in the small restaurant near the hospital. On all three dates—such as they were—they had fun.

Three dates of that sort was just about the amount of time possible for a busy senior resident to give to his girl. Except for about six hours' sleep out of the twenty-four—not six hours consecutively always—the rest of Red's time was spent "on the floor."

Busy—and contented to be busy. The old rut, he told himself, felt nice and comfortable.

After the letter he looked back wistfully upon its comfort.

It was the first of the month and payday, otherwise the letter might have stayed in the mail room for a day or so. But Red—any resident, in fact—never forgot to pick up his pay check.

There was an ad for a seminar in modern art, with beautifully lithographed enclosures. There was a letter from his mother . .

Red said, "Hi!" to someone who spoke to him. At this hour of payday the downstairs corridor was very busy.

He stuffed his mother's letter into his pocket along with his pay check. Then he looked at the third piece of mail. It was a long envelope of pebbled bond; the address was typed on an electric machine, beautifully clear and neat. But what . . . ? Frowning, Red reached into his breast pocket and took out the scissors which he carried there, along with his pen and thermometer and ophthalmoscope. He held the envelope to the light, then trimmed off the end; he squeezed the envelope enough to let him draw out the letter. He shook it open, glanced at it, read it.

And he stood frozen.

There in the middle of the busy main corridor, with people hurrying past him, brushing against him, speaking to him, he heard nothing, saw no one, and spoke to no one.

He looked only at the letter. . . .

Then, suddenly aware of the people—nurses and doctors, two nuns, a sharply uniformed delivery man, three women fearfully come to the hospital to await the outcome of surgery, a Gray Lady with a cart full of flowers—Red hunted a hole. He ducked into one of the small interview rooms and closed the door, standing against the wall where he could not be seen through the glass. This move was purely instinct. To hide, to protect himself.

He drew a deep breath and again unfolded the letter. "It

can't be," he said under his breath. But there it was.

The neat letterhead:

M. LUTHER MARESCHAL
Attorney at Law
Norfolk, Missouri

Red frowned. Norfolk? Yes. He remembered, in planning the drive to Bridgeton last month, noticing the name on the road map. Yes, it was just beyond Old Pardee.

Probably larger than the pleasant little town where Red had spent his week. Would it be in the same county as— where was it the Lockettes had lived? Red could not remember.

Two hundred people in their town, Graham had said.

Sighing, Red let his eyes travel again across the letter's sentences, its neat paragraphs.

M.—for Martin, surely—Luther Mareschal was acting in behalf of Carrie Lockette. (How strange the name looked typed out on this sheet of pebbled white paper! The letters had no meaning—there was no image of the girl! But there it was.) Luther Mareschal was acting in behalf of Carrie Lockette, at the instance—what a word, *instance!*—at the instance of her guardians.

Paragraph.

This same Luther Mareschal, attorney, was hereby preferring a charge . . . for performing . . . an operation without the permission of Carrie Lockette's parents . . . executing surgery without their consent . . . on a minor . . . which performance . . . and execution . . . on a minor . . . amounted to assault.

Red groaned and leaned his shoulders heavily against the green wall. Out in the corridor three men went past the door, talking loudly.

This damned same Luther Mareschal understood that Redding Cahill, addressed herein, now held, and on 26–27 December past did hold, the position of resident surgeon at Lincoln Hospital . . . Luther Mareschal also understood that Dr. Cahill's post-graduate certificate—or any post-graduate certificate—authorized the holder to practice medicine only in the hospital specified and under the supervision of said doctor's sponsor.

Red's hand dropped, the letter rustling against his leg. His other hand brushed across his eyes.

Under the supervision of . . .

In the *shadow* of—his sponsor!

Well, as of now, said Redding Cahill needed that shadow! Large, black—and protecting!

He would at once go to see Enns and talk to him. This letter—Red folded it, hating the very feel of it, and put the thing into his pocket. This letter sounded like big trouble!

Without speaking to anyone, without seeing hall or elevator or the floor desk, Red was opening the door of the Chief's office and going in. "Would you read this letter, sir?" he said abruptly. "I am afraid it means trouble."

Dr. Enns gave his senior resident an intent glance, then he put on his dark-rimmed glasses and picked up the letter. He read it carefully, folded it, and returned it to the envelope, which he laid to one side of the desk. "Yes," he said gravely, "I am afraid this does mean trouble."

Red leaned toward him, his forearm across the corner of the desk. "What do they *want*, sir?" he asked anxiously.

Dr. Enns took off his glasses and swung them back and forth. "They want money," he said readily. "Of course. That's what all malpractice suits want."

"That letter doesn't say anything about—"

"No. This is a first letter, a feeler. But if you don't re-

172

spond properly, the next letter will be more specific."

Red sank back into his chair. "It could mean my M.D.," he said morosely.

"Well . . ." Dr. Enns drew a deep breath "We'll see what we can do about that, of course." His face was grave, but his voice betrayed no panic.

"But," said Red, "can they . . . ?"

"Sue for malpractice? Oh yes, Red. Almost anybody can sue any doctor for malpractice. On that basis I would say that this Mareschal has a good case. It is going to be much easier, you know, to prove that there was that assault he mentions than for you to prove that there was not."

Red got to his feet, walked the length of the small room, and came back. "But, Dr. Enns," he cried, "I am innocent! I only helped a girl—I kept her from dying. Isn't the burden of proof of any *guilt* on *them?*"

Dr. Enns was shaking his head slowly, firmly.

"No," he said emphatically, "that isn't the way things go in these cases. You have to prove you were, and are, innocent. If you can."

Red beat his clenched fists together. "It hasn't happened!" he protested. "It isn't happening! It just cannot be!"

The Chief's eyebrows went up. "It is happening," he said mildly. "It happens all the time. Have you reported this to the Center's legal office or to the insurance authorities?"

"No, sir. I came straight up here to tell you."

"I meant during the past month."

Red looked puzzled. "No, sir. I told you about it when I first came back."

Dr. Enns nodded. "Yes, I remember your telling me that you had operated, under difficult circumstances, for a subdural hematoma and spinal compression. But I do not recall that you told me you did all that without authority."

"I had to save the girl's life, sir! She was convulsive. What should I have done? Left her at the side of the road to die?"

"Now, let's take one thing at a time, Dr. Cahill," said the Chief. "You knew—I hope you knew—that you should not have undertaken surgery without consent."

"But we couldn't find the parents. And it was an emergency."

"All right. It was an emergency. Didn't you also know that you should have reported the thing immediately to the insurance company? You knew it was irregular, and you should have known that you had breached various regulations."

Again Red slumped down into the chair. "Yes, sir," he agreed. "I suppose I did know those things." He was recalling a lecture which he had attended only weeks ago about the avoidance of malpractice suits. Then he had been in hot water about the battered little boy.

This . . . This was more serious.

"There have to be rules, Dr. Cahill," Dr. Enns lectured him. "Doctors are entrusted with a great deal of responsibility. Human lives are in their hands, and human well-being. But doctors are not above the law!" His voice rang out strongly. "If there were no restrictions upon us, chaos would result!"

"I know." Red sat, head down on his chest, the image of gloom.

"Well!" said Dr. Enns briskly. "How are the morning's post-operatives doing?"

Red looked up, frowning. "I suppose all right, sir."

"Don't you think you should *know?*"

"Yes, sir, but—"

"*I* think you should get on with your work, Dr. Cahill!" said the Chief firmly.

Red got to his feet. "Go back to work," Dr. Enns said again, "and do not talk about this matter." He tapped his forefinger on the letter from Attorney Mareschal. "Do not discuss it with anyone, Red, until you have seen the Center's lawyer."

Red took a deep breath. "Yes, sir," he said meekly. "How soon . . . ?"

"Should you see him? Why, as soon as you possibly can. About a month ago would have been best."

13 ✿✿✿✿✿✿✿✿✿✿✿✿✿✿✿✿✿✿✿✿✿✿✿✿✿

ON the next day's posted schedule **Dr. Redding Ca**-hill was given a two-hour period free of call. He also had received a message that the hospital's lawyer would see him at eleven the next morning.

This hour coincided with the beginning of his free two hours. So the conference was set up. Red ate his breakfast and worked in surgery with a heavy feeling of doom impending.

At ten Dr. Enns, meeting him in the hall, murmured, "Come by the office before you go downstairs, Dr. Cahill, please?"

"Yes, sir."

So the conference would be threefold at least. Maybe bigger than that. Dr. Enns had kept the Mareschal letter and no doubt he had shown it and talked to the lawyer Probably to the Administrator as well.

Red suspected that this was not strictly a hospital case but he was an employee of the Center, Dr. Enns was hi sponsor, and he was covered, through the hospital, wit insurance.

Yes, it would be folly to think that the trouble was his alone.

It was a sunny day, with a cold wind whistling around the corners of the tall buildings. When Red went to his room to shave and put on fresh whites, he wished that he could change to street clothes and go up and tell that country lawyer a thing or two.

He could not.

He must go downstairs. Probably the Chief of Medical Services would be there, too! And Red must face all those men and explain why he had done as he had done—and which, he told himself, he would, as sure as hell, do again!

Checking in the mirror, he caught the pugnacious set of his square jaw, and he rubbed his hands down his cheeks. If he wanted to appear to be any sort of a doctor, self-control was of prime importance. He need not smile—which was a good thing. He could not have made it.

He went out into the hall, was stopped twice—once to sign an order, once to answer a question. He spoke to a patient, and he knocked lightly on the door of the Chief's office, then turned the knob and went in. Dr. Enns was sitting in his wheel chair, and Red was surprised. For two weeks the man had got along, defiantly, on crutches.

"I thought you could ride me downstairs, Cahill," said the Chief at once. "I am going with you."

"Yes, sir." Red held the door open, and Dr. Enns wheeled through. He was wearing a gray flannel suit with a tie as blue as his eyes.

"Just take it easy, Red," said his Chief quietly.

"I'm afraid I can't, sir."

"No. Would you have rather talked to Mr. Randol alone?"

The elevator came and Red put his foot on the sill while Dr. Enns wheeled in and turned the chair.

"I'd rather forget the whole thing, sir," Red told him, laughing a little. Not humorously. He pushed a button and leaned against the wall.

Dr. Enns said nothing.

On the first floor Red put his hands to the wheel chair and guided it deftly between the people who always thronged down there.

"To Mr. Randol's office?" he asked. "I don't know the man personally. I've heard him lecture on Forensic Medicine. I know him by sight."

"He's a smart man, Red."

"I hope." On sight alone, Randol was not Red's type. He was a big man, and pudgy. He talked a lot and told jokes when he lectured to the medical students and interns—jokes that fell a little flat, but which he always announced as funny. He . . .

They had reached the office, and Dr. Enns leaned forward to open the door. Red bore down on the wheel-chair handles. It would be a fine start to have the Chief pitch in on his nose!

The secretary said they were expected. She smiled at Dr. Enns; she beamed at Dr. Cahill. She was a cute girl. She got up and opened the inner door.

"Dr. Enns is here, sir," she said formally, "and Dr. Cahill."

The inside office was a large room and rather untidy. Mr. Randol's desk was stacked with papers, letters, and even three five-dollar bills thrown casually atop the mess.

Red coughed and looked at the man behind the desk and at the second man who sat to the left of it. Mr. Ovian, the hospital Administrator.

178

These men spoke to Dr. Enns, and he replied, then he tipped his head toward Red. "My senior resident, gentlemen. Dr. Cahill."

There was a murmur of names. Red sat down in the chair to the right front of Randol's big desk and adjusted the leg of his trousers. His hands were perspiring a little. He took a deep breath and looked at Mr. Randol, who was looking at him.

"I thought I had you pegged, Cahill," he said. His voice was soft and a little breathy. He offered cigarettes around the group. No one took any, but he lit one for himself.

He moved papers around on his desk, then he leaned back in his chair. "Dr. Enns brought me a letter yesterday, Dr. Cahill," he said in a tone of discursive reminiscence. "I have discussed its contents with Mr. Ovian." He glanced toward the Administrator.

"Yes, sir." Red sat quiet, one of his palms cupping and rubbing the arm of the chair.

"My first reaction," said Mr. Randol, "was to decide that these people—these Lockettes—have found themselves a very good lawyer." He shot a glance at Red. "And then I decided," he continued, "that you, Dr. Cahill, had given that lawyer a very good case."

Red bit his lower lip. "I was also a good Samaritan, sir." His tone was bitter.

Dr. Enns stirred in his chair.

"Yes," agreed Mr. Randol. "I understand that you were. Would you care to tell us the circumstances under which you took on that role, Doctor?"

"Yes, sir. I—"

"Briefly, Doctor."

Red hated this man's guts! He nodded. And in as quiet a voice as he could manage, he went over again the details of the trip north and the freezing rain. He told of the wreck —the dead driver and the girl thrown out, her head striking the edge of the gas-pump island. He had called an ambulance; he only mentioned the hospital. He briefly told of his examination and diagnosis. He told of the efforts to determine the girl's identity, of the phones out and the lights. In twenty words he told about the surgery and the discovery that the optic nerve was damaged.

"But the girl lived," he concluded. "Now she is making an excellent recovery."

As he talked, briefly as had been requested, his audience had sat silent. Now Red sat back and again waited.

Mr. Randol patted his finger tips together and looked up at the ceiling. "And you were the good Samaritan," he mused.

"I was there, sir. The girl was hurt. I was a doctor."

"Yes. I think Mareschal would concede those points. He might even go along with the good-Samaritan bit, had you administered first aid and then taken the injured child . . ."

"Girl," Red corrected, his jaw tight.

"Fifteen. Yes, a girl. You could have sent—or taken— her to the nearest doctor. Still being a good Samaritan, you see?"

Red sighed and waited.

"Dr. Cahill." The attorney tipped his chair forward and looked earnestly at his victim. "Do you know that twenty-one states of this country have passed good-Samaritan laws designed to protect doctors like yourself who stop at accidents to help the victims."

"To protect them, sir?"

"Yes! To protect men like you. In the past, you know— though maybe you don't know—many doctors who have saved the lives of these injured people have later been sued on the grounds of malpractice by these same ingrates."

Red wanted to get up and walk out of the room. He was licked. He was through.

"The doctors have needed protection," said Dr. Enns quietly, probably detecting Red's impulse and his mood.

"Yes," agreed Mr. Randol. "As a result of these suits—and they are many, Dr. Cahill—lawyers like myself, and insurance companies, advise their doctors to keep traveling whenever they encounter a wreck."

"You mean, I should have stepped over that girl and gone to my room. To bed."

"Well, had you done that, we would not be sitting here this morning trying to decide how to handle the matter of this letter from Mr. Mareschal."

"Had you taken her to another doctor . . ." contributed the Administrator.

"But I did!" said Red. "I had the ambulance called, and I took her to the nearest hospital. I went with her, but the *ambulance* took her. It took us an hour to drive that mile or so. The storm was terrible, gentlemen! The hospital, when we reached it, was small. A good hospital, but small. And the surgeon, though he was good, too, said he could not undertake brain surgery. There was no chance to come back here to the city.

"Besides, I was *there!* I knew how to save her life—and I could not let her die! *I could not!*" He got to his feet and walked, in agitation, around the room.

For a minute the three older men watched him. Then Dr. Enns spoke quietly, firmly. "Come back here and sit down, Red."

Red obeyed. His face was dead-white. "What would you have done in my shoes?" he demanded.

Dr. Enns shrugged. "Maybe the same thing you did,

Red," he admitted. "And I'd be in the same kettle of hot water you now enjoy."

Red snorted. Leaning to one side, he fished a handkerchief from his trouser pocket and blew his nose.

"Now," said Mr. Randol, "suppose we get down to business. Tell me: have you made any record or report of this case? and did you sign any such record?"

Red considered this. "I wrote orders on the patient's chart, sir," he admitted. "And I probably initialed them. I do here."

"What sort of orders? Medication—therapy—stuff like that?"

Red looked hard at a framed engraving of Mark Twain. "Yes, sir," he said.

"Do you yourself have a detailed case record containing all the pertinent facts, including the patient's name, the date of the—er—incident, and a brief description of the surgery and treatment?"

Red shook his head. "I could work one up, sir."

"Well, a late one would be better than none. So you do that. We can put it with whatever legal papers may be served on you."

Red could think of nothing to say.

"When that worst comes to the worst," continued Mr. Randol, "doctors are asked always to gather immediately all records, reports, and other evidence that might be needed by the defense attorney."

I could go up to Old Pardee, Red thought, *and get the hospital record. Graham would give it to me, or a photostatic copy . . .*

"Every scrap of recorded evidence becomes important," the attorney was saying, "including hospital records and X-ray films. And I may not need to add this warning, Dr.

Cahill, but in no case should existing records ever be destroyed or altered."

Red's jaw fell. "There would be no reason to do that!" he cried.

"Good! However, I felt it my duty to warn you. Now let's see. What next?" Then he smiled.

"I guess a conference with the insurance agent will be next," he announced. "You and me, and him, Doctor. So I urge you to be prepared to be completely candid with him and detailed in your discussions with him."

"But I have been candid!" Red shouted.

"Good!" said Mr. Randol, probably not believing him. The man was a sadist; he was enjoying himself. He liked to see a worm squirm on a hook. "Entire frankness must be your watchword.

"Now, tell me this—if you didn't sign anything up at this hospital—"

Red's mind flashed to that night and to little Dr. Robinson. Dr. Cahill had offered to sign a statement releasing the Old Pardee Hospital from all responsibility for the surgery he was about to do. No such statement had been presented or signed, but both Dr. Robinson and Dr. Graham could witness to his offer. Should Red tell Randol about this? Later, perhaps . . .

"Did you in any way make a statement to the family of this girl, Dr. Cahill, that could be misconstrued as an admission of your irregular medical conduct?"

Red stiffened. "I told them that Carrie had been critically hurt. That immediate surgery had been the only thing possible to save her life."

"And that you had done that surgery without consent?"

"The father knew surgery had been performed—and that I had done it. And since he didn't even know his daughter had been hurt until twenty-four hours after the accident, he also knew that his consent had not been obtained. He must also have known why, Mr. Randol."

"Don't get hot, Red," murmured Dr. Enns.

Red sat back in his chair and tried to compose himself. *Not get hot!*

"Did you tell the parents that their daughter was blind?" persisted Mr. Randol suavely.

"Yes, sir."

"Did they blame you?"

"I—yes, sir, they did. But we—Dr. Graham and I—told them that I was not to blame for her blindness, and we also told them that I had saved the girl's life."

"Did they believe you?"

"I don't know, sir. They were people of small experience and little education. Dr. Graham called them backwoods people."

"Ah-huh. Well, personalities are not significant."

They would be to Red. An ignorant man often mistrusted and resented the gloss of education on another man.

Mr. Randol was talking again. "Did you," he asked Red, "in the course of your conversation with the parents or with the patient, ever brag, or even comment to them, about the possession of liability coverage?"

Red could only shake his head. He was beaten. These men in this room—all of them—thought he had acted the complete fool, that he deserved a suit for malpractice.

"Well," said Mr. Randol briskly, "you and I will talk to the insurance people, Dr. Cahill. And we'll hope to avoid the publicity of a lawsuit. Where it is at all possible, you know, the company agrees that a justified claim should be settled promptly. And I promise you that I shall do what I can to settle this matter out of court."

184

Red could not believe his ears! "You wouldn't fight it?" he cried.

"Not unless I'd have to," Mr. Randol assured him.

"But what about me?" asked the young doctor. "I'd want to be vindicated!"

"Tell him, Bill," said Mr. Ovian.

Dr. Enns nodded. "He really doesn't need telling," he assured the other men. "Red is well trained and experienced as a doctor. Just now he is shocked at what a well-meant offer of assistance seems to be costing him.

"As for vindication, his position as senior resident in Neurosurgery here in this hospital center has already vindicated him in the eyes of his profession. So far as a public vindication goes, I need only remind him that once a doctor is publicly charged with malpractice, there is *no* vindication. His usefulness as a doctor is reduced to nothing."

Red put his two hands to his head and shook it hard. "You have decided that I am guilty!" he cried. "You think—"

"It doesn't make any difference, Red," said Dr. Enns firmly, "what we—what I decide or think. We have to consider the possibility of a court trial. And the surety that to the public, where a doctor is concerned, there is little difference between an indictment and a conviction. *That* is why Mr. Randol hopes to get this thing settled out of court and as quickly as possible."

"But it isn't fair!" Red groaned. "I never did—I never will do—better surgery."

"It isn't fair," Dr. Enns agreed. "But we have to face things as they are. And you must co-operate with us."

Red sighed. "Yes, sir," he said morosely. "I'll try . . ."

"I guess the thing to tell you, Cahill," Mr. Randol said, not unkindly, "is for you to wait for word from me.

Otherwise do nothing, say nothing. Don't talk about this to anyone! Understand? Because you can be quoted and the press would grab a chance to make a sensational story."

"I'll be careful."

"You be damn more than careful, son!" said the attorney, his voice roughening. "A simple statement could convict you! These people—Lockette and his lawyer—seem out to ruin you and possibly the other doctors involved."

Not Dr. Graham! Red's face showed his dismay and his protest.

Randol nodded. "O.K.!" he said. "If you won't save yourself, think of them!" He stood up. "I think that should do for now, gentlemen."

Red took Dr. Enns up to his office, and once in, he closed the door behind them.

"You had better get your lunch, Red," said Dr. Enns kindly. "I mean to have mine."

"Yes, sir. But first I have to ask you—"

Dr. Enns frowned. "Randol was quite specific."

"Yes, sir, he was. But there is this: I want to know what my position will be while this matter is being handled."

Dr. Enns wheeled his chair around and looked earnestly at his senior resident. He loved the boy, and the events of the past hours had hurt him just about as much as they had Red. But he knew that ethical decorum was his best protection and Dr. Cahill's as well.

"I should not have to state your position, Cahill," he said sternly. "As senior resident on Neurosurgery, you have the authorization of all surgery performed on this service. Don't you know that?"

"Yes, but now . . . that authority will not be withheld?"

"I see no reason to suspend you and withhold it."

Red stood for a minute, not knowing just what to say. Then he turned to the door. "Thank you, sir," he said uncertainly. He went out into the corridor.

The nurses at the station looked at him curiously. Red glanced at his watch, went to his room briefly, then downstairs for some lunch. He would not go on duty for another twenty-five minutes. In the cafeteria he spoke when spoken to, but shortly.

That afternoon on the floor—making rounds, supervising the care of an emergency—he had nothing to say beyond professional directions and comment. He did not join the three-o'clock coffee break. By then the wards, the whole service, were buzzing. Vince Sebaja came up to N.S. with the intention of asking Red what was wrong. He went back to his own wards, shaking his head.

By dinnertime everyone was asking what was wrong with Cahill. He was doing his job, but he hadn't said ten words to anyone all day. Gutzell voiced the opinion that Cahill was grumpy "because something's eating him again."

Red would have agreed. At ten o'clock he went to bed, expecting as always to be roused during the night—he had better get some sleep.

But he could not sleep. He lay on his back, the noises of the hospital faintly about him. A bell rang, the elevator sighed to a stop, someone spoke loudly, feet whispered along the tiled floor. Light came through the blinds at his window and made a striped glow of radiance on the ceiling. Red flopped over on his stomach and pounded the pillow.

For the past month he had felt himself, working, liking people, sleeping well. And now this thing had hit him. The hospital was behind him. He need not feel that he must

187

fight this battle alone. But he felt exactly as he had felt over Ronald. Both times he had been put into shock for doing a job which he knew he could do and really had been doing for three years.

The next day was Sunday, a crisp, cool day; the sun was shining, and in the afternoon Red had a few hours free. He called C'ele.

How about a walk in the park? he asked her. He needed some fresh-air exercise.

She agreed at once. She would meet him at the corner of the Boulevard.

He put the phone down, feeling satisfaction. C'ele would be good for him; so would the air and the exercise. Tonight perhaps he could sleep.

He went downstairs, striding through the lobby, out to the steps of the hospital. People—visitors—were all about. Various doctors and nurses spoke to Red. He answered absent-mindedly and went on to the sidewalk, turning north.

C'ele was waiting, a thin white scarf snug to her head, the hem of her red coat blowing a little.

"Hi!" she said, tucking her hand through his arm.

They waited for the light, then crossed to the park. They had a pattern for these walks. They would go along one length of the park, then cut across, through the zoo, around the lake, past the rink, and home. Four or five miles, with plenty to see. And plenty to talk about, if one was in the mood.

Today Red did not seem to be.

Briskly they walked along Lindell, past the fine homes there. A poodle wanted to adopt them. A child rode his tricycle pell-mell at them; Red drew C'ele to safety without comment.

She made an attempt or two to talk. "It's a beautiful day . . ."

"I'm going to want a hot dog at the end of this safari . . ."

"Did you hear about Dr. Schonwald's wife?"

Red answered in monosyllables and again fell silent.

When they turned and began to walk back toward the hospital, C'ele took a quick step or two and got ahead of him, where she could turn and face him. "What's wrong with you, Red Cahill?" she demanded.

"Nothing's wrong with me, C'ele." He would have walked around her.

She backed up. "Yes, there is too something wrong," she insisted. "And I want to know what it is. Can you be fuming again about that battered-child business?"

Red grasped her arm and walked her along the road.

"I know you have been upset about it," C'ele told him, trotting to keep up with his stride. "And outraged that there are no laws to protect such children."

"Laws!" growled Red.

C'ele clung to his arm. "That's right!" she encouraged. "Let's talk about laws."

"I would if there were any," he said morosely.

C'ele smiled a little, a little smugly.

"Aren't there enough laws, Red?" she asked coolly.

"Not in my field. The kids aren't protected, and the doctors aren't. Though, if I thought sacrificing myself for Carrie's case would do it, I'd make that sacrifice. And secure a way to help all Carries."

He was talking!—though C'ele didn't understand a word he said.

"What sacrifice, Red?" she asked quietly. "How could you help?" And, she asked herself, *who* was Carrie?

He hadn't told her about anyone with that name, though, of course, doctors had a way of discussing a case without identifying the person. If she could keep Red talking, he would tell her who Carrie was.

He did. First he reminded her of the accident when he'd taken that trip a month ago. She remembered?

Yes, of course she remembered.

"Well, the girl—the one who was so terribly hurt, you know—she was—she is—a lovely thing.

"She had the most beautiful red hair, C'ele. A true copper-red. It shone. Her eyes were a dark, purplish blue and set into her head in a way . . . her hands were childish . . ."

He had no thought of disobedience to Mr Randol's specific orders. He was only remembering Carrie and telling C'ele about her.

"How old is she?" C'ele asked softly, thinking that again Red had one of his "battered" children.

"Fifteen," Red answered. "Almost sixteen—but that's what got me into trouble."

"What trouble, Red?" C'ele spoke quietly.

He turned and looked at her, as if he had forgotten she was there and that he was not talking to himself.

"You are in trouble," C'ele persisted. "Aren't you?"

Red nodded. "Yes . . ." he said slowly. "I am. I knew better. But—that night—I thought only of that young girl. Of saving her life."

"And you did."

"Yes. Yes, I did."

"But—then—*how* did you do anything wrong, Red?"

He shook his head. "There are rules—ethics." His voice flattened.

C'ele shook her head impatiently. "I am not talking

about that. I mean—did you do anything *wrong?* Really wrong."

"There are those who think so. They think that it was wrong to be a good Samaritan. To try to save a life when there was no one else to do it . . ."

"And you did save it?"

"Yes."

"All right! Keep that in your mind. You are a doctor, and you did a good job of doctoring. There isn't anything else, is there?"

Red put his hand on her shoulder and drew her close to his side. For five minutes they walked along this way. He was half smiling and thinking. Now and then he would nod his head.

He was examining his past and present feeling. Something C'ele had said had brought him to a stage where he was no longer worried about himself. Where he knew that he could do a good job . . .

"I know that my judgment is better with each experience . . ." he said, consideringly. "Now—well, I'll see what I can do. I won't just give up! If I am going to be a doctor . . . I am! I already am one!"

Then his step quickened; he and C'ele continued their walk in good spirits, though Red didn't want to talk any more about Carrie. "I've got all that straight in my head," he told the girl. "Let's go get your hot dog."

They got it and ate it, watching the skaters. Before long, Red promised, he would skate there with C'ele. He didn't have time today. He must go on duty at five.

He left her "at the corner" and went on to the hospital, in through the wide glass doors and across the lighted lobby, into the elevator, and up.

He stopped at the desk to ask Miss Greenberg how

things were. Dr. Enns came out of his office.

"Don't you ever go home?" Red asked him.

"I've been waiting for you. We got ourselves an accident case while you were gone, Doctor. The young man's in seven-fourteen. There's a hematoma to attend to. Will you do it?"

Red began to take off his jacket. "Sure," he said, starting down the hall. "Wait until I change—"

The Chief watched him go into his room. The Chief was smiling.

14 ✿✿✿✿✿✿✿✿✿✿✿✿✿✿✿✿✿✿✿✿✿✿✿✿

IN the middle of the month Red had a whole day free. That morning he was to appear in Common Pleas Court as a witness in the trial of the woman who had, last fall, poured pepper down her child's throat and was now accused of manslaughter.

Red had been on e.r. duty when Thelma was brought into the hospital, dead. His testimony should not take long, and it had been promised that he would be called this day. Then, if he should get away from court early enough, he had plans. . . .

He stopped for a haircut and went on down to the courts building, enjoying this change from the hospital routine of surgery, rounds, and emergencies. He had dressed carefully; both Dr. Enns and Mr. Randol had talked to him briefly about his testimony and his general "attitude."

Red would keep their advice in mind. These days his behavior was important, and both men were trying to help him.

Within thirty minutes of his arrival at the court Dr. Cahill was called. He was sworn and took the witness chair.

The jury looked him over and saw a big young man—around thirty—with an open face and an honest and confident manner. He was quiet and spoke quietly, though concern for the child, Thelma, was evident.

Dr. Cahill was thanked; he was excused, and he went, on a half-run, out of the building, to the parking lot. He turned his car toward the Freeway and drove, as closely as possible to the speed limit, to Old Pardee. This trip, he knew, would be entirely against the Chief's advice and Randol's, had he asked their advice.

The day was fair, windy, and not very cold. He passed the Northland Motel with a reminiscent glance and went on, down the hill, up the second hill, and into the old town, to the hospital. It was not yet noon, but when he came in through the back door, trays were being served.

The floor nurse welcomed him warmly. "Doctor," she said, was upstairs in the dressing room. "He'll be glad to see you, Dr. Cahill."

Red grinned at her, waved to Maurita at the desk, and took the stairs three at a time. He wanted to see Dr. Graham, first and maybe only. After all, he had been told not to talk.

Dr. Graham *was* glad to see Red. He must stay for lunch —could they go out to the house? Rachel . . .

"I haven't much time," said Red. "I must be home and back on the floor at five this evening."

Dr. Graham closed the door into the hall. "You're being bothered, aren't you?" he asked quietly.

Red laughed a little at the mild term. "I don't have enough experience to feel that a lawsuit is just a bother, sir."

"We hardly ever reach that degree of sophistication. Can I do something for you?" Dr. Graham sat on a stool, a

194

strong, quiet man in a white coat.

"Is this hospital being 'bothered,' too?" asked Red.

Dr. Graham shook his head, and Red sighed with relief.

"I expect we could be," Dr. Graham continued. "And Dr. Robinson is sure of it."

"I'm sorry."

"For his jitters? Well, yes, I can take a bit of sympathy on that count. He is a worrier—even a nagger. He seldom if ever waits to see if a thing will happen."

Red nodded. "I didn't anticipate this charge," he confessed. "I am glad you're not in on it, but I do wonder why they picked on me."

"The Lockettes and Mareschal decided you were rich."

Red stared at the other doctor, then he laughed. "Where did they ever get such an idea?"

"I'm afraid that Maurita told around that you had to be.

Now Red laughed aloud. "Because of my car?" he asked.

"Because of your car."

Red shook his head. "Did you tell them what a resident gets paid?"

"I haven't told them anything, Red. They came to me and wanted the records, and I refused."

"Could you?"

"Maybe not. But it worked on the first try. I told them, which is true, that it is not permissible to furnish medical information about a patient without his consent, except under court order."

Red whistled silently.

"Yes. Then I went on to explain—rather stuffily, I thought—that the physician-patient relationship is a highly confidential one. When an insurance company, or anyone else, seeks to obtain information improperly, it is the doctor's duty to protect his patient by not furnishing that information without the patient's consent."

Red was shaking his head in awe. "And they bought it?"

"Yes, they did. For the time, at least. Certainly I am not going to be the one to remind them that Carrie is a minor, and—" The big doctor shrugged.

"They'll come to. Our legal light says Mareschal is a smart lawyer. And certainly the records could be produced at any hearing or trial. My handwriting and initials are on the chart pages. I wrote orders. And I wouldn't think of denying that I tried to help Carrie."

"Of course you would not. Er—Dr. Robinson, I am afraid, told Mr. Mareschal that you had released the hospital from all responsibility."

"Yes, and I offered to sign such a release, but the matter was never pursued."

"Robinson was sure you had signed such a paper; he nearly tore the place to shreds hunting it. He and Maurita finally got into a noble row about it."

Red smiled. "How *is* Maurita?"

Dr. Graham laughed and shook his head. "Didn't you see her as you came in?"

"Yes, I waved to her."

"She'll catch you on the way down. Can't you come out to the house for lunch, Red?"

"No, I'll mooch a sandwich from the kitchen as I leave. But I've a few things I want to do . . ."

"You want to see Carrie, don't you?"

Red nodded. "I thought you'd never ask."

"She's not here, Red. Her father took her home last week. She seemed to be making good progress. I—well, of course I couldn't hold her."

"No, of course not. Will you tell me how to reach their house?"

"Do you think you should go there?"

"I think I have to go there."

"Yes, I suppose you do. I'll take you down for that sandwich, and while you eat it, I'll draw you a map."

Maurita, at the front desk when the two men came down the curving stairs, at sight of Red was out from behind the counter, squealing with joy. She seized his shoulders; she put up her face for a kiss.

"Oh, Dr. Cahill!" she cried. "I had gone into despair about ever viewing you again! Of course, there is the trial —but that would be so different, wouldn't it? Oh, let me observe you! Look, Miss Gardner . . ." She hailed a passing nurse and explained lavishly who Red was, how she and he had met. She told what *old* friends they were . . . She was going to have lunch with him!

Red listened, smiled, and tried to disengage himself from her grasp.

"Aren't you going to be nice to me, Red?" she pouted.

He shook his head. "I haven't time," he said firmly. "Sorry."

"She won't like this," said Dr. Graham as the two men went on to the kitchen. "She considers you her special property."

Red shrugged. "Why do you keep her?" he asked.

"Maurita? Well, she keeps good books, Red. The town knows her, discounts her stories. Besides, Maurita has a mother to support. The girl wouldn't last ten minutes in a city office."

"No," Red agreed. "She would not. She is evidently planning to come to my trial or whatever."

"And fully expects Raymond Burr to be there."

"On whose side?"

"Oh, I don't think she cares. She considers *you* very cute."

Red smiled wryly. "*I* don't consider this very much of a joke," he told Dr. Graham, thanking the cook for the plate set before him. "But Maurita may well provide the needed light touch."

Red had, with Dr. Graham's sketched map, little difficulty in finding the tiny town of Sublette where the Lockettes lived. A woman in the combined general store and post office directed him to the Lockette home, which he found to be a modest white frame house; the grounds about it were as neat as a pin. There were trellises and flower boxes and a wagon wheel, all painted a bright pink. Red parked his car in the driveway and considered the choice of a side door close at hand or going around to the front door.

While he stood there, four cats appeared from nowhere and rubbed against his trouser leg. And then the side door opened, and Carrie's mother looked out around the storm door.

"You want something, mister?" she called. "The judge ain't to home."

Red walked toward her. "I wanted to see your daughter, Mrs. Lockette," he said firmly. "I am Dr. Cahill."

By then he was up the steps and able to prevent Mrs. Lockette's closing the storm door in his face. He reached around her and pushed the inner door back against the wall.

"I don't figure you got business here," she attempted.

Red went on into the little porch. Beyond it was the kitchen. "It isn't a matter of business, Mrs. Lockette," he said in his kindest way. "I just want to see Carrie. How is she?"

"All right, I guess. 'Course she can't see, but *you* know that."

"Yes, and I am sorry."

"She don't seem real sick otherwise, Doctor," Mrs. Lockette told him. "But she don't eat well, and at night I hear her cryin'."

"Oh, dear. Where is she?"

"Well—her pa ain't goin' to like your bein' here."

"We needn't tell him, perhaps."

"He's got ways o' knowin' things. Somebody'll drive by, see that red car sittin' out there—he'll know."

"But that risk is already run. So let me see Carrie and—"

"Well—all right. You can come this way."

On another day and in another mood Red would have found the Lockette house a marvel of gimcracks, knick-nacks, gewgaws. Never had he seen so many vases and pitchers and china dogs.

There were bright cushions in every possible corner of the massive, overstuffed furniture in the living room. Hand-hooked rugs in fearsome colors lay atop the carpeting. There were fluted doilies on the small tables, crocheted blind pulls, and tiebacks at the windows.

Red's mind reeled to think of the time spent on all this handwork, the making of it, the maintaining of it in its present shining and dustless condition.

Carrie's small bedroom was down a short hall from the living room. Red found the girl sitting in an upholstered chair; a small electric heater made the room stifling hot.

"Carrie," he said cheerfully, "I am Dr. Cahill, and I came to see how you were doing."

She jumped at the first sound of his voice, then she

seemed to shrink down into the chair. She was wearing a blue corduroy robe. Her hair was beginning to grow; there was still a band of gauze and tape on her head.

"You're not afraid of me, Carrie," said Red, putting his hand on her shoulder.

"No . . ." But she still cowered in the bright slip-covered chair. Red picked up a small side chair and set it close to her. He sat down in it and took her hand.

"Your wrist healed nicely," he said.

Carrie sat with her chin down.

"Look at me, Carrie," he told her.

"I can't see . . ."

"But you can look at me. If you want to. Don't you want to?"

"I don't want nothin' these days."

"That's the way she is," said the mother from the doorway. "And you'd better go, Doc. If the judge or my son should come in, they would throw you out bodily."

Red could feel Carrie's hand tremble. He tightened his grip on it. "There are ways to handle your blindness, Carrie," he said to the girl, his warm voice steady. "Things you can learn to do. You can dress yourself, learn your way about the house—and out into the yard when it gets warm."

"But I won't see nothin'."

"Oh, but there are ways to see other than with the eyes. For instance, feel my sleeve. You can 'see' if I am wearing a white coat or not. Here, try it."

He put her fingers upon the tweed of his coat; she even rubbed the cloth a little. Then, without warning, she was weeping terribly, sobs shaking her, and great tears rolling down her cheeks. Red took his handkerchief and wiped her face. She took the wad of linen in her hand and held it to her cheek.

"It smells like you," she sobbed.

Red chuckled. "And how do I smell?"

"Clean," she said. "Soap—and ironed cloth—and a little medicine—some tobacco, but not much . . ."

"That's seeing me, Carrie," he told her gently.

"I've a mind to call the judge," said the mother belligerently.

Red glanced around at her. "I'll leave if you insist," he said.

He stood up, and Carrie's hands clawed at him—at his hand, his arm. She strained upward. "Don't leave, Doc!" she cried. "Don't leave now. Tell me more about seein' without no eyes."

Red sat down again. The mother stayed in the doorway, but Red ignored her and soon forgot her. He talked to the girl, gently and firmly. Eventually he saw the girl's head lift; once she even smiled. And she said, shyly, that she was glad he had come. Would he come again?

"If I could. But your family doesn't like me as much as you do."

"I know." Her head drooped again.

"Carrie," he said with determination, conscious again of the starched print skirt visible out of the corner of his eye, "you don't believe that I would hurt you, do you?"

"Oh no!" It was a mere whisper.

"You know that I tried to help you when you were hurt in that car wreck?"

"Yes."

"I took you to the hospital, and I operated on your head. I fixed it so you could breathe—and walk and talk. But I couldn't fix your eyes, Carrie. I am sorry that I couldn't do that. But I couldn't, any more than I could bring Johnny

Trigg back to life. Do you understand that?"

She nodded and lifted his hand to her cheek. "I'm sorry," she murmured.

"Oh, we're all sorry, dear. But there are those who think —at least, they say—that I hurt you."

"No . . ."

"No, I didn't. Now, do you understand about hospital records, Carrie?"

"You can tell me."

So he did tell her, carefully, and ignoring the impatient sounds made by the mother still in the doorway. He told how the charts were kept and orders written down. Everything about Carrie's injury, everything that the doctors had done, was written on those records.

"Now," he continued, "some men, some lawyers, want to keep me from working any more as a doctor. They think that if they can get your hospital records, it will help destroy me."

"They gone to court, ain't they?"

"Yes, they are doing that. Would you consent to their having and using your records to hurt me?"

"No, Doctor, I would not!"

"All right, then. Remember that. Remember that you don't want your records used against me."

"She ain't nuthin' but a chile!" said Mrs. Lockette in the doorway.

"I was sixteen last week!" Carrie reminded her spunkily.

"Well, good for you!" said Red heartily. "That's certainly old enough to know what you want to do and do it."

"Dr. Cahill . . ." said the girl fearfully. "Do you think I could ever—well—get out of this room—and do things?"

"But of course you can, Carrie. You'll learn to walk

around your home, to feel things, and listen to things. It won't be easy, but you can *learn.*

"You'll do it all yourself, really, but I'll help where I can. There are talking books I can send to you. They are records, you know. Of whole books. And a machine to play them on. There are guide dogs and schools where you can learn to read and write Braille."

"But I can't do all that! Go to school and all."

"Why can't you? If I help you?"

"You mean that, Dr. Cahill?" the girl asked intently.

"I do mean it," Red assured her. "Certainly I do."

"It ain't right to raise her hopes this way," said Mrs. Lockette, the voice of doom.

"Oh, Mamma, shut up!" cried Carrie. "He does mean to help me, and I mean to let him."

Soon after that Red departed, still planning on the things he would do for Carrie. He thought he may have helped his cause by the visit; he was sure he had helped Carrie's. And this first step would quickly be followed by others.

With that hope in mind he was in good spirits and drove home with his thoughts busy but not troubled. He didn't know how long it would take to bring the matter of the threatened lawsuit to a head, but if delay occurred, he still would set the wheels in motion for Carrie. He could make every reasonable try to improve things for her.

He put his car away and came on up to the hospital entrance, stopping to buy a newspaper at the door-side box. He flapped it open, wanting to learn the outcome of the trial where he had appeared as witness that morning. It seemed weeks ago!

Yes, there it was! The mother had been found guilty of first-degree manslaughter and sentenced to from one to twenty years in the women's prison. Well! Her other children would be safe from her, and long enough—he hoped —to . . .

His eyes drifted across the page. Russia—Vietnam— Heart Fund . . . He stopped, read, gulped, and read again.

Well, that was that! There he was in the headlines. Not across the top of the front page, but prominently enough in a two-column inset on the lower part of that same page.

LINCOLN HOSPITAL RESIDENT
ACCUSED OF ASSAULT ON MINOR

Wheee! It did read bad! Had the following name been other than his own, Red would have immediately made some sound of disapproval. Resident surgeons should watch their step, he would have thought.

He read the article, word for word, then he folded the paper and tucked it under his arm. Having done that, he thought about the hospital corridors and the people he would meet. He unfolded the paper and laid it back upon the pile in the box, smoothing its pages. If he decided that his attitude was to be one of forbidding "No comment" —and he had better decide that!—he should not appear with this thing in his hand.

He took a deep breath, looked at his watch, and went into the hospital.

As he had expected, the place was in a turmoil. Everyone he saw stopped talking, looked at him curiously, spoke to him oddly, and then, after he had passed them, talked fast and furiously to each other.

Eyes front, jaw set, Red went upstairs. He checked in; he went to his room and changed; he called the scheduling desk to get the upcoming surgical program; he went to the chart desk, then down for his supper. He greeted everyone who spoke to him, but he had nothing to say about his own affairs.

A dozen came to him and said something like, "Hey, Red! What gives?"

After a half dozen such questions he achieved a fishy eye and a bland face. "I couldn't say," he answered coldly.

Inside he was churning. Outwardly he managed icy calm. He wouldn't, he determined, say a word to anyone.

About nine o'clock Vince Sebaja came up to N.S. and cornered Red in the small floor lab.

"*Did* you operate on a girl of fifteen without her parents' consent?" he demanded.

Red shrugged. "The newspaper says I did." His lips clamped together.

"Won't talk, eh?"

Red said nothing.

Vince nodded. "Well, I'll say this much: I don't believe you did any such thing—ever."

Red laughed shortly and shook his head. "Get out, will you?" he asked.

As he passed him, Vince clapped his shoulder. "I'll quote you," he promised.

For a minute Red sat staring at the door which had closed behind his true friend. A steel door, it was, with the glass window covered by a wire-mesh screen. . . .

He would have liked to talk to Vince. It would have cleared his mind. But he could not talk to his colleagues. Nor must they talk—the order probably was already posted. Conferences of interns and residents were probably being scheduled. No comment on this development, they would be told, must be made to anyone, out or in the hospital.

Had Red already talked to many people about Carrie? He had mentioned the trip and the emergency surgery, but, except for C'ele, he did not think—

205

C'ele! He had spoken of Carrie to her! Walking in the park . . .

Abruptly Red got up from the lab table. He snapped off the lights and went swiftly to a pay phone booth at the end of the long corridor. He wedged himself inside and put the coin in the slot, dialed, then reached up and twisted the overhead globe until the light went out. In his white clothes, here in this booth, he was entirely too conspicuous.

C'ele answered quickly and gasped with relief to hear his voice. "Oh, *Red!*" she said.

"Mhmmmmmnnn. Look, C'ele, I called to remind you—or tell you—not to talk about me and my affairs. Not one word, my dear. Not—one—word!"

"But, Red," she protested. He could see the way her mobile face would be twisted with emotion, worry and protest.

"It's my career, girl," Red said sternly. "You wouldn't want to hurt it, but you could. So just keep the lips buttoned. O.K.?"

"Oh, Red, I am so *mad*. Can't you come over? I *have* to see you, Red!"

"No, I can't come over. I am on duty until midnight, and anyway, it isn't such a good idea. Not just now."

"Well . . . You can't talk, either?"

"No."

"It's just awful, Red. Don't *you* think it's awful?"

He chuckled. "Good night, C'ele," he said gently, and hung up.

He would make last rounds, check orders, and go to bed. The day had been a long one.

The night was a fairly busy one, too, with little chance to discover whether he could sleep or not. However, he did get to bed around four, only to be awakened at a few minutes past six by the telephone.

He sat up and reached for the thing, all in one motion. It was his mother calling; she had got the early news, and did Red know what she had *heard?*

Well, she *was* upset! Did he have any idea of what it did to a mother to learn, over her breakfast coffee, that her son . . . ?

She would not be put off. So Red told her, briefly, what he had "done."

"Well, I don't see anything wrong with that!" said Mrs. Anne Cahill Sutcliffe. Red could fairly see her indignation.

"Unfortunately, others do not agree with you."

"If you are in trouble, Red, maybe I should come out there. Or at least send my lawyer. Maybe I should do both."

"No, Mother."

He finally succeeded in dissuading her. He told about Mr. Randol and the insurance company. No, he said again, he had done nothing wrong. The matter lay in the interpretation of the law. This thing would be settled. Oh yes, he was certain of that!

"I'd like to believe you, Red," she said, her voice wavering between hope and fear. "I'd want to be with you if you needed me."

"Of course you would, Mother. But there isn't a thing you could do, and I'll be fine."

She sighed. Red could picture that too. She would still be in bed; she always turned on the early-morning news while she had her orange juice and coffee. She would be wearing a bed jacket, and her black poodle would be somewhere in the folds of the satin comforter and the white wool blanket.

"I am glad you do think you will be all right," she was saying. "I'm booked on the *Caronia*, and I have all my clothes, but—"

"Good!" said Red heartily. "It's the best thing you could do, to go around the world again. Are you sending me a schedule of where you will be?"

"Yes. And, Red, dear, I'll put some money into your account at the bank, so that—"

"Oh, Mother, don't do that!"

"But, darling—"

"Look. My best defense may be that I am a poor resident doctor and it would be folly to sue me."

"Red?" His mother's voice trembled. "Are you teasing me?"

"Well, just a little. But I won't need money, dear. You go on your trip and enjoy yourself. I'll keep in touch with you if you send me your itinerary."

"I'll do that, of course! And I'll call you, Red."

She finally hung up and Red decided there was no use going back to bed. He smiled ruefully about his mother. She would want to help him, but he guessed no one could really do that. He . . . He frowned. Money! He had never cashed his first-of-the-month pay check! He had picked it up the same day that he'd got the letter from Mareschal, and . . .

In Pete's name! He had been in a twit! For two weeks! Not to cash . . . He scrambled wildly among the papers on his small desk. Habit would have made him empty his pockets. Yes, there it was, along with that unopened letter from his mother. He only hoped his enemies didn't learn about this evidence of his disturbance.

208

15 ❋❋❋❋❋❋❋❋❋❋❋❋❋❋❋❋❋❋❋❋❋❋❋❋❋

SURPRISINGLY things went along. The first day was got through, and the second. The first week was passed, and a second. Red's determination not to talk about his troubles made for loneliness. He drank his coffee alone, sat alone in the cafeteria. Once he tried a date with C'ele, but it didn't work out well.

People talked at him and about him. Once Red let himself get furious with what he heard Iserman saying, then realized, just in time, that Iserman had meant for him to overhear. And hoped he would react.

Dr. Cahill worked in Surgery; he attended to his patients and the affairs of the service. His relationship with Dr. Enns was courteous, but neither man sought an opportunity for further discussion of the senior resident's personal affairs.

Then, two weeks and two days after the newspaper announcement of the lawsuit, Red was summoned to a meeting in the hospital Board Room, at 4:15 that afternoon.

Well! He put the phone down. This was it! He was going to be fired.

Within hours of the news release he had expected to be. As time went on, this expectation had leveled off into a numb waiting. Now the time had come. He would be fired.

Did he care?

It was hard to say, hard to know. His reaction had become one of not feeling anything. The past two weeks had been difficult. Certain patients—newspaper readers, of course—had given trouble over Dr. Cahill's attendance on them. At least one attending doctor had questioned his service in o.r.

The hospital had handled these problems and others. The hospital, as a whole, had been kind to Red, but, as a whole, the hospital had its troubles too.

So now there was to be this meeting in the Board Room, and Red was glad that, finally, something would happen.

He shaved and put on fresh whites, then asked Polly if he looked all right. She smiled at him gently and said he was "beautiful."

"That should do it," said Dr. Cahill.

He told the desk where he would be; he looked into Dr. Enns's office—he was not there. Probably gone down before him. Red caught the elevator and went downstairs.

He had been in the Board Room before this. He remembered how many pleats there were to each window curtain; he remembered the great oval table with its ash trays and pencils, and . . .

He lifted his chin, straightened his shoulders, and opened the door, stepped inside.

He was shocked for a moment to see only three—no, four—men in the room. Seated at the far end of the long table, they all were faced toward him, their eyes upon him in his white clothes.

Red hesitated.

"Come down here, Dr. Cahill, please," said the Administrator.

He was there, Randol, the hospital counsel, Dr. Enns, and a man Red knew only by recognizing him from a picture which hung in the front lobby. James V. Pyder, chairman of the board.

Feeling like an actor doing his first stage walk-on, Red went around the table. Mr. Ovian introduced him to Mr. Pyder who was an extremely handsome man, with thick gray hair and the keen-honed look of an aristocrat with money.

"Sit down, Doctor," said the Administrator, and Red pulled out a chair, one removed from Dr. Enns. Instinctively he set himself apart from the group which was there —for what?

To reprove him? Question him, certainly. And then probably dismiss him from the hospital. Red took a deep breath and held his face rigidly free of all emotion.

"Mr. Randol?" said the Administrator. "Will you begin?"

"Yes." Randol put a leather folder on the table, unzipped its sides with a sound which set Red's teeth on edge. Enns frowned at the noise, and Red thought, "Why, he's as nervous as I am," and he pitied the man.

"I don't think we need do much of any recapitulation of the situation we find ourselves in, gentlemen," said Mr. Randol. He wore a soft white shirt with French cuffs and plain gold links; as he talked, his pudgy hand lifted the corners of the pages before him. "Dr. Cahill is being sued for assault on a minor and the malpractice of medicine. Dr. Cahill is a resident at this medical center. He—we—must seek means of defending him from the charges."

He looked around the group, seeking Red's eyes last.

"Yes!" said Mr. Randol. "Now I have, I think, achieved some progress in this matter. Perhaps we can even call it a gain."

Get on with it, man! Red thought tensely. *Talk! Tell us!*

"I'll get straight to the point," said Randol, as if reading Dr. Cahill's mind. "I am quite pleased to report that I have secured a preliminary hearing on this case. To be held *in camera*."

In camera. The phrase was not entirely strange, but just what did it mean? Red frowned, trying to think . . .

Dr. Enns asked the question, forthright as always.

"Will you please explain the term, Mr. Randol?" he asked. "Will this hearing take the place of a trial?"

The board chairman nodded. He too wanted to know exactly.

"A hearing *in camera*," Randol explained, "is held before the trial. It may, under favorable circumstances, take the place of the trial." Mr. Randol smiled. "Favorable, in our view, would be for things to go our way. But, nevertheless, we have arranged such a hearing. Which will be just what it says: a hearing of all charges made against Dr. Cahill, and a hearing of the pleas for his defense. Present at this hearing will be the insurance company and its attorneys, the family of the allegedly injured patient, and their attorney. There would be a limited number of witnesses."

"And us," said Dr. Enns.

Mr. Randol laughed aloud. "Well, of course, *us*."

Mr. Pyder looked down the table at Red. Then he smiled and nodded to the Administrator. "I would say that our attorney has done some noble work in securing such a hearing. The hospital at least appreciates it. I should think Dr. Cahill—"

Red nodded. "Yes, sir. It seems I should appreciate his efforts as well."

Mr. Randol made a show of modesty. "I was just doing my job," he told the men in the room.

He shuffled the papers in his case and brought forth a thin sheaf of papers stapled together. He laid this on the table and took a fountain pen from his pocket, uncapped it.

"This proceeding as arranged is something of an experiment," he said weightily, "and here is an agreement drawn up by me and the attorney for the Lockette family. We were advised by the court which has jurisdiction. If all who are concerned in this litigation find themselves in accord to the extent that they will sign this agreement, any decision reached at the hearing can be binding."

Red frowned and stirred impatiently in his chair. Since acknowledging his introduction to Mr. Pyder he had sat so rigidly that his thigh muscles now ached. For so long a time he had been silent about his case—and he had accumulated so many questions to ask . . .

He looked at Mr. Randol. "Is that a good thing?" he asked, his voice a little harsh. "To settle matters in such a hearing?"

"It may be," said the counselor. "Yes, in our case it well may be. So I suggest that you sign this agreement, Dr. Cahill. You have quite a few things on your side, and they are things of a sort that would perhaps show up more plainly—and favorably—in such a hearing than they would in court.'

Red looked at the other men; they evidently were still "appreciating" Mr. Randol. Well, perhaps he was a cagey guy, this lawyer. Red hoped so. And, yes! A private hearing would definitely be preferable to a trial in open court.

"I'll sign," he said gruffly.

"I must tell you," Randol then said expansively, "that I do not deserve the first credit for securing this hearing. I did the legal work, all right, but before I could and did start that, Dr. Enns, your Chief of Service, and Dr. Graham, from Old Pardee, laid the groundwork for getting us such a hearing. They developed the idea, and it was a good one."

"Dr. Graham?" asked Red. He turned to look at Dr. Enns. "You've met him? You . . ."

"He came to see me about two weeks ago," said Bill Enns quietly.

"You—"

"No, we didn't say anything to you at the time. We wanted to see if we could make a real effort to keep this thing out of court. You know about it now."

Red tried to imagine the two doctors together. "What did you think of him?" he asked curiously.

Dr. Enns smiled. "I found him everything you said he was, Red."

"Yes!" Red sat back in his chair. "He really is a good man," he told the others. "A good doctor, and a good man. He runs a tight little hospital." Red's voice was eager.

Dr. Enns smiled at him, then glanced apologetically at his colleagues. "Er—yes," said the Chief of Neurological Surgery Service. "But before we doctors got into this thing, gentlemen, Miss Carrie Lockette had made her own special appeal to Dr. Graham."

Now Red *was* stunned. "Carrie did?" he asked, dazed. "How . . . ?"

How had she managed, handicapped as she was?

"I don't myself know how she accomplished such a thing," Dr. Enns told him, his manner kind. "Perhaps she used the opportunity afforded by a regular medical examination.'

Red nodded. Yes, Carrie could have gone to the hospital for a dressing, and then . . .

"Next they brought me into the thing," Dr. Enns was telling. "Graham came to see me. He found that I also wanted to help you. And the three of us—"

"You—and Carrie—and Graham?" Red was sure he was dreaming. He lost all awareness of Mr. Ovian and Attorney Randol and Chairman of the Board Pyder, all of whom, in truth, were listening in fascination approaching his own.

"We three," Dr. Enns agreed, "had what I understand was the effrontery to go to the judge of the Circuit Court up there—"

"It was most irregular," murmured Mr. Randol.

Dr. Enns's blue eyes flashed him a glance. "We were told that it was. The judge said he felt that our side was bringing undue pressure to bear. He was quite stern with us."

Red could make a picture—the big blond Dr. Graham, the elegant, handsome Dr. Enns, and the blind girl with her lovely face, her sightless blue eyes, her feathery red hair . . .

"He also knew, Red Cahill," Enns was saying, "that you had been up to see Carrie and had exerted pressure on *her* not to let her records be used."

Red flushed crimson. "I was trying to find out *why* these people should be doing this thing to me!" he cried. "I exerted no pressure."

"Yes. Carrie told the judge that you had not. You see, he talked to the girl and let her talk to him. Of course, he already knew Dr. Graham and respected him."

"Yes." Red would expect that.

"And he even gave *me* a chance to point out the damage

215

which a public trial could do to a doctor at the beginning of his career. I made as good a speech as I could on that subject. I have decided that he listened to us only because both sides seemed to be represented."

"Maybe he thought I had a good case," suggested Red.

"If he had considered the merits of your *case*," said Mr. Randol sharply, "he would have refused to talk to any of those people. However, he did talk to them. Then he asked that the attorneys meet and draw up an agreement for a hearing. Which we have done." His hand brushed across the papers on the table.

"Could you tell us," Dr. Enns asked, glancing reassuringly at Red, "just what to expect at, and even of, this hearing?"

Mr. Randol nodded. "The first part of your question is easier. I myself would like to know as of now how things will develop. But as for what the hearing is and will be, it amounts to an examination before public trial. Both sides appear and are sworn in. No judge presides. A transcript of the hearing will be made and sent to the circuit judge. Counsel—that is, the lawyers on both sides—will conduct the hearing. The prosecution will start, and the defendant will present his side second—as in a trial. Exceptions to questions and behavior will be recorded, or granted—"

"Will there be a jury?"

"Oh no. But there will be witnesses. For instance, I'll call people to testify as to the storm and road conditions of the night in question—witnesses, you see. I should think that the local court would be represented, to hear both sides.

"Of course we are hoping that there will be no indictment, but if there is one, then there will be a trial with jury—the works. We plan to keep reporters out of the hearing, and it is my personal feeling that, things being where they are, such a hearing cannot hurt Dr. Cahill and may help him. If we are careful of how we handle matters."

"We shall be," said Dr. Enns grimly.

Red held out his hand. "I'll sign your paper," he said.

16 ❊❊❊❊❊❊❊❊❊❊❊❊❊❊❊❊❊❊❊❊❊❊❊❊

DR. CAHILL was amazed to find that there still were two months to be lived through before the hearing would be held. He declared that he could not manage such a delay. Then he found that he could and that he did.

The life of the hospital went on around him; he himself listened to gossip, laughed at jokes, talked a little. Interns, residents, nurses—and patients—fell in love and out of love; they quarreled and schemed. His friends met with success and disappointments. . . .

Red Cahill worked.

He found that work would provide him with a shell within which he could dwell in some peace. He found that he could depend on his rigorous training and practice, that he would know, almost instinctively, what to *do*. He asked for a certain knife; he held a scalpel in a certain way and used it in a certain, prescribed way. He cut and cauterized and clamped. He set a suture, his fingers lightning fast and skilled, from practice. He handled tissue, bone and nerves and vessels, all in a certain way. He found surgery somewhat easy because there were fixed rules of technique and routine things to do and say.

The examination of a patient and diagnosis were more difficult because the patient was an unknown factor. His own judgment and occasional self-doubt sometimes threatened to shadow his automatic performance. But still there were rules on which he could rely. Certain symptoms of appearance and reflexes, temperatures and response and pressure could be added together and an answer computed.

It was not easy to work so, without any of the sure, personal joy of being capable, but one could so work. Red did. Physically tired at night, arising unrefreshed in the morning, and going to work again.

In this way the days passed and were endured.

Feeling the shell hardening about him, Red sometimes made a real effort to escape from it. But he found it hard to be himself or to seem himself at gatherings of any sort, however small. He could not talk about his trouble, and his trouble was what everyone wanted to talk about to him and around him.

Even with C'ele and with Vince he found himself forced to be silent—and therefore irritable.

But when, finally, he was told that the hearing would take place the next day, he wished that he still had time. To prepare himself, to talk to people, to—to get things in line. He could think of no excuse to offer for what he had done on that icy December night.

He couldn't even rely on the term good Samaritan. He had not been one, caring for an injured child on the side of the road. No! He had taken that "child" to a hospital, then he had insisted on contriving ways to do a complicated amount of surgery. Under the circumstances he had, in a sense, worked "at the side of the road," and such surgery, in such a place . . .

He had no case. He would tell Randol so and settle the

thing out of court! But by the time he could get down-stairs, Randol had gone for the day.

The next morning he must attend the hearing. At ten.

The hearing was to be held in the conference room of a hotel at the edge of the city. Red knew that a list of possible witnesses had been made—C'ele was on that list, for some reason unknown to him. He had told her to stay at home; she couldn't possibly be needed.

Feeling entirely unlike himself, his nerves taut, his eyes aching from his efforts to look straight ahead, his jaw stiff from not talking, he came into the hotel and into the hearing room, a big young man in a dark flannel suit, a narrow tie dark against his white shirt. His hands were clenched at his side. He must appear guilty on sight.

As a matter of fact, he looked like an especially well-controlled man, well dressed, skin clear, eyes steady. He was neither late nor early.

He was directed by some unknown man to a seat at the far end of the long conference table, reminiscent of that in the hospital Board Room. This table was oblong, but there were similar ash trays set out and chairs were ranged around it.

Dr. Enns sat in the chair to Red's right, with Mr. Ovian, the hospital Administrator, beyond him. Dr. Enns told Red who the others in the room were.

At a small table beyond the big one sat three circuit judges. "One from Old Pardee, one from here in the city, and an outsider, acceptable to both sides."

No one asked me to accept him, thought Red.

"They will listen," Dr. Enns continued, "but probably will take no part in the proceedings."

Red nodded. The scene was quite a lot like movies which

he had seen—and enjoyed—of courts-martial proceedings. He looked at the others in the room. Mr. Lockette was there—*Judge* Lockette. Rangy, ruddy-skinned, dressed in a tweed sport jacket and brown slacks, he had a jovial greeting for everyone. He even came up and, ignoring Dr. Cahill, introduced himself to Dr. Enns. He managed to tell a joke or two.

There were a dozen or more people seated against the wall. Witnesses? Perhaps just interested observers? With a nod to Red, Dr. Graham took a seat down the table from him and to the left. Rachel had come in with him, and she took one of the chairs against the wall. Red hoped he would get a chance to tell her how glad he was to see her.

The room was filling rapidly. Randol arrived, his brief case bulging. He stood for a minute and talked to the lawyer for the Lockettes, laughing and friendly.

The Lockette lawyer, Mareschal, might be the "smart man" Randol had told Red he was, but he looked like a pipsqueak to Dr. Cahill. He was a slight man, his blond hair and skin all one color. His head was narrow, his nose beaklike, and his eyes close-set. He was neatly dressed and no more than thirty-five years old.

Red coughed a little. This thing of judging a man by his appearance was pure folly. He . . .

He stiffened. C'ele had just come into the room, and Polly Ferris was with her. Both women looked trim and attractive, Polly in a dull green linen suit, with a netlike thing on her hair. C'ele wore a print dress in black and white, and her small hat was white. Red wished they had not come, and yet he was glad, too, that they were there, that they had wanted to come.

The chairs against the wall were now well filled; Red

supposed that these were the possible witnesses. Though Polly couldn't be. However, there were other hospital doctors present. The motel manager—what was his name? Dean? That was it. Maurita Smith was there, dazzling in a yellow and white dress, full-skirted, low-bosomed. Her hair was a mountain of black, studded with tiny yellow bows. She twiddled her fingers in greeting to Red, and he smiled faintly, apprehensive of the possessive demonstration she was capable of staging. Rosie Steckman, the o.r. nurse from Old Pardee, had come with Maurita, the woman almost unrecognizable in street clothes.

Red's eyes came back to the table. Dr. Graham's big, clean hand lay on it, lifting and dropping, lifting and dropping. . . .

All these people—some of them would know that Dr. Cahill had wanted only to help the girl who now was being led to a chair beside her father.

Red looked yearningly at Carrie. She wore a simple summery dress, pale green in color. Her hair now was well grown out, and it shone like the coat of a fine Irish setter. She was composed, her violet eyes wide. As she sat down, she had fumbled a little with the chair, but once in it, she sat quietly, waiting.

Red wished he could go to her and reassure her. He could not.

Someone was rapping for attention, for silence.

The judge from the Old Pardee Circuit rose to his feet and identified himself. He was a handsome man—theatrically handsome, with a thick mane of gray hair and a skin as freshly pink as a baby's. He would, he said, explain the nature of this hearing.

A hearing was not unusual. In matters of crime and possible grand jury indictments a hearing was desirable, and in instances mandatory, to determine if a case were at hand which would require trial and the judgment of the Court. Such a hearing now was to be given the matter of a suit for damages against Dr. Redding Cahill. The judge went on to explain that all damage suits were injurious in the eyes of the uneducated lay person.

To accuse a man was, too often, to convict him. This was astonishingly true in matters where a doctor was accused of malpractice and abuse. The least breath of accusation against a doctor always reduced his standing in the community, before ever a chance could be given him to establish his innocence or, for that matter, for the claimant to establish his position as accuser.

So, said the jurist, a hearing was a very good thing in the case particularly at hand. Such a hearing would afford a reasonable accounting of facts, of circumstances, motives, and performance.

He then went on to outline the means of procedure, much as Randol had outlined them to Red in the Board Room two months earlier. The opposing counsel would conduct the hearing; a transcript would be made. The prosecution would begin; the defendant would then have his chance to present his case. Exceptions could be offered. The Courts presently represented would be interested listeners and would intervene only by mutual consent of both counsel.

The judge explained that both sides had consented to this procedure, which he felt to be an admirable step. The judge sat down.

There was then a little flurry of papers and whispered conferences and moving about, during which Red looked around the room in which they sat. The walls of this room were of a gray-tan color, and there were inset, arched panels of shining brocade in red, gold, and brown. The room was not especially pleasant or interesting, but it would serve its purpose.

Randol touched his arm, and Red glanced at him in question. "Listen," said the attorney.

Red nodded. He was ready to listen.

Down the table length a man was standing with a paper in his hand. It was the same man who had shown Red where to sit. A law clerk or some such, he supposed. Anyway, his chair was beside Mareschal, who was watching him as he began to read the charge.

Like all legal documents, the wordage could have been cut in the interest of information, though the information was there to be heard. Red heard it. He found that he was being charged with the "sudden and inadequate care of a minor without the consent of . . . guardian . . . resulting in injuries . . . brain damage . . . loss of sight . . ."

"And he slit her throat, too!" said Judge Lockette loudly, when the list of injuries did not promise to include that item.

Mr. Randol's head snapped up—faster than Red would have said the man's fat neck would accommodate—and Mareschal leaned toward Lockette, whispering urgently. Lockette sat back, glowering and muttering. Carrie twisted a handkerchief in her fingers.

The clerk, or whatever, resumed his reading. ". . . and lack of services for which said guardian is prepared to ask that damages be paid."

The clerk sat down, and a copy of his text was passed along the table to Mr. Randol.

Everyone was looking at Red Cahill. He had expected this and had previously determined on his hoped-for pose. He would remain as calm as he could; he would listen to the questions—he was prepared for any number of these and of all sorts—and he would answer directly. Above all, he would not lose his temper.

He hoped.

Mr. Randol had talked to him a little about the interrogation. But now, when asked, he could truthfully say that, no, he had not received instruction as to his testimony.

"I am afraid you will rather continuously be in the witness chair, Dr. Cahill," said Mr. Mareschal courteously. "It would be my method to call a witness to reply from where he now sits and always be able to refer to you for corroboration, denial, or whatever is required. Would that be satisfactory?"

Randol answered for his client. The method would be satisfactory—with agreement that he, in turn, could question.

"Oh yes, certainly!"

One of the judges wrote something on the pad of paper. Dr. Enns and Mr. Ovian had similar pads, their pens at the ready.

Red was sworn and asked to identify himself—name, age, present employment. He told where he had been born and raised, where he had attended school, college, medical school. Where he had interned, and where he now was senior resident in Neurosurgery.

"Was there some reason for you, an Easterner, to take up your residency at Lincoln Hospital?"

"Yes, sir. I wanted to train under the best surgeon and teacher in my field."

"I see."

Mr. Randol then asked if there was competition for such positions. There was. He determined how long Dr. Cahill had served as resident and as senior resident. This was his third year.

Then the matter of duties and hours was gone into.

"Will you tell us why you were in Old Pardee on the night of December twenty-seventh, Doctor?"

"I took an injured person to the hospital there."

"Where had this injury occurred?"

Red wanted to say that everyone in the room knew that! He glanced down at the table and his hand. He spoke carefully.

"The injury occurred in and during the wreckage of an automobile in front of the motel where I was staying for the night."

"Were you on some sort of vacation from the hospital?"

Red wanted to rub his hands together. He could feel Randol and Enns and the Administrator all tense before his answer.

"I," he said, "had been allowed a few free days in which to go to Bridgeton to look into the matter of a staff position which might be open in the new hospital there; this was looking forward to my next year's location."

"But you stopped overnight at the motel outside of Old Pardee."

"Yes, sir. There was a freezing rain—what is known as an ice storm. The road conditions were extremely hazardous both because of ice on the road and the danger from fallen wires and trees. I felt that nothing would be gained by my forcing my way on to Bridgeton that night."

"I see. You stopped at the motel, engaged a room, and thus you were in the motel when the accident occurred in which Miss Lockette was injured."

"No, sir, when the accident occurred, I was not *in* the motel. I had gone outside to check on the storm, and I happened to be something like a hundred feet away when the girl was thrown out of the careening car. I *saw* the accident."

"Er—yes. Thank you, Dr. Cahill. We shall come back to you. Now I would like to talk to William E. Dean, if he is present."

Mr. Dean half rose from his chair. "I'm right here, Mr. Mareschal," he said in his eager manner.

Randol told Red that he was doing fine. "Let's see how we do here," he added.

Mr. Dean milked his brief minute of prominence. He told importantly that yes, he was the manager of the motel. "Two miles from Old Pardee, sir." He told of its virtues, services, "elegant" rooms, air conditioning, and electric heat, the restaurant.

Yes, Dr. Cahill had come to his establishment on the afternoon of December 27. Oh, the latter part of the afternoon. Three-thirty, perhaps. Oh, certainly, the weather was bad! Mr. Dean elaborated. He endorsed Dr. Cahill's good judgment in stopping for the night; he volunteered that Dr. Cahill had been—and was—a nice young man, friendly. He drove a fine car.

Yes, he thought probably that the doctor was outside when the Trigg boy wrecked his car. "He was driving much too fast, you see, and skidded—"

Mr. Mareschal suggested that they stay with the matter of Dr. Cahill's location in the driveway of the motel.

He probably was there, confirmed Mr. Dean. He had spent some time in the restaurant, and earlier Mr. Dean had seen him talking to the attendant of the filling station. He was a friendly young man—he had talked to the folks in the restaurant.

Mr. Randol established that Dean, and the "folks," had learned of the stranger's profession. "Had he not been outside at the time of the impact," he asked, "would you have summoned Dr. Cahill from his room to attend the injured girl?"

Mr. Mareschal said this was asking for surmise, and Mr. Randol argued about it. Evidently the "summoning" of the doctor was an important item. The judges all made notes of the interchange. Finally, to laughter, Mr. Dean managed to say that he "sure as the devil" would have called some doctor.

Next Maurita Smith was addressed. Red held himself tense while she identified herself as a resident of Old Pardee, "over twenty-one"—she was coy about this. She told where she lived, where she was employed.

Did she know Dr. Redding Cahill?

"Oh, definitely, yes!" Maurita's hand felt of her hair structure.

Would she tell under what circumstances she had become acquainted?

It took a little time. She made an elaborate explanation of why she was at Northland's the afternoon of December 27. She was in search of a certain book, she said, in a small, paperback edition. They had a good rack there which was kept up to date. Since she was to return to duty at the hospital within an hour or so, she also decided to eat a hamburger.

Yes, she was having chains put on her car. The weather, she said, was "inclement."

Red swallowed a smile. Inclement, indeed!

Maurita said she was in the restaurant, seated at the counter, when Dr. Cahill arrived. "In this long car—*really* long—bucket seats, and four on the floor. You know?"

Yes, she had learned at once that he was a doctor. "He talked to me, you see. He bragged about who he was. And he asked a lot of questions. He was a man on the make; a girl like me gets to recognize that type on sight."

Red could only gape at her.

Maurita told that he had talked to her for an hour or so. "He asked where I lived, and when I informed him that I was employed at the hospital, he asked a lot of questions about that. He made fun of our nice little hospital, and—"

Red sat up straight. He had done no such thing! What was Maurita up to? He glanced at C'ele. She was sitting, eyes down, her hands clasped tightly together.

Maurita was still talking. She said that on the afternoon in question she had returned to the hospital where she was in charge of the office, and since the weather was so bad— she still called it *inclement*—she thought there might be accident cases brought in . . .

Red said something below his breath to Mr. Randol, and that attorney asked permission to address the witness.

Maurita resented the interruption but finally agreed, under his probing, that her hours of employment were divided. Yes, one would designate that system as split-shift. She said the word delicately and with obvious distaste.

She brightened when Mr. Mareschal asked her if any accidents had come to the hospital on that inclement night. Oh yes! There was a woman who had fallen and cracked her elbow, a man with a badly skinned knee and shin, and then!—she was *present* when that poor child—she waved her scarlet-tipped fingers toward Carrie—was brought in. She waxed vivid in her description, and untruthful as well. Red sat back, biting his lip.

Carrie had *not* sobbed and screamed. She had not protested! There was some matted blood in her hair, but nothing like Maurita's gory description.

"I was immediately cognizant of the child's condition,"

said Maurita.

Mr. Randol leaned forward. "May I?" he asked the prosecuting counsel.

Mr. Mareschal nodded.

Maurita looked warily at Mr. Randol.

"How old was Carrie?" he asked.

Down the table, Carrie herself answered. "I was fifteen," she said clearly. "I am sixteen now. My ma's first baby was borned when she wasn't but sixteen."

There was a crystal drop of silence in the room.

Mr. Randol sat back.

After a minute Mr. Mareschal told Maurita to continue, to tell what had happened that night at the hospital.

"Well, I was delaying my departure for home, and I was present when the case came in . . ."

Red didn't think she was, but he really could not remember. He *thought* she had been sent for to try to locate Carrie's family. Which lawyer, Red wondered, had she decided was Raymond Burr? Certainly she was playing *her* part to the hilt.

Dr. Cahill, Maurita was telling, came in, ready to operate at once. He refused to wait, the way Dr. Graham wanted him to do. He insisted on doing the surgery immediately! The men were at the point of quarreling . . .

"Maurita!" It was Dr. Graham's deep, calm voice.

"You did want him to wait," said Maurita, her voice rising and sharpening. "You *know* you did, Doctor!"

"We discussed the possibility, but we never approached a quarrel."

"Oh, you doctors don't know when you are quarreling and when you are not!" cried Maurita, her brassy voice ringing. "You disagree with each other—you and Doc Robinson do all the time—you know you *do*, Dr. Graham!

Why don't you be honest about it and *call* it a fight? Just the same as when you argued with Dr. Cahill that night. I can remember if you cannot, and frankly, Dr. Graham—"

Dr. Graham stood up. "I am afraid, Miss Smith," he said coldly, "that you are being *frank* with the wrong person."

"Dr. Graham," said Mr. Randol, "did you argue with Dr. Cahill that night?"

"Not about what was needed to help Miss Lockette, sir. I did remind him—unnecessarily, I am sure—that we should make every effort to locate her family." He swung about. "And *that* is what Miss Smith was set to do. That—alone!"

Dr. Graham sat down.

Maurita regarded him sulkily.

Mr. Mareschal adjusted his papers. "Miss Smith," he said, after a pause, "did you make an effort to locate the injured girl's family?"

"Well, we didn't have the least idea who her identity would be," said Maurita in an aggrieved tone.

"You didn't know her?"

"Oh no, Mr. Mareschal. In fact, no one connected with the hospital remembered ever seeing her before. Which was a novelty, of course, because we are very congenial people in our part of the state, and we customarily know one another."

"Yes. Now will you explain the means by which the young girl was eventually identified? I assume that she was unconscious and unable to identify herself."

Maurita pursed her lips. "I have to assume that myself, Mr. Mareschal," she said delicately. "Because, as you have had a demonstration of, I am not entrusted with medical detail." Red saw Mr. Mareschal smile slightly and shake his head in patient resignation.

"Will you please . . . ?" Mr. Mareschal asked again.

"Oh yes, sir. Well, I did just about everything. I called around—to the police station and the highway patrol. I called Mr. Dean and asked about the car license, but the license number could not be determined until morning, and no one seemed to know the boy either. He was killed, you know. As poor Carrie might as well have been."

Mr. Randol's head went up, but it was Mareschal who rebuked Maurita. She was asked to tell only about things which she had seen and done, he pointed out. Conclusions and opinions were not desired.

"Well . . ." said Maurita, seeming to search among all the things she wanted to say to find something she would be allowed to say. "I remember that night very well," she told Mr. Mareschal.

"Yes. Then you can tell us the measures used to locate the injured girl's family."

"But I *am* telling you! I phoned around—until the phone went out. It did, you know. And the lights were extinguished also. By then the surgery was being done, and I decided to return to my home—my mother was alone. And I really could not endure to remain. I had done everything I could to persuade the doctors to wait, but it was no use. Dr. Cahill was determined to do surgery."

"You say *you* tried to dissuade him?"

"Oh yes," said Maurita. She blinked her beaded eyelashes; she smiled alluringly. "In any way I could. Most men—"

"Look!" Red leaned toward Mr. Randol. "That woman is lying in her teeth!"

Mr. Randol nodded. "You can say so later. Meanwhile, she isn't helping her side too much."

"I just wish you had listened to us, Dr. Cahill," Maurita now said, loudly and unexpectedly addressing him. Hos-

232

tility now was naked in her eyes and in her voice. "Dr. Graham was older than you, and I have worked in a hospital longer than you have—you should have listened to us and trusted our greater experience. Then today you could be back at your medical school learning some other things that you also probably need to know. You should learn a little about girls, too, Dr. Cahill. And not be unwise enough to build them up to a big let-down. As you see now, the girl may be the one to let *you* down!"

Red sat stone-faced, shocked—and shamed. He would not have hurt this woman; he had given her no right to think that she had any claim upon him. Did she really think he had—well—jilted her? Perhaps she did.

"Miss Smith!" Mareschal had to speak three times. By then his clerk had his hand on Maurita's bare arm and was attempting to lift her from the chair. "We are excusing you, Miss Smith," said Mareschal. "I have your agreement, Counselor?"

Randol waved his hand. "Yes, of course."

"But," protested Maurita, "I was only endeavoring—"

"Yes. But you seem to misunderstand your function as a witness. Dr. Cahill is not on trial, nor are you the judge. Good-by, Miss Smith, and thank you. Mr. Elsea will see you to your car."

"Well!"

She walked the length of the room to the door, every eye upon her. The bows in her hair trembled; her hips swiveled; her ankles wavered at each ringing step taken by her high bronze heels.

Red sighed.

Surely having passed Maurita in the hall, Vince Sebaja then came in, Sylvia with him. Red was surprised to see them. He glanced down the line of witnesses. All these hospital people—who was minding the store back at the Center?

In his check of the witnesses his eyes had lingered briefly upon C'ele, who still sat, eyes down, looking embarrassed about Maurita. And why not? The spitting, vindictive cat! Red wished C'ele had not come! What had she expected? To be pleased and proud of him? To hear people praise him? Maybe he should send her a note to go home. What could she be witness to, anyway?

On her part C'ele would have welcomed such a note, and in that minute she might have obeyed it. Maurita's performance, and Red's anger with the lying woman, had deeply upset her. Though she had always known how much he hated dishonesty, phony pretense. So she sat, eyes down, and feared for herself in Red's eyes.

The hearing proceeded, sometimes slowly, with too much being said and repeated, sometimes rapidly with not enough time for all to be said. There seemed to be no plan, though there must have been one.

The witnesses moved into prominence and withdrew again to the ranks of listeners and watchers.

The Lockette family—father and son—were bitterly vindictive, their speech larded with profanity, which they seemed surprised to have suppressed, and localisms which needed translation.

"Just what do you mean, Judge Lockette," asked Randol courteously, "when you say your farm is located in a 'scope of woods'?"

"Well, I mean what folks do mean when they say that, mister. Our farm is—well, in a place where there are trees. All sorts of trees."

"A wooded area."

Judge Lockette lifted his bony shoulders and smiled, his

false teeth popping into prominence. "If that's your way of talking . . ." he conceded.

"Thank you. Now, you were explaining that you had lost Carrie's services on this farm. Will you explain what they were, previous to her accident?"

"Yes, sir, I will. She made herself right useful. She had a way with animals, you know. Any ill calf or bull gentled down for her."

"An *ill* bull?"

Judge Lockette was exasperated. "Cranky! Ready to take out after you. *Ill!*"

"Could you mean ill-tempered?"

"I could," drawled Judge Lockette, glancing around the room to gather smiles from his friends.

"What did Carrie do for the animals?" asked Randol.

"I told you once. I told Mareschal here and you should-a listened. She took roundings."

"Will you explain that, please?"

"Ef I need to, and seems I do. Well, the girl would drive the beasts out-a the woods to the barn lot. Saved us usin' a hand—a man—to do the same job."

"I see," said Mr. Randol.

"Well, I'm glad of that, mister. Doin' what she did made Carrie damn useful to us. More'n just the hep she was to her ma in the house, you see."

"Carrie was not in school?"

"Like she told you, she was nigh sixteen."

"I see. This party she was planning to attend on the night when she was hurt—you gave your consent to Carrie's going?"

"Her ma thought she should go. And you can't ride kids with too tight a rein, mister."

"But—considering the weather, and the hills to travel—

she did go with your consent?"

"I knew she was goin', if that's what you have in mind."

"It is."

"What I can't figger," said Judge Lockette, in a conversational tone, "is why you didn't find Carrie's purse that night. She sure had one—got it for Christmas—black, and big enough to hold a week's wash. Where was it that night? It would-a told you who she was. But I don't reckon your young doctor even looked for it. He just grabbed her off the road and cut on her. Now she's blind and no good to anybody—nor herself neither."

"Are you saying that Dr. Cahill deliberately blinded your daughter?"

"No, I don't say that. It's enough that he bungled the job that he set out to do, and I claim there should be some protection against doctors like him who jump in with a knife given any chance at all."

"Even under emergency circumstances, Judge Lockette, you don't think the surgery should have been performed?"

"It ain't only me that thought that. You heard that black-haired woman say that Dr. Graham didn't think it should. And that he argued with Dr. Cahill about it."

"Dr. Graham? Would you care to speak on that?"

"Yes, sir, I would," said Dr. Graham. "First, on the matter of the purse, it probably was left in the car and burned in the fire. Carrie did not have it with her when thrown out or when she was brought into the hospital. Second, my discussion with Dr. Cahill that night amounted only to urging him to be sure that we were faced with an emergency which required immediate surgery. He was a capable surgeon; I knew it at once, and this opinion was later verified by his performance."

Someone then mentioned lunch, and the Old Pardee

judge said that provisions had been made for one o'clock, should the hearing still be in session at the time.

Now witnesses were asked to testify as to Red Cahill's character. In turn the hospital people were asked about his reputation and performance in the hospital. Red listened, wondering how Iserman had been kept out of this.

The first three witnesses said that Dr. Cahill was a nice guy, well liked, and a good surgeon. Smart. No, not nervous or anything like it. Nice to work with.

"So far so good," murmured Mr. Randol.

Red relaxed—though what had he expected?

"Is Dr. Vince Sebaja present?" Mr. Mareschal was asking.

Vince half rose from his chair. He was asked to identify himself. Yes, he was a friend of Dr. Cahill's. Yes, he said, he worked with him in hospital. Psychoneurology and Neurosurgery were closely allied services. Dr. Cahill, he said, was as good as they came.

Were the two men friends?

"Yes, we are. Have been for three or four years."

"It's been told that Dr. Cahill drives a sporty car."

"Well—"

"You've ridden with him in this car?"

"Yes, and the one which he had before. His mother gave them both to him." Vince's face was stern.

"Lucky man," said Mr. Mareschal pleasantly. It was impossible to tell what that attorney was thinking. "Does Dr. Cahill drive pretty fast?"

"I've never felt in danger."

"Answer the question, please."

"Well, yes, Red drives fast."

"To your knowledge, or when he and you were together, has he ever been cited for speeding?"

Vince's eyes were angry. "Yes," he said tightly.

"How often? Just to your knowledge, Doctor."

"Twice!"

"Thank you, Dr. Sebaja."

Vince looked across at Red, who shrugged ever so slightly. He didn't know what it suggested either.

Now Mrs. Vince Sebaja was addressed. What on earth would Mareschal find to ask Sylvia?

She said yes, she was Dr. Sebaja's wife, married for four years. She worked—she had two children. Her mother lived with them. Oh yes, she knew Dr. Cahill. Certainly they were good friends! He was her older child's god-father.

Yes, he came to their home. Yes, she and her husband went to parties and things with Red. Where he was, she meant. Oh, hospital parties for the doctors and interns and nurses—those were the big parties. Sometimes the parties were small, Dutch-treat affairs. Last fall there had been a wedding . . .

Oh yes, Dr. Cahill was fun at parties. A real kook, she said. Without a quiver to indicate that she knew she shouldn't have said that, Sylvia continued smoothly, "But the main thing about Red is the good doctor he is. All the hospital people know *that!*"

"Thank you, Mrs. Sebaja."

Red did not risk looking at her or Vince. He frowned and watched his hand playing with a match book, tipping it to one edge, then another. He let it lie flat when C'ele's name was spoken.

"For Pete's sake!" he muttered to Randol.

"Take it easy," said that attorney. "Your friends are do-ing all right for me."

238

But Red was not sure. He folded his arms and looked straight ahead of him.

C'ele's voice came, shaking a little at first, then firming. Her gray eyes would be steady, and her sensitive lips would respond to Mareschal's manner to her. He had better not get smart!

Red glanced down the table at him, his chin jutting.

C'ele was saying that yes, she knew Dr. Cahill.

"Well?"

"That depends on what you mean."

Score one for C'ele.

"Does he date other girls? Or only you, Miss Davidson?"

"He may date other girls. I just know about his dates with me."

"You are not engaged?"

"Oh no!"

"But you see him often? Date him, I mean."

"That depends on what you mean by *often*," said C'ele reasonably. "A senior resident doesn't have a lot of free time. Dr. Cahill's work comes first, you know. He never misses a duty—has not, since I've known him. That's almost two years."

"But he does like to go to parties?"

"Well, of course. He's young and enjoys a good time. But his work still comes first. I understand that, and it's always been fine with me."

Now Red could smile a little. C'ele's earnestness must have come through in her testimony.

Polly Ferris next testified that she worked closely with Dr. Cahill and found him always to be both capable and a conscientious surgeon, certainly concerned for the well-being of his patients.

Next Dr. Enns was addressed. He sat at Red's right and

where he faced the three judges as he talked. He would make a strong impression, Red was sure, however his testimony came out. He was not at all sure of that testimony. Dr. Enns had sternly told Red that he should have secured permission for surgery—Red could think of a dozen times when Dr. Enns had criticized his senior resident. . . .

Dr. Enns identified himself; he explained his relationship with Dr. Cahill.

"He is an excellent doctor," said the Chief. "Four years ago I selected him as a resident in my service as the best of fifty-three applicants for the position. I have never regretted my decision. He has learned quickly and in turn teaches well. In fact, he performs notably in all phases of his chosen work."

"You say he has learned well, Doctor," said Mareschal smoothly. "Had he been taught to gain consent before surgery?"

"Yes!" said Dr. Enns crisply. "He has been thoroughly indoctrinated with all the ethical and medicolegal formalities. And has observed them."

Red sat and looked down at the buttons on his coat. Not many doctors—young ones—were given a chance to hear such testimony, such a summation of his achievements.

"Dr. Cahill is no machine of medicine," Dr. Enns was saying. "One of my few criticisms of him as a doctor has been that he can become too personally involved with a patient and takes the patient's affairs too intimately into his own concern. I am sure he did not act in a thoughtless, irresponsible manner in his care for Miss Lockette.

"Last fall this same young surgeon went into a spin because of his concern for what our profession is calling the 'battered child.' This has to do with children abused in the home by their parents or guardians and brought to the hospital suffering from injuries inflicted by the people who should be trusted to care for them tenderly.

"Because I have witnessed Dr. Cahill's deep concern over those children, I am as sure as if I had been present that he was neither hasty nor heartless in his care of the girl whom he found injured at the side of the road last December. He was acting only as a true Samaritan, and I am certain that the help he offered—the help which he gave—was *good!* Competent surgically, and goodhearted in the basic sense of that term!"

"Thank you, Dr. Enns. Will you admit prejudice on the subject?"

"I certainly will!" said Dr. Enns quickly.

Well! That should do it!

But of course it did not. The glow of all this praise had only begun to fade when Red realized that the two lawyers were involved in an argument.

Something must have been said about his not having waited until proper and complete tests could be made. Mr. Randol was retorting that "the way medicine is being practiced in this country, physicians are ordering costly procedures not so much because they are convinced that they need them as because they want to be covered in the event of a lawsuit." There was an interchange about that.

Then Mr. Mareschal asked suavely if his opposing counsel would advise the acceptance of a single professional opinion in a case such as they had at hand.

Mr. Randol retorted that if a dozen professional opinions were brought in, and this case went to trial, the jury's sympathy still could typically be with the plaintiff.

Under the cloud of all this argument Red sank into a state of bewildered discouragement. What definite decision could come out of all this? He wished he were a hundred miles from there—or even ten miles! Back at the hospital, going into a patient's room and out again, into the next room, then the ward, noticing people, recognizing their needs, helping them—people who needed Dr. Cahill and neither hated nor distrusted him.

He looked up at a stir throughout the room. "We are breaking for lunch," said Mr. Randol, "and the judge has asked that there be no discussion of the case. We'll be back here at two."

Red nodded and turned to assist Dr. Enns.

17 ❀❀❀❀❀❀❀❀❀❀❀❀❀❀❀❀❀❀❀❀❀❀❀❀❀❀

AT two, even as the hearing room was again settling down—Vince Sebaja and Sylvia had been excused and gone home—there appeared, and was introduced, the specialist over whose testimony the lawyers had hasseled earlier.

He was a famous man. Red was amazed to find that he would take time to appear. He was identified, and some minutes were expended in determining that he had never previously seen Dr. Cahill. He knew Dr. Enns by name and reputation, but he had been contacted by Dr. Graham of Old Pardee, who had sent him a transcript of the hospital records on Carrie Lockette. From this record he discussed his knowledge of the case, going into technicalities which had Judge Lockette restless and on the edge of his chair, nervously whispering questions to Mr. Mareschal, half rising once to shout, "He *cut!* And my girl is blind!"

The visiting specialist waited; he then said that he had examined Miss Lockette, and he testified firmly that any injury to the spine with compression of the spinal cord required that the patient—any patient—be operated on as soon as that patient could be prepared for surgery.

Yes, the records indicated that in this case such speed had

been necessary.

Would the surgery have made her blind?

No, it would not. It was his opinion that the injury to the optic nerve was due entirely to impact at the time of the accident. Though, yes, where there was a hematoma—a clot or tumor—within the dura—the lining of the brain—lengthy surgery was required to halt hemorrhage from the ruptured blood vessels and to evacuate the hematoma, then some damage might result.

Oh yes, he would call the surgery successful. There was no paralysis, no speech difficulty.

Only the blindness.

Brain and spine injury often involved much more loss of tissue and function.

"You say that you have studied the records? Were X-rays taken before surgery?"

"They were. I had the plates to read."

"Would you say that the equipment at the Old Pardee Hospital was adequate as a preliminary to such involved surgery?"

"The records which I have had to go by would indicate that the equipment served its purpose. Since the results were good."

The specialist was thanked, excused, and he departed, escorted by Dr. Graham. Red, at lunch, had visited a little with Rachel, talking about the farm, the flowers, and their cook.

Rachel was going to send Red a country ham "when all this is out of the way."

Randol jogged Red's arm. Mareschal was asking him if *he* thought the X-ray examination of Carrie had been adequate.

Red thought about his answer. "It was a surprisingly good machine," he said slowly. "With the patient already convulsive, I could not have delayed for the more elaborate proceedings of dye and fluid tests."

"Such as would be done in your big hospital, you mean?"

"Yes, sir, I do mean that."

"In your big hospital would you have operated without formal consent from the family?"

"In as great an emergency, yes, sir, I would have."

"Then being a so-called good Samaritan would not have been an item?"

"In this particular case it was a very great item, sir. For instance, had I not been present at the scene, Carrie could have been handled in such a manner as to preclude saving her life by surgery."

Here Judge Lockette asked to have the word "preclude" explained. He said that city folks talked funny theirselves.

"Now," said Mr. Mareschal—he still did not look like an attorney-at-law. More like the Mad Hatter in the Tenniel drawings, Red thought. "We are back to the matter of consent, Dr. Cahill. That night were you aware that Miss Smith was attempting to locate the injured girl's family?"

"Yes, sir. She kept making reports to Dr. Graham."

"For how long, would you say, did she make these efforts?"

"That night? The family wasn't located until the second day, you know. But that night—I would say that after she came to the hospital she worked for a matter of an hour or two. It seemed much longer then, because I knew that every second of delay was dangerous."

"You *knew* that?"

"Yes, sir, I did."

"What did you do while this search was being conducted?"

"I—well, of course blood tests were made, a spinal tap, the X-rays which I have mentioned. There was a general prep for surgery." He explained that term.

"We—" said Mr. Mareschal. "We, as you say, have discussed the matter of X-rays. How about the other equipment of the Old Pardee Hospital?"

"The lab and the instruments, you mean? Well, it was not completely what I have at hand in N.S. at the Center. But I managed very well. I have no apology to make for the surgery done that night." Red pressed his lips tightly together.

"Doctor," said Mr. Mareschal smoothly, "in brain and spinal-cord surgery, doesn't the proper equipment feature rather largely?"

"Yes, sir, it does. With such difficult and lengthy surgery every assist is of value. But what I had to work with was adequate—and in the emergency which certainly existed I had to use it and was glad to use it."

"You will testify that an emergency existed."

"Yes, because it certainly did exist, sir. Surgery was immediately necessary to save that girl's life."

"Because of the injury to the brain?"

"No, sir. There definitely was subdural bleeding, but if the spine had not been compressed, we could have waited a while on the hematoma." He glanced at Dr. Enns and then at Dr. Graham, who had returned. "I think your expert witness so testified, sir," he said courteously, "that the spine condition was what required immediate relief."

Mr. Randol asked that the specialist's testimony be read back.

After this was done Mr. Mareschal resumed. He asked

Red to tell how he had determined the presence of spinal injury so great that . . .

"I have mentioned that Carrie was in convulsion. I made a spinal tap—and determined that the pressure in the spinal fluid was elevated to the point of grave concern. And—well—compression in the spinal cord made immediate surgery imperative."

"Or else?" asked Mr. Randol.

"Or else," said Red firmly, "there would have been death. At best, complete paralysis."

Down the table, Judge Lockette rose to his feet and leaned forward. "So you chose blindness for her!" he shouted.

The law clerk and Mr. Mareschal sought to quiet him. The man finally did sit down, but he sat glaring at young Dr. Cahill.

"I did not *choose* blindness," said Red quietly, feeling his finger tips tingle. "It is my opinion that Carrie was blind before she ever went into surgery."

Mr. Mareschal turned over a page of his papers. "Now, Dr. Cahill," he said, in his quiet—and even pleasant—manner. In other circumstances Red thought that he could have liked the man. "Let us go back to the night—the day—of December twenty-seventh. Will you tell us again why you were out on the highway that afternoon? Why you were so located that, during a storm, you took refuge at the Northland Motel. Why were you traveling at all on that day?"

"I told you," said Red patiently, "I was planning to go on to Bridgeton. They have a new teaching hospital at the University Medical School there, and I'd learned that the position of neurosurgeon was open."

"Were you planning to leave the Center?"

"Not until my term of duty was finished, sir."

"You had not been dismissed?"

"No, sir!" cried Dr. Enns. "He had not!"

"Please let Dr. Cahill answer."

Dr. Enns sat back. "I'm sorry," he muttered. "Go on, Red."

"There had been nothing said about dismissal," Red told. "I was given the time off—and I went to Bridgeton. I started to go there. I never made it."

"Were you on suspension from your hospital duties?"

Red bit his lip. The talkative shadow of little Iserman was large in the conference room.

"I had been given a week's vacation," Dr. Cahill said tightly.

"Is such a vacation usual for resident surgeons?" No! Red could not possibly like this man.

"They are not usual," he said sharply. "But perhaps they should be!"

Beside him he heard Dr. Enns chuckle. The hospital personnel along the wall were smiling too.

"You were on your way to Bridgeton to inquire about a new job," said Mr. Mareschal. "You could not have been resident at Lincoln for another year?"

"He could be," said Dr. Enns. "He has not applied."

"Dr. Cahill?" said Mr. Mareschal patiently.

"No, sir," said Red. "I have not applied. Not yet."

For the next fifteen minutes Red was subjected to questioning on the matter of his training. Mr. Randol brought out every item, though Mr. Mareschal had instigated the subject. Where had he gone to school? To college? Had he had military service? Where had he done his pre-med work? What were his grades? His standing in class?

The same things were asked about medical school—Randol led to the listing of prizes and awards. Where had Dr. Cahill interned? And again his reasons for coming to the Center were explored.

The whole system of resident doctors was outlined by Dr. Enns and repeated by Mr. Ovian. Yes, it was a good system. The hospital and the patient were all served, and the young doctors gained the experience which they needed to have. Yes, it turned out specialists. Yes, Dr. Cahill could be so considered. A specialist in the brain and nervous system. A surgeon.

"Have you ever engaged in private practice, Dr. Cahill?"

"Oh no, sir."

"You have just worked in the hospital. Do you diagnose a patient's ailments?"

Red's big hand brushed the smile from his lips. "Yes, sir, I do."

"Under supervision or alone?"

"My decisions are reviewed."

"Yes! Now what about surgery? In the interest of time let us narrow this down to the surgery which you did that night in Old Pardee. Had you done this type of surgery before?"

"Many times."

And then came the expected question. "Had you done it under supervision? Assisting? Or alone?"

Red's tongue licked across his lip. "I had not done it alone in the sense I was alone that night, sir. In Old Pardee I was my own man, and I truly thought that what I was doing was right—both surgically and morally."

"How about ethically?" asked Mr. Mareschal. "Did you think about that? Was the matter of consent brought to your attention?"

Red glanced across at Dr. Graham. He wore a blue bow tie that day and dark-rimmed glasses. Since the lunch break Rachel had been sitting at her husband's shoulder.

"Yes, sir," said Dr. Cahill firmly. "Dr. Graham pointed out to me that we should have consent. But I knew that for myself. I had been taught legal medicine."

"Had you, on that night in question, been reminded specifically of the consequences which have resulted for you and of the situation now in debate, what would you have done, Dr. Cahill?"

The room was in dead silence. Every eye was on Red. Some leaned forward to see and hear more clearly.

He placed the palms of his hands flat on the table and seemed to lean upon them. "There was an emergency, Mr. Mareschal," he said quietly. "A young girl's life was in danger. Had I been able to foresee in particular this legal action, I still would have performed the surgery which I did perform."

There was an audible sigh across the room; people leaned back. Polly Ferris took a handkerchief from her purse. The flutter of white caught Red's attention, and he smiled at her—a little.

One of the judges—the one from the city—asked if he might be permitted a question, a little outside the line of inquiry?

Mr. Mareschal assented, and so did Randol. Red nodded, since his agreement seemed to be desired.

"Dr. Cahill," said the jurist. He was a large man, beginning to gray. "I feel that I need not ask if you realize what this inquiry and the possible trial signifies. But I would like to ask if you have plans, Doctor? In case this matter goes against you—or, even, in either case? Do you have plans, and if you do, could you tell us . . . ?"

Dr. Enns had turned in his chair to look at Red, to watch him. Was he also curious? Or only wary? Hoping that his gaze would warn his protégé . . . ?

But Red was quite calm. He was not a man easily panicked by a present danger or even one to deal particularly with future and possible danger. His training had been to cope with circumstances of the present. He had met danger before, risk, and had fought death itself at close hand. In o.r., of course, that was, not in a room of this sort, with people watching him, waiting on his word, his decision.

"I hope," he said quietly, "that I can go on in Neurosurgery. Perhaps I would still apply for that position in Bridgeton or for a staff position somewhere. If I can work . . .

"If I cannot work, I am going to fight to change the laws which handicap a doctor under certain extreme conditions."

The judge leaned forward. "Did you say *fight*, Doctor?"

"Well—work."

"Does that, perhaps, mean the same thing to you?"

"Yes, sir, it does. In this case. I know there must be laws. And I am sorry if I broke them."

"And you did know, specifically, the risk you ran?"

"I know the story of the good Samaritan, sir," said Red quietly. "I know there was one man who spread his cloak . . . That night, in Old Pardee, I knew that I should have consent to operate on that dying girl." He turned his head to glance down the table at Carrie. She sat with her face lifted toward the sound of his voice.

"If I hadn't known that I needed consent," Red continued, "Dr. Graham was there to remind me. But, gentlemen, this was an *emergency!* It was! The nature of the injury, the weather, my being on the scene and able— There are

251

privileges in such circumstances, under such conditions!

"I knew the girl was young—Dr. Graham and I discussed her youth, guessed at her possible age. I didn't think of the assault possibility. Such an item did not come into my mind. I only wanted to help Carrie—and I did help her. I saved her life."

For a minute he was silent in the waiting, silent room. Then he lifted his head. "Then, too," he said quietly, "there was another law in effect that night. I didn't consciously consider it. But it was there. A law. A rule. The Golden Rule. I suppose that is what it would be called." His cheeks flushed bright red.

"Yes," he said tightly, "it *was* the Golden Rule! That's old-fashioned, isn't it? People today stand aside, keep out of things. They have no feeling of community integrity, with all that it implies in the sense of concern, kindness, and responsibility. In the bigness of city life it is easy to lose that. We leave things to the police, to the authorities. There seems to be a missing ingredient in our life. No one wants to take a risk; no one wants to step out and *do*. But that night in Old Pardee—I knew I was taking a risk; it still was something I had to do. For the girl who was helpless, the girl who lay at my feet, the girl *I* could help."

C'ele was afraid she would sob, make some sound. She bit her lips and reached for Polly's hand.

Red, probably not knowing that he moved, got slowly to his feet. He stood there for a brief moment, tall, his head up, his eyes narrowed, his hands still. He was a big man, clean-cut, and earnest.

He was showing up well—even Judge Lockette must have thought so. Others in the room did.

"If ever," he said, slowly and speaking clearly. His voice was not loud, but it struck like a clean-hitting hammer, each word a telling blow. "If ever I were hurt on an icy road, and there were a doctor close by, I would hope that he would help me as best he could. And no questions asked. If I should be hurt tonight and the question of consent were asked, who would there be to consent? My only relative is my mother, and she is in the Indian Ocean somewhere, on a world tour. Should I then be allowed to die for want of a paper signed? No! An emergency would exist, and I would be helped. I should be helped!"

Every face was thoughtful. And as each one thought, hope brightened those faces.

"Tell me this, Dr. Cahill," asked the questioning judge. "Under approximate circumstances, would you help again?"

"Yes, sir." Red sat down. "Yes, sir," he said quietly, "I would."

The judge nodded. "No matter what today's—or a trial's—judgment might be?"

"Yes, sir, I think I would. If allowed to be a doctor, I'd do the same thing, and even if I were not allowed, I think I would still try to help. Because I would still have my training, you see, my knowledge, my judgment of such circumstances." Red sighed, as if he were, at last, weary of all this. "Perhaps," he said slowly, "I didn't have the right . . ."

"There!" shouted Judge Lockette, suddenly on his feet, waving his arms. "*That's* what I ben a-waitin' for him to say! That's what I wanted to *hear* him say!"

There was a silence in the room. A deep silence, in which one might even have heard a heartbeat.

If all this had been only to hear so simple a statement . . .

If a man's career had been put into peril by another man's frightened anger and false pride . . .

Red spoke as if there had been no interruption. "I have another thing to say," he said, still speaking quietly, "and that is to state, to remind those of you who do not know it, a doctor, any doctor, all doctors, must make many decisions, little ones and big ones. Often he must make a big decision in a hurry and—er—under pressure. In order to make these decisions, a doctor must, first of all, be trusted. And he must trust himself. Without that a doctor could scarcely work at all."

"Dr. Cahill." Mr. Mareschal was resuming control of the hearing.

"Yes, sir?"

"Do you think that there should be no laws other than ethics to constrain and regulate doctors?"

"No, sir." Red's answer was quick. "I do not! But I am forced to realize that a law can be good at one time and harmful at another."

"Yes. But let us take this law of consent. Do you think there should be such a law?"

"Yes, sir, I do."

"Even though you violated it and say you would violate it again?"

"I did violate it—I would violate it—only under certain circumstances, sir. I—well, it's like a soldier who is liable for harsh punishment for going to sleep at his post. It isn't much like—" Red's familiar grin flashed. "But there is a similarity. What I mean to point out is that there can be mitigating circumstances, and I think provisions should be made for them."

"Would you suggest such amendment of the laws, Doctor?" In his turn Mr. Mareschal was earnest.

"I don't know specifically what should be suggested. But there must be some solution to this thing. As for my finding it—me, personally—I am still learning my own profession."

"You said you would fight," the judge reminded him, his voice and manner kind.

Dr. Enns and Dr. Graham exchanged glances. Red had made a good showing, and the older doctors were glad. He could so easily have been belligerent, antagonistic, or even conceitedly ready to defend his superior training and education against the "country" people who had ventured to attack him.

The insurance company's man cleared his throat warningly. This was no time for overconfidence. They had better listen to Cahill's answer.

"I did say I would fight," Red was telling the judge. "That is, I shall try very hard to do something. Perhaps the first thing that I'll do will be to talk to older, and wiser, doctors and lawyers, see if they think there might be a solution to this problem. Perhaps they would suggest what I might do."

The insurance man now exchanged his own glance with one from Mr. Randol.

"By solution, Doctor, do you mean other *laws?*"

"Yes. If only more explicit statements of the present laws. I can think of a few such statements."

"I see."

The judge who had been talking leaned to his right and conferred in rumbling whispers with the other two jurists. After a few minutes of this they asked Mr. Randol and Mr. Mareschal to join them at the small table.

"I think the witnesses may leave if they wish," said one of the judges.

Some did leave. Polly remained, and C'ele, and one or two others of the Center personnel. Dr. Graham and Rachel

255

and the o.r. nurse, Rosie, who had driven to the city with Maurita, continued to sit in their chairs, as did Judge Lockette and Carrie.

Red remained seated in his group of advisers—Dr. Enns, Mr. Ovian, the insurance representative.

After another ten minutes Judge Lockette was called to the conferring group. Mr. Ovian's eyebrows went up. Lockette's whispers were pretty loud. Once he said, "Jest so it's known that he . . ."

Red was uneasy, more so then he had been all day. Why couldn't they have gone into another room—or sent everybody not needed out of this one? This standing by, watching and listening to a half dozen men decide anything so vital as his career . . .

He clenched his hands and struggled to maintain calm. It seemed as if all the testimony had been against him. Now the only decision needed would be when to hang him and how high.

When Judge Lockette returned to his chair, smiling smugly, Red felt anger and protest build within him. He wanted to go down the room and take Carrie away from that vindictive old fool!

He wanted to help Carrie—he meant to help her—and how could he, with her father standing ready to oppose anything?

Red growled something, and Dr. Enns smiled. "You expected some trouble out of all this, didn't you? Well, you're getting it."

"I suppose." Red slumped down in his chair, prepared for a long siege.

And then, of course, the small-table meeting broke up. Mr. Randol came back to his chair, nodding to Dr. Enns's

256

inquiring look. A nod which could indicate a dozen things —or nothing, Red thought.

Mr. Mareschal, meanwhile, was rebuffing Judge Lockette's wish to talk. He indicated that one of the judges meant to speak.

He did—the one from the Old Pardee-Norfolk Circuit Court, the handsome man with the flowing silver-gray hair. His skin was pink; he had a courtly, Old-World manner.

Now he waited until everyone was seated and the room quiet again. Then he cleared his throat.

He thanked all concerned for their patience; he thanked everyone for their testimony and their wish to help the Court in this hearing. He then said that the listening Court had conferred with one another, and with the counsel present, and had reached a conclusion which was acceptable to them but which the accused and the accuser now must hear and consider.

He looked at Dr. Cahill, then he turned and looked at Judge Lockette. That gentleman waved his large, gnarled hand. "Anythin' you say, Jedge," he said magnanimously. "I heerd the young whippersnapper say he done wrong!"

Red felt that the bottom had dropped out of his world, but he determined not to let anyone know how badly he was hit. His face like a mask, he nodded to Mr. Randol.

Randol evidently approved of his conduct, which made Red feel one pin point better. He looked steadily at the judge from Old Pardee.

"We are glad that we attended this hearing in person," said that jurist. "It can save a great deal of time. Our day has been well spent. I am also happy to have the opinions of my distinguished colleagues. Now!"

He glanced down at the pad of paper before him.

"We have listened carefully," he said, "to all the evidence presented today. We have judged the responsibility and competence of those who have testified. All items are represented in our conclusion. There was, during the testimony, some discussion of the wisdom of allowing one expert opinion to influence the Court. We are not doing that. We feel that several experts, each in his own field, have testified for Dr. Cahill in this case, but we are going to quote from the testimony of Dr. Horstmann, the specialist who was asked by Dr. Graham of the Old Pardee Hospital to go over the records and form an opinion as to the surgical care given to Carrie Lockette on the night of January —no, *December* twenty-seventh last."

For God's sake, say it! Red's hands ached from their fierce clenching.

"Dr. Horstmann," continued Judge Steward, "was accepted by both sides as being an eminent authority in his field. Therefore we have leaned upon his opinion that while the—the hematoma might have waited for surgical correction, the spinal pressure could not. In that case an emergency did exist."

Red's hands fell limp, and tenseness dropped away from him like air from a balloon. He felt weak—giddy—with relief.

"In conference," said Judge Stewart, "we have agreed that there is, in our joint opinion, no case here for a trial in court. There has been presented to us no evidence which would indicate an intent to do injury, nor is there any evidence of laxity. Therefore we feel that we have no basis for a suit for damages because of such injury or laxity.

"However, since the girl, Carrie, is and was a minor, the matter of assault has some standing. And it is our recommendation that a fair and accepted payment be made for the loss of the girl's sight, the money to be placed in a trust

258

fund for the girl's care and education. No punitive damages are to be allowed or ever claimed."

Red frowned. What had been said?

"The insurance company will reach a settlement," Dr. Enns murmured in his ear.

"We also specify that an injunction should and will be laid upon all public discussion or publication of the charges filed against Dr. Cahill. Such publicity being detrimental to his professional career, it is our judgment that no such damage should be inflicted. We believe that Dr. Cahill acted with youthful intensity and enthusiasm which"—the Judge's mouth twisted wryly, and his voice grew wistful—"we doubt will happen again."

He turned to face Judge Lockette. "Do you understand what I have just said about publishing the matters dealt with in this hearing?"

"We understand completely, your honor," said Mr. Mareschal firmly.

"Good! Dr. Cahill?"

"Yes, sir."

"I—we—are going to advise you, sir, to learn the laws governing you in the practice of your profession. If you have already studied them, study them again. And having learned them, you are enjoined to stick to those laws as written. Perhaps some day you can effect changes in them, but until that day comes, obey them."

"Yes, sir," said Dr. Cahill quietly. Perhaps, some day, he would change the laws.

The hearing was over. Red wanted to speak to Carrie, but no one seemed to think he should. If he could only have smiled at her across the room! He could not, and the fact of her blindness struck a new blow.

He walked slowly down the length of the room. Randol was talking to Judge Stewart; the insurance man was with them. Dr. Graham had pressed Red's arm, and Rachel had told him to come to see them. Then they had left. Each one who spoke to Red said that he had done a good job in his own defense.

Had he? If so, he had done it on his own. If so, he surely could now consider himself his own man. Others had helped him—certainly they had! But their help, their backing, in no way had shadowed him. Did C'ele know that?

Where was C'ele? All day she had been sitting with Polly, but Polly was now over in one corner of the room with Bill Enns.

Bill was talking very earnestly to Polly. Red would go out to the car, lest it seem that he was eavesdropping. He need not, because he could guess what was being said. Something like, "Well, that's nicely settled. . . ."

Which was exactly what Bill *was* saying to Polly.

"I'm so glad, Bill!" she told him.

"Well, of course! I could have killed Red for getting into the mess, but I will say he did a good job of getting himself out again."

"But you'll never tell him so?" Her steady eyes probed his.

"Oh, not for a time. I do feel, however, that all we needed to do was to confront Red—at his best—with that awful Lockette—at his worst."

"He was an old coot, wasn't he? What about that daughter of his? Isn't she lovely?"

"Yes, and I'll count on Red's having plans for her."

Polly looked startled. "You don't mean . . . ?"

Bill's hand pushed the idea away. "Of course not! But he's already sent her talking books. Next will be a guide dog perhaps. He'll stay with it."

He touched Polly's forearm. "I wish," he said earnestly, "our affairs would—and could—be settled as well as Red's were today."

"Oh, Bill."

"I do wish it."

"I know—but there is nothing I can say or do."

"Nor I. Except to go on loving you. I do, you know. And I even hope—"

Polly shook her head. Tears came into her eyes. "That isn't enough, Bill," she said softly. "You should have more."

"It's all I can have, isn't it?" Bill asked intently.

Polly nodded. "Yes. Yes, it is, Bill. I can't even say I'm sorry. So—let's go home, shall we?"

"Red came with me."

"I know. And I brought C'ele Davidson."

"She's Red's girl?"

"I hope so. He'd be lucky."

18 ✿

THERE was to be no publicity. There was none, except for a brief statement in the city's newspapers, later to be quoted by a news service and several medical journals, that the damage suit against Dr. Redding Cahill—resident in Neurosurgery—had been dropped.

Perhaps it was too much to expect that the hearing would not be discussed in the little town of Old Pardee. It was certainly too much to expect of that hotbed of talk, gossip, opinion, and surmise which was the Lincoln Medical Center.

But nobody made much of an attempt to talk about the matter to or around Red until the evening at the end of the week when he went over to C'ele's for an hour or two with her. Her apartment was near the hospital; Dr. Martin and his wife lived in the same unit; Dr. Sebaja had heard Red say he was going to see C'ele that evening if he could, so he and Sylvia dropped in.

Dr. Schonwald saw Red's car parked at her door; he picked up his pal Adams, and they came in. . . .

By nine o'clock a full-scale party was in progress. The Sebajas had brought pizzas; the Martins fetched beer. His friends sat on the floor and talked about Red, about his case, about the outcome of it. Red was helpless before the talk. He drew C'ele down to the arm of his chair and listened. . . .

"I had hoped for a cozy evening alone," he told her.

She shrugged. "They won't stay."

"I hope."

But while they stayed, his friends talked.

"What would you have done in Red's shoes that night?" This was always the first question, the beginning of any talk about the situation. It was tonight.

And tonight the talk moved to a second question. What would you do now? What was Red going to do?

"I hear you are going to change some of the laws," Clyde Martin challenged him.

The others laughed and watched Red, teasing him—in the friendliest sort of way.

But Red could only be solemn. "I do mean to do something along that line," he assured his friends.

"What, Red?" asked Schonwald. "*What?*"

He could have thrown them a gag answer.

He did not. Somehow the past months had brushed the shine off the old line.

"Well," he said slowly, "I am hoping to find some way—somehow—to protect the battered child."

Dr. Adams groaned. "Not *that* again."

Vince Sebaja told him to shut up. "Wait till you meet up with it, son. You'll be passing out laws yourself."

"But what can you *do?*" asked Dr. Martin. "Now parents aren't *allowed* to abuse their children."

The other doctors looked patiently at each other.

"Now," said Vince, "you have to identify abuse. Then you have to connect it to an adult—and you have to keep

263

yourself free, out of a lawsuit for damages resulting from your accusations."

Dr. Martin gaped. "Well, excuse me!" he said.

"Certainly, Doctor. Any time. So—tell us about your law, Red."

Red shrugged. "It won't sound like much, but it would be a start. And, as a matter of fact, I have already talked to our representative—in the State House, that is—urging him to present a bill at the next session which would require all physicians—repeat, *all physicians*—to report *all* suspected cases of child-beating."

"But," cried Sylvia, "isn't there already such a law?"

"No," said Red.

"Such a law would eliminate the damage-suit thing . . ." one of the doctors mused.

"It would," Red agreed. "The bill I have in mind would exempt a physician from being sued if, in good faith, he reported an injury suspected to be the result of child-beating. Also, it would require that the physician report such injuries within twenty-four hours to the Prosecuting Attorney."

"With a penalty for not reporting it?" asked Sylvia.

Red shrugged. "I haven't got that far. There would need to be a penalty, I suppose."

"Of course there would! What else, Red?"

"Well, the main thing would be to make it a misde-meanor to inflict any cruel or inhuman corporal punish-ment on children under seventeen resulting in serious in-jury. It just seems to me there must be such a law!" His face was a little pale with his earnestness.

"Aren't you being too intense about all this?" asked Dr. Adams. "I mean—"

"I am as solemn as a judge about it, if *that's* what you

264

mean!" Red testily assured him. "Vince here told me to find out what went on with the battered child. He said it wasn't enough just to get mad and flail around, accusing people. So—I did. I found out that doctors have to have immunity against reprisal lawsuits before they can exercise their consciences in these things. But somebody has to protect the kids! And I mean to get my bill before the legislature in this state. I'll want you guys to help me too."

"Vince will," said Dr. Adams slyly. "He started all this."

"He told me to do something else," Red continued, ignoring the irony. "He told me to find out *why* a child is battered."

"And did you?"

"I did. I've tried—and I've come up with some answers."

"I've known parents," said C'ele, "who were terribly strict with their children, but only because they loved them and wanted—"

Red nodded. "The Prussian papa," he identified the example. "But he doesn't seem to feature in the battered-child syndrome. Because, for one thing, he seems to be fading from the American picture. Few parents around here now beat their children because they love them."

"It's still beating, isn't it?"

"No, and the children seem to know the difference."

"You've really been studying this?"

"I sure have. I've done a lot of reading. I've studied hospital cases, court records, social service reports. Vince has helped."

"What did you find?" asked Bunny Martin. "Are the parents hardened criminals?"

"Psychotics," offered Dr. Schonwald.

Red nodded. "Some of each; also some parents are from the depressed socio-economic classes."

"The words that man knows!" marveled Dr. Adams.

"You should go the course," Red advised him. "Get firsthand the words I learned, the things I saw and heard about. But I found that the parents—some of them, of course, were criminal, psychotic, and even the product of their environment—but most of them, the ones guilty of sudden and horrifying attacks on their children, were just average parents. People—mothers and dads—just like the people we know. People like the Sebajas and the Martins—like the people we'll become, Adams, when we marry and have kids."

"It's a sobering thought," said Dr. Adams, and Schonwald punched him.

"It is more sobering than we realize," Red assured him. "These parents seem to get along well in their communities, in their neighborhood, and at their jobs. But, of course, at some point they violently attack their children."

"All their kids, Red?" asked Sylvia.

"Sometimes. But, no—usually it is one child in the family who is selected for abuse."

"Why?"

"That's been looked into too. Locally and nationally it has been found that a number of common characteristics exist among battering parents."

"Mothers *and* fathers?"

"Sometimes both. But usually singly; the number of abusive mothers about equals the number of abusive fathers. And a great, great many such cases are found in families where the parents were very young at the time of their marriage and are relatively young at the time of the abuse.

"Marriage strife is common, and outside pressures, financial difficulties, discord with relatives, unsatisfactory living conditions—all these may be present."

266

"And they take it out on a kid," mourned C'ele.

"Yes, they do. Often the circumstance of the battered child's birth may be unhappy. In cases of a first child, often it was born too early in a marriage. At five or six months, I mean. When it is a third or fourth child, the new baby may place a too-great financial burden on the family, or it strains the parents' ability to keep domestic order.

"But the real common denominator of battering parents seems to be the misery of their own childhood."

"All this and Neurosurgery, too!" breathed Dr. Adams.

"Get yourself into trouble," Red advised. "You learn a lot on the way out."

"Ignore him, Red," said Sylvia Sebaja, "and tell us more about what you learned."

"Vince knows it all; he could tell you."

"For all Vince tells me professionally, he might as well sell ladies' millinery."

Everyone in the room laughed at the picture, even Red. "He'd be good at that, too," he decided.

"Are you saying the parents, in their own childhood, were beaten?"

"Some were; some were physically and emotionally neglected. The social service worker's term is: their baby needs were never met."

"It sounds a little," said Dr. Schonwald, "as if the battering parent and the battered child might get confused or seem to merge into one and the same person."

"But they do!" cried Red. "And that's why it is so important to protect a child where and how we can. It isn't just the broken arm, or the blacked eye—or even the child's terror, as awful as that can be. There's an over-all effect on such a child which must be considered.

"Excessively severe and continued physical punishment

has two major effects on such children. First—and this is the more usual—the child himself will become extremely aggressive, taking out his anger and frustration on other children and animals. Or, second, he becomes cowed and fearful.

"In both cases the child becomes isolated and anti-social. When he grows up, he will lash out at society, or will expend his anger on his wife, or vent his rage on his own child.

"Now, his own unhappy and abused childhood may be a reason for his attacks, but it is no excuse. Legally or morally, an adult has no right to commit felonious assault on a child. The syndrome does, of course, indicate that the situation is the result of social breakdown and emotional disorder rather than cruel and calculated viciousness."

"Then it can be treated!" said Dr. Martin.

Red nodded. "It can be treated. First, such children must be located—"

"And the doctor protected."

"Oh yes. He must have anonymity and immunity. But of course the child must also have protection immediately and during the rehabilitation of the home and family into which he has been born and should, ideally, grow up."

Vince started to say something, but the telephone rang, and everyone waited—the women each stiffening with anticipation until they knew which doctor would be called.

It was Dr. Schonwald. He had, he said, putting on his shoes, a hot appendix. "And it better be real hot," he grumbled. "Adams, you listen, if Red says anything more. Come I find me a battered child, I want to know how to proceed."

He departed, and the others settled down again. "How

do you proceed, Red," asked Bunny Martin, "when you find such a child? Call the police?"

Vince glanced at Red.

"No," he said. "When a child comes into Admissions— he's fallen downstairs, broken an arm. Maybe he has a black eye. X-rays show the broken arm, but it also shows rib fractures in various stages of healing. The mother can't explain this at all!

"Maybe the radiologist raises the first flag of suspicion, and we decide we have a battered child. But still we must move slowly, examine for brittle-bone and so on. However, it should be the radiologist's moral responsibility to report the unsuspected fractures to the attending physician, and also—I feel—he should be required, both legally and morally, to interpret the probable cause.

"All right. Say that several medics arrive at the painful conclusion that a child has been 'battered.' Then the social worker should move in; she must find out all she can about the parents and the home—and, if at all possible, find out what happened to the child. By now we are into several problems—psychological, social, legal, and of course medical.

"What next? No, we cannot hang the parents, but once we have determined that the battering parent of today was the battered child of yesterday, we must be free to make some sort of wise and cautious approach to the whole syndrome. We must try to prevent our present pitiful and bruised child from carrying such emotional scars that when he is adult he will reach a point of violence where he will re-enact the whole shocking scene on his own child."

Red fell silent. Sylvia Sebaja blew her nose and wiped her eyes. C'ele rubbed the shoulder of Red's coat; he

269

caught her hand and held it.

"Where do I sign, Doctor?" asked Adams, his voice gruff.

"I'll show you," Red told him. "We all can 'sign'—we all can do something for these kids."

"Could we protect the good Samaritans, too?" asked Adams slyly.

"Something should be done to protect us battered medics," Red admitted. "If these high and wide suits could be handled before they reach a jury with its power, irresponsibly to assess damages—"

"The legal eagles are too ready to pounce on a doctor's mistakes, or—even worse—their inability to effect a cure every time." Adams slapped at his knee.

"That's the way we doctors see the lawyers," Red agreed. "But they see us as ready to cover up one another's mistakes, slight or gross, and they accuse us of a conspiracy of silence in refusing to testify against each other in malpractice suits."

"Well, what do they expect?"

Red shrugged. "They wish a solution could be reached, and so do some doctors."

"Can it?"

"I think so. That was the subject of a seminar I attended. In fact, the hearing given my case was a test of just such a plan."

"How?"

"Well, it is a plan on a co-operative basis which could prove helpful. It would consist of a continuing panel of leading medical practitioners and lawyers who would screen malpractice claims against doctors of their area. Such a group, working in a confidential manner, could discourage claims that have an insufficient basis and thus save the physician from harassment and damage to his professional reputation. Where the claims are judged to have reasonable grounds for finding negligence or error, such intra-professional panels could encourage settlement of those claims or, should the case go to court, provide medical testimony for the plaintiff.

"That was Lockette's weak point, you know. He could not get any adequate medical testimony as to wrong-doing in the case."

"He only wanted you to say you had made a mistake," said C'ele bitterly.

"I know that's what he wanted. But *he* meant a medical mistake, like a bungling knife. When I admitted *my* mistake, I meant a mistake in judgment—about operating without consent."

"Could such panels as you describe really be set up to be effective?" Vince asked thoughtfully.

"I think they could by law—yes. I think any law should be subject to change, to smoothing out. Certainly if the big medical centers would help get such adjustments and provisions, the thing could be done. If they won't, I— we—maybe can do something."

"About good Samaritans, too, Doctor?" needled Adams again.

"That?" said Red. "Oh, sure, we can do something about *that!*"

Vince stood up. "It sounds like a lot of very busy work," he decided.

"But worth while."

"Yep. Worth while. Come on, Sylvia. We have kids at home, and tomorrow is another day."

The group broke up. Red started to pick things up for C'ele, but she stopped him. "Let it wait, Red," she told him.

"You look tired."

He sat down on the couch, and she put a pillow behind his head.

"I wish the gang hadn't come in," he confessed.

"They are your friends."

He shook his head. "They have been. Now—they seem so damn young, C'ele."

"So are you. Young."

"Me? I'm a hundred years old."

"Oh . . ." Then she looked at him. And nodded. "I suppose it is time . . ." she agreed.

Red gazed at her, then he nodded. "Aren't you going to miss the kook?" he asked.

"Aw, Red! Don't blame Sylvia for that."

"I don't. But—answer my question."

"No, I won't miss the kook. But I have missed *you*, and often, these past weeks."

"Mhmmmn." Red stretched his long legs. "You're a very smart girl, aren't you?" His eyes slid to her face.

She sat serene. "No," she said readily. "Just a girl in love."

Red reached for her hand, and they sat quietly. Calmly. The girl in her pink and white dress, her dark hair smooth, her eyes brooding. The big man, thinking, thinking. . . .

This was nice, he thought. I'm glad C'ele loves me. She will help me, always. She's not a Carrie, maybe. She probably never will shake me as my first sight of Carrie did. Carrie's hair—her wide-set eyes—her childish, appealing hands . . .

No, I'll never know that sort of heady, ballooning emotion with C'ele.

But then there will always be C'ele. A woman who I know will do what she has to do.

272

And it was this woman who loved Red Cahill. A woman who would be loyal to him—C'ele had been loyal. She was a fine girl, and she had believed in Red. Not blindly, but trustingly. She had already gone through a lot with the man she loved.

That kookie business—she had joined Red in all the wild things he had ever thought up to do and say; she had ridden the roller coaster with him, maybe not liking it, but trying to make herself like it if that was what he wanted.

She had stood by him through the trial. Well, never actually a trial . . . But from the first word that he was in peril, her faith in him had never wavered.

Maybe she even guessed how he felt, and sometimes dreamed, about Carrie. And she had decided that she could go along with that too.

She would do it. She would let him help the girl—and once helped, he and C'ele would remember Carrie all of their lives.

Red sat up straight, gazing ahead of him, not seeing the picture on the wall or the arch into the dining nook . . .

All of their *lives!* he thought. For now there was going to be a life. It stretched before Red. Work—surgery— white ducks—a child in a crib—a man able to talk and to work. The battered child protected, the good Samaritan with a fighting chance—C'ele—a home—and a family . . .

For Red was going to be a doctor! His shoulders still felt the narrow squeak through which he had passed. If the Lockette case had ever come to trial—a jury, and the publicity, would have riddled him!

But now . . . He sighed.

He must go to see Carrie soon. And take C'ele with him. The last time he had seen the girl, to take her the machine and the talking books, she had said to him, as he left, "You

273

should might ought to come back early, Dr. Cahill." Now he smiled gently at her way of speaking.

But he would "come back early"—and often. Now he was his own boss. Even C'ele thought so.

He turned to look at C'ele. Waiting on his thoughtful mood, she seemed not to have quivered an eyelash.

"A doctor," he said aloud, "should have more to contribute than a bedside manner and a knowledge of genetic chemistry."

C'ele blinked and turned squarely about to look into his face. "You're going to be that doctor?" she asked coolly.

"Why not?"

"No reason," said C'ele, settling back against his shoulder again. "No reason at all, I guess."

He put his fingers under her chin and tipped her face so that he could look down at it. "You sound as if you didn't like the idea."

Her eyes met his. "How should I sound to convey the impression . . . ?"

"Oh, gosh, C'ele! From the way you used to talk—"

She stroked her hand up the back of her hair. "Used when?" she asked. "And how did I talk then?"

He sat shaking his head. "Maybe I should go back to the hospital. Just walk out of here, and go back . . ."

"O.K.," said C'ele. If that was what he wanted.

But it didn't seem to be. "Seriously, C'ele," he said, rubbing his head against the pillow, "if— Why, girl, you can't have forgotten all you used to give out concerning a man's being his own man—not just the shadow of another man."

"Oh, that," said C'ele, indifferently. "I am sure glad to find out that I wasn't the one to advise you to be a stuffed shirt."

He was watching her.

She nodded. "Lately I've begun to worry," she assured him.

He sat straight up then and turned to look directly at her. "What *is* all this?" he asked. "What's up, C'ele?"

To a surprising degree she was not being the smooth, and quiet, C'ele he was used to, agreeing with everything he said. He leaned forward and looked at her more closely, a bubble of excitement rising in his veins, then another . . .

Her eyes were shining, as if she saw, and knew, exactly what was happening.

"I might as well say it," she said brightly, "since I am going to chop a hole in the boat anyway."

Red's lips parted—he could only gape at her.

She shrugged. "I can't go on this way any longer, Red," she told him. "Being dishonest with you . . ." A crimson flush smeared itself painfully across her face, and he put his hand on her arm. The girl was trembling.

"I'm ashamed of the way I've gone on, Red," she told him passionately. "Telling you I was a college girl, lying about my family. I know you will despise me for the lies I've told, but—"

"Hey, hey!" cried Red. "What kind of way is that for you to talk about my girl? What sort of foundation are you laying for our marriage?" He drew her into his arms and kissed her. Tonight his kiss was different from any kiss he had ever given her—or received from her. Tonight their kiss was *good!*

C'ele laughed in joyous excitement. "And you just said that you would be your own man," she taunted.

"I am my own man," Red promised her. "And I shall be."

"We'll see."

"Bet your life, we'll see."

"The right kind of man, Red? Chemistry, and all that jazz?"

He laughed. "I like my girls foolish," he assured her.

"I'm dead serious."

"So am I. And I'll be everything you know I want to be. Oh, I may make some more mistakes, but I do hope, C'ele, that, stuffed shirt or not, I'll always be on the side of what is morally right."

"And legally?"

"That, too. I hope. Because laws *are* necessary—"

"You've finally decided that?"

"I better had," he said emphatically.

"You talked so well tonight, Red. To the gang, I mean. I was proud of you."

He nodded. "I do feel that things can be done, C'ele. Even if we can't—even if we don't—change the laws, maybe we can change the way people use the laws."

C'ele's eyes rounded. "Do you think *that* will be good?"

"I think I'm about to try and find out."

She nodded. "Well," she conceded, "that will suit me. In fact—you know? I believe it suits me fine!"

Red chuckled and smoothed her hair. "It would 'suit you fine' if I'd announce I was going over Niagara in a barrel."

"Oh no!" she denied. "At least, don't test me."

He rubbed his cheek against hers. "Don't you ever change, C'ele," he said. "Don't you—ever—change!"

"Nor you, Red," she answered contentedly. "Because I like us, just the way we are."